DEATH IN DARKNESS

Molly Sutton Mysteries 8

NELL GODDIN

Beignet Books

CONTENTS

৯ছ I ঽ

2007

"**W**atch out!" Molly shouted, as she looked up from pulling weeds in the front border in time to see an impending disaster—Constance on her bicycle, Bobo the dog, and a small truck all converging at high speed at the end of the driveway.

The driver of the truck slammed on the brakes. Constance jerked the bike to one side and landed in the ditch; Bobo ran to her and licked her face.

"Are you okay?" Molly said, running over. She waved and smiled at the truck driver, who she hoped was bringing the first load of materials for a new renovation project at *La Baraque*, her two-year-old *gîte* business.

"Yeah, but no thanks to that dude," grumbled Constance, as she brushed off her jeans and then looked at the front wheel of her bike, which was no longer perfectly round. Her hair was pulled into a tight ponytail, her usual get-down-to-business hair-style, and her young, fresh face went without makeup.

"Go inside, get something to drink, and relax. I've just got to talk to Boris for two seconds and then I'll be right with you."

Constance glowered. "I'm supposed to be on a day-trip with Thomas, you know. He wanted to drive over to Bordeaux and show me off. His words, isn't that *so* adorable? But I told him no way can I miss changeover day, Molly is counting on me."

"And I appreciate that, Constance. Nothing's broken, no sprains? Go on in, I'll be there in two seconds. Then let's have a little gab before we start work."

The prospect of a bit of gossip and hanging out in Molly's living room cheered the housecleaner up a bit, and she went inside without further grumbling.

"So," said Molly, turning to Boris, who was patiently waiting in the cab of his truck. "Bonjour! You nearly gave me a heart attack just then. My dog— like most dogs, I suppose—is not that smart when it comes to cars and trucks."

"Bonjour, how are you?" said Boris, and without waiting for Molly to say how she was, which at the moment was rather irritated, added, "Tie it up, then," gesturing to Bobo.

She opened her mouth to tell him what she thought about people who don't like dogs, but then closed it again, realizing that her opinion was hardly going to change his mind. She took a breath and tried for better footing. "I'm having the old stone barn rebuilt, it's back that way," she pointed, "behind the house...it might be better to go back to *rue des Chênes* and then drive across the meadow from the road. Of course, the closer you get to the worksite, the better."

"Is there going to be a separate driveway for the barn?"

She hadn't thought of that. "No. At least I don't think so. The building will be divided into three *gîtes*, and the parking is here," she said, gesturing to the large area between her house and the cottage.

"People won't want to carry bags that far," said Boris.

How annoying it is when people you don't like say sensible things! Molly thought.

"All right, well, I'll sort all that out later on. For now, please go down the road to the left, away from the village, and go about two hundred meters or so. You can see the ruined barn from the road, though it's so covered with vines it looks like a big green lump. If you get to the small stone building close to the road, you've gone too far. It's been fairly dry and the meadow drains well in any case, so I'm not worried about the truck getting stuck or even causing ruts."

Boris saluted and backed up onto *rue des Chênes*. That salute—it had to be ironic, right? Smirking? Molly felt like chasing after Boris and giving him a piece of her mind, but she squared her shoulders, called Bobo, and went to find Constance. They were old friends by this point, Molly having hired the younger woman to help with cleaning when Molly first arrived in the village several years earlier.

The main house at La Baraque was very old, by American standards, as well as rambling, having been added onto over the centuries in a haphazard way. But Molly had instantly fallen in love with its disorganized charm when she saw it listed on an internet real estate site, and had hustled over to Castillac and bought the place, just like that. What followed had, thus far, been the happiest years of Molly's life: she had made good friends and solved a handful of crimes, and unexpected—and unlooked for—romance had bloomed in that sensual Gallic atmosphere.

Constance was lying on the sofa holding a glass of lemonade. "Who *was* that guy?" she asked, reaching down to rub her knee somewhat theatrically, and groaning softly.

"Never met him. He's delivering materials for the work on the barn. Hey, I thought you knew everyone," said Molly, pouring herself another cup of coffee though she had drunk two already.

"Pretty much," said Constance. "I do have news on that score," she said, throwing out a little bait and grinning.

"What score? About Boris?"

3

"No, silly, about someone new to Castillac. Two someones, actually. No, make that *three*."

"My heavens, the floodgates have been opened! You've met these new people?"

Constance shrugged and sipped her lemonade, which Molly took to mean no.

"Well, who are they? What have you heard?"

"I can't believe you're not more *plugged in*," sad Constance, wanting to prolong the pleasure of Molly's ignorance.

Bobo stood by Molly's chair and Molly fiddled with her soft ears while waiting patiently for Constance to get on with it.

"Okay," Constance said, unable to hold back any longer, "I'll tell you even if you won't beg. Ben hasn't said anything at all?"

"Constance!"

"Okay, okay! What I hear is: Maron is out, and we're getting a new chief!"

Molly's eyes widened. "What?"

"Well, it's no big surprise. You know the *gendarmerie* rotates people around all the time. They don't want the gendarmes getting too cozy with the people who live in their district or whatever."

"Right. I just…I was finally feeling like Maron and I were on pretty good terms."

"You mean he let you muck around in all the interesting cases," said Constance with a cackle. "You'll be very lucky if the next person lets you get away with that."

"You're probably right," said Molly, her spirits sinking. "I don't think this is good news for Dufort/Sutton Investigations."

"Why isn't your name first, anyway?"

"Alphabetical order. And because Ben is the one who knows everybody, so it just made sense."

"Does it bug you though, having to be second?"

"No! I swear, Constance, sometimes I think you work overtime just trying to stir up trouble." Bobo jumped up in Molly's lap, causing coffee to spill onto the arm of the chair. "Honestly, Bobo, you're not a puppy anymore! Okay, who else? You did say three new people?"

Constance tapped her chin, thinking. "I'm not positive about that. Could be more. Let's say: three with an asterisk. Because it's a family and there might be children. My information is a little sketchy at the moment. You know that manor out rue de Fallon? It's back from the road behind some trees, so you might not have noticed it. Really nice place though it could use some TLC."

"That's the new family's house?"

"Am I so hard to follow? For an ace detective you can sometimes be a little slow on the uptake, Molls."

Molly stood up and wrenched the stained slipcover off the armchair, the irritation she had felt at Boris coming back with a vengeance. "Okay, fine. I'm getting started. It's already ten, and you know how guests are, they can show up at unpredictable times."

Constance finished her lemonade, feeling equally annoyed. It was disappointing when you had some juicy tidbits and they went completely unappreciated.

"You hear anything about who the new chief is going to be?" Molly asked, as they gathered up pails, vacuum cleaner, and mop.

"Not yet. Sure wish Ben would take the job again. I mean, I didn't hate Maron. But he wasn't likable either, you know? You never had the feeling you knew what he was thinking."

Molly shrugged. Dufort/Sutton Investigations solved an important case back in June, but there had been precious little going on since then. The news about Maron's leaving put her in a sour mood, and she flung herself into cleaning as though getting every last speck of grime off a window would magically bring a friendly chief to the village, someone cheerfully disposed to collaborate with her and Ben.

But she was quite clear, even as she thought it, that it was only a wish, and unlikely to come true.

❦

IT WAS the same routine every Saturday, at least when Molly had new guests coming, which was most Saturdays now that business was steady. The changeover cleaning was onerous, the way any job was when there was no getting out of it and it repeated on an endless loop. But it was also satisfying, partly because the Saturday cleanings gave a rhythm to the weeks rolling by, and also because Molly found that making the spaces clean and welcoming provided a distinct pleasure. In a world that could be difficult, with so much tragedy in the news day after day, at least she could give her guests the felicity of a room with fresh flowers and a bottle of wine, crisp sheets and sparkling surfaces.

Constance's performance with the vacuum had improved since Molly first hired her. It was still necessary, most weeks, for Molly to ask her to revisit a few of the rooms, where on final inspection dust bunnies were found still lurking. But the rooms were no longer strewn with used rags or empty bottles of cleaning fluid tossed aside and forgotten.

Most weeks, the two women enjoyed each other's company, but on that particular Saturday Molly was glad to see Constance wobble out of the driveway on her bike, and Constance was just as glad to go. At this point, it's almost like she's family, thought Molly, as she did one final room check before any guests showed up. And family is going to get on your nerves some of the time, that's just how it is.

Molly was no longer nervous on changeover day, worrying about whether anyone would show up and how to act around them. All of that was old hat, and she found herself instead looking forward to meeting the new people. Let's see, she said to

6

herself, sitting down at the computer to check the reservations so she'd know everyone's name.

She heard the taxi in the driveway accompanied by Bobo's barking, and after raking a comb through her tangled red hair, went out to greet the latest guests of La Baraque.

Christophe drove a Peugeot, and not a big one. But as Molly walked over, more and more people climbed out of it until there were five altogether, practically like watching a clown car at the circus.

"Bonjour," she said, reaching to shake a big man's hand. "I'm Molly Sutton. Are you...did you all meet at the train station?"

Christophe just shook his head, smiling, and went to the trunk and began taking out bags.

"It was just good luck," said a small woman whose pronunciation of French was very precise. "Todor and I were just leaving the station and we saw only the one taxi-cab, but this fellow here—excuse me, *monsieur*, I've forgotten your name already—"

"Arthur," said a young man, brushing off his pants.

"Yes, of course, Arthur. As I was saying, Arthur had already engaged the taxi but we overheard him say 'La Baraque,' and so, though we knew we were being impolite, there was only the one taxi, so we asked the young man—Arthur, yes, I have it now—and just as we were getting our bags into the trunk, along come the Jenkinses and they too were headed right here to La Baraque, and so—"

"In other words," said the small woman's husband, "we shared the taxi."

"Wonderful," laughed Molly. She turned to Mrs. Jenkins. "I thought you were going to be driving a rental car? Am I confused?"

"No, no, our plans changed. Actually..." Mrs. Jenkins's pleasant face colored just a bit. "Actually, I lost my license just before we left the States. I was driving to a meeting, I was late, I was going too fast..."

"And the cops nabbed her," her husband said cheerfully. "My wife's got a record as long as your arm, and this last time she crossed some kind of line, and they suspended her license." He shook his head but was smiling. "If you're ever in a hurry, put ol' Deana at the wheel. But if you want to stay clear of the law, maybe not."

Mrs. Jenkins's face got redder. "Billy," she said. "You don't have to air all our dirty laundry the instant we meet someone."

Before an argument had time to get going, Molly jumped in. "Well, I'm so glad you're all here! Mr. and Mrs. Jenkins, you're in the *pigeonnier*, down that way. If you could wait a moment, I'll get the others settled before walking you over."

"Please, call us Billy and Deana," said Mr. Jenkins.

"I will," said Molly. The sight of the Americans made her a little homesick, though she did not recognize it as the cause of a little stab between the ribs. Something about the way they dressed and their facial expressions were so American and familiar —Billy wearing a pair of khakis with boat shoes from L.L.Bean, and Deana in a wrap skirt printed in pineapples. Meanwhile, the Frenchman was beginning to look annoyed at having to stand in the driveway so long. "You are Arthur Malreaux? You'll be in the annex, attached to the main house. And you must be the Mertenses?"

Todor and Elise Mertens nodded, their bags at their feet. They were both quite short, and looked to be in their seventies, with rosy cheeks and white hair. All of the guests were eager to see their rooms, and in a brisk half hour, Molly had all five settled in their accommodations.

So far, no one had any special requests, or had left anything critical at home, or presented any sort of problem for Molly to solve. It was an auspicious beginning for a somewhat large group. As Molly turned her attention to some overdue housework in the main house, she was thinking about having the new guests over for an *apéro* possibly the following evening, and enjoying the lack of drama and calm of a beautiful September in Castillac.

There was the matter of the new chief of gendarmes, and how important a good relationship with the person in that position was to Ben and Molly...but no use worrying about the future, she thought as she buffed up a side table in the living room. Anyway, how bad could it be?

B en Dufort was up early as usual, and had gone for a run and showered before most of Castillac had opened one eye. He was not a tall man but quite fit, with a brush-cut Molly liked to run her hands through, with faint crow's-feet on his perennially tanned face. Ben was often one of the first at the Saturday market, and this week was no different. He had bought a few things he knew Molly would like: prunes stuffed with *foie gras* never failed to make her whoop and dance around the room, and a new vendor had sold him a collection of flavored salts in small glass containers that he was pretty sure would be a hit. He was meeting a potential new client at the Café de la Place, and took a seat at an outdoor table, looking around for Pascal, the exceptionally good-looking waiter whose mother did the café's cooking.

The café was packed as it usually was at the tail end of market day. Ben recognized most of the other diners and noted a few strangers, always glad to see Castillac graced by some tourists since they brought much-needed cash to the small village. Pascal was laughing with a table of teenage girls celebrating something over bowls of ice cream. A large family was finishing a late breakfast at the next table, the children well-behaved and in their seats.

Leaning back in his chair and staring into the middle distance, Ben mentally reviewed his notes on the potential client. Bernard Petit was from Bergerac. He'd agreed to the fee without hesitation, but refused to provide any detail on what the job in question actually entailed. Ben wasn't sure whether he was encouraged by this display of discretion or worried about what he and Molly might be asked to do.

No point worrying about it either way, as the man was due to arrive any minute and would surely fill in the blanks. Ben's mind jumped next to his dwindling bank account and he felt a slight chill, though the day was sunny and warm. Molly was kind-hearted to a fault, so the chill was not so much about fearing he would go hungry as about pride. It is not a foolish kind of pride that propels a man to want to be not only self-sufficient but able to provide for a wife, he said to himself, watching a large man make his way down the sidewalk and guessing correctly that he was the mysterious prospective client.

Ben stood up as the man headed to the terrace of the Café. "Monsieur Petit?" he said, and when the man nodded, Ben introduced himself and stuck out his hand. But Monsieur Petit ignored the hand and Ben let it drop, wondering what the man could possibly be offended about.

"This is terribly...public," Monsieur Petit said. "Is this any kind of place for a personal conversation?" It was true that the Castillaçois were renowned busybodies, and Ben acknowledged to himself that Petit had a point.

"Let's enjoy lunch," Ben said, "and afterwards we can take a stroll together and discuss whatever it is you would like me to do. We certainly don't want to ruin Madame Longhale's delicious cooking with any talk of work."

Monsieur Petit shrugged. He pulled out a cigar and proceeded to go through the elaborate process of trimming and lighting it. Taking a few deep puffs, he plumed the bluish smoke over the heads of the large family at the next table. The mother shot Petit a dirty look, gathered up her children, and left.

The man chuckled. "Works like a charm," Petit said.

Ben kept a poker face but internally was grimacing. There's no rule about having to like the client, he said to himself, though it didn't make him feel any better.

Pascal made it over to the table and took their drink orders, but had too many tables to stop for much of a chat.

"Is anything good here?" Petit asked.

Ben took a deep breath.

"Madame Longhale is quite accomplished in the kitchen. Her confit is excellent, as is the cassoulet—"

"It's far too warm to eat anything like that. It may be September but there is no chill in the air whatsoever. It would be ridiculous to eat a hot stew on a day such as this."

Ben took another deep breath, trying to disguise his irritation by briefly holding the menu in front of his face. "Obviously, order whatever you like. I'm going to have the cassoulet followed by salad and cheese." He hadn't had a thought of ordering the cassoulet—and indeed, he would have agreed that the weather wasn't especially suited for it—but Monsieur Petit had been so smug in his dismissal of Madame Longhale's dish that now he was determined to have it.

"So how did you hook up with the American, anyhow?" asked Petit.

"In Castillac, as you might imagine, it is easy to meet the people who live here. Eventually everyone crosses paths."

"I heard she showed you up. Solved a case right under your nose, and when she could barely speak French on top of it."

He was not usually so easily ruffled, but Ben had to hold himself back from leaping up and punching Petit right in the nose.

"Molly is a very skilled detective," he said, using a lot of will to keep his teeth from clenching. "I am very lucky that we are on the same team."

"How's her French now? Gotten any better?"

"I should say so. She's been here almost exactly two years."

"Eh, we both know people who've come over and gotten nowhere in that amount of time. They stick to their own kind, watch English television shows, make no effort at all."

"I'm not sure I know anyone like that. But you are certainly not describing Molly. She has thrown herself into village life with much enthusiasm."

Petit squinted his eyes in what Ben took to be a skeptical manner. The prospective client had not quite insulted Molly, not enough to excuse storming off from the table. But he was right on the edge, and Ben waited, perversely hoping Petit would say something so awful it would put Ben completely in the right for telling him to shove it and walking away.

At that moment, Pascal appeared with a plate of crudités, small toasts, and a generous pot of his mother's pâté.

"Thank you very much, Pascal," said Ben. "I could eat your mother's pâté for lunch every single day and be a happy man."

Pascal grinned and made a graceful bow. "I'll tell her. Sorry to rush off, but we are packed today and the new waitress hasn't shown up—"

Petit, as Ben knew he would, hmphed his disapproval of the missing waitress. Then he dipped the short knife into the pâté and spread a thick layer on a piece of toast.

Ben busied himself with a stalk of celery while waiting for his turn with the knife, making a point of not asking Petit what he thought of the pâté. The two irritated men did not even try to make polite conversation.

"Oh the hell with it," said Petit with his mouth full. "I'll just speak low enough that those people over there can't hear me."

Ben leaned towards him, curious in spite of himself.

14

"I have quite a nice house in Bergerac. Just a block from the church. Expansive backyard with a garden and a small pool. One of the best—if not *the* best—houses in town, if I do say so."

Ben barely succeeded in not rolling his eyes.

"Someone is stealing from my house. Pilfering, I should say, if that word connotes stealing of a smaller monetary value."

Ben needed to finish chewing before asking, "What kinds of things have been stolen, and how long has this been going on?"

"The first time was about six months ago. I noticed the shoe trees in my closet were missing. I have some expensive pairs of shoes and I take very good care of them. No point paying all that money and then simply tossing them down and allowing them to become misshapen and unsightly. It only takes a little bit of care and attention, you understand, to put them away with trees inserted.

It would be impossible to dislike this man any more than I do, thought Ben. "And how many shoe trees are missing?"

"Seven pairs."

"All right, and then? When did the next theft take place?" Ben had pulled out a small notebook and was taking down the information with a fountain pen.

"I failed to write down the exact dates of any of this, which I realize was a mistake. But I had no idea it would come to this, that an actual investigation by a professional would be necessary. I suppose I thought once I fired the old hag who cleaned the house and got someone new, with impeccable references, things would go back to normal."

"But they did not?"

"No. Probably three weeks later, I went to get in bed and found my pillowcase missing. When I looked around in other bedrooms, the pillowcases on the guest beds were missing as well. They were not in the laundry or anywhere to be found."

"Odd."

"I'll say it's odd!"

"Does anyone live at the house with you?"

"I have two children, a son and a daughter. They are grown now, attending universities far from Bergerac."

"And their mother?"

"Must you pry so dreadfully? Their mother and I divorced long ago. I don't keep up with her movements any longer."

"Do you know if she lives in Bergerac?"

"No, she does not. Last I heard she was *finding herself* in Tibet, or some such nonsense. If anyone wanted to find *her*, just follow the scent of incense when it rolls by, and eventually it'll lead to her. Last place I saw her reeked of the stuff."

Ben nodded his head slowly, looking carefully at Petit. He had a big head, big nose, wide mouth, and ears that were nearly half as long as his head. Everything about the man was oversized, like a cartoon drawing. His eyebrows were dark and thick, his lips fleshy...only his eyes were on the small side, though that may have only been the effect of being swamped by such large features.

Ben tried to imagine this man at home, with a wife and children, but struggled to make the image come alive.

"All right," the detective said, flashing a sudden smile at the sight of Pascal headed their way with a heavy tray. He waited to finish his thought until Pascal had served them and gone off to deal with the teenage girls. "All right, so am I to understand that you want us to find who is stealing from you, and if possible to recover the items?"

"Yes. Brilliant conclusion," said Petit, tearing a leaf from an artichoke with a degree of savagery. "I would like your full attention on the matter, and will pay accordingly."

Dufort allowed himself an inward smile at that news, though the prospect of working with Monsieur Petit was unappealing to say the least.

I'll probably smell like cigars until the case is over, he thought.

But at least I'll be motivated to wrap it up as quickly as possible, and hopefully other cases will soon come along.

And with a mostly satisfied sigh, he dug into the bowl of steaming hot cassoulet, his mouth watering at the sight of several nuggets of *confit de canard* and the whole thing covered with a thin and delectable layer of goose fat.

"Simon, I do *not* understand why you insist on coming into the house looking like that. You know it's disturbing to me. Would it really be such a bother to rinse off first?"

Simon Valette grinned at his wife. He was a good-looking man with bright blue eyes, the crow's-feet having the effect of conferring wisdom or kindness. His hair was thick, dark, and unruly. Along one cheek was a scar that gave him an air of mystery. "Oh, Camille," he said, moving to touch her face but she pulled away from him. "I really like it here," he said, still grinning.

"Apparently," said Camille, with the very faintest hint of a returned smile. "I'm glad you've found something to do that you enjoy, truly I am. I certainly never would have guessed when we lived on Boulevard des Capucines and you were working at Byatt Industries that you would take to building stone walls like a common laborer, but you have, that's it, and I have nothing to say against it. Except that you are bringing a cloud of dust inside with you every time you come in for a drink of water, and the girls' allergies are going to be absolutely insane, not to mention who do you think is going to be running the vacuum every five minutes to keep on top of it?"

"Tell me," said Simon seriously. "Are you feeling better? I know we've barely gotten here and still have boxes to unpack. But I'm hoping...hoping that already you feel...less stressed? Lord knows Castillac seems to be an easygoing place, as far as I can tell."

"Oh, it's easygoing, all right," Camille muttered. She was dressed in a long cashmere cardigan in a particular shade of brownish gray that was popular that year with important Parisian designers. Her slacks were well cut and her jewelry quietly impressive, not ostentatious. She was pretty, in the way that plenty of money can polish a person up, but her severe bun made her look stern and her expression was tense. As she stood talking to her husband, her fingers plucked at one of the buttons on her cardigan.

Simon wanted to take her hand and hold it to make her stop plucking, but he'd learned that it only made things worse. "Well, so far I think the decision to leave Paris was brilliant. My father seems calmer, wouldn't you say? And the girls are having a wonderful time! Who would have guessed that playing in a little grove of bamboo with some sticks and an old blanket would be so much fun?"

Camille waved her hand in the air as though to erase that particular vision. "If Andrea could see them..."

"But that's the whole point, *chérie*. We left the city partly to get away from people like Andrea."

"Andrea is my closest friend."

"She is a viper, Camille, for God's sake." Simon's face was reddening and he smacked his dusty hands together. "Well, we've talked about this a hundred times. We're here now, that's what matters, and I think it's going to be good for all of us."

Camille stood with her arms folded, looking up at a stain on the ceiling. "I didn't notice that when we came to look at the house. Was it in the inspector's report? Look at it, Simon! Clearly there's a leak in the roof, we're probably going to have to rip the entire thing off and start over. It will cost a *fortune*. And you with no job." She stood rooted to the spot, her eyes pinned on the small stain, a path of gray that extended about four inches down the wall, soiling the wallpaper.

"It's not a worry, darling. Yes, it was in the report—it's old damage and the roof was new just a few years ago. We can paint the ceiling, have new wallpaper, whatever you like."

Camille shook her head, staring at the stain.

"It's ancient history," said Simon soothingly. "The damage is over and done with, and we don't have to worry about it. And not only that—if a storm whipped through tonight and the roof was torn clear off the house? I have plenty of money, Camille. I'll simply buy us a new roof and that's it."

The sound of shouting came in through the open window and the couple looked out. Their two daughters, aged ten and six, flew past as though being chased by demons.

"I don't think they should be running with sticks," said Camille. "They could easily lose an eye playing like that. Where is Violette? She should be keeping a closer watch on them."

"I'll talk to them," said Simon, glad of an excuse to go back outside, having no intention of saying anything at all to the girls.

Camille spent another few minutes inspecting the stain before going upstairs to her bedroom. The house was an old manor, though not a particularly grand one as manors go. The bottom floor consisted of a living room, dining room, kitchen, library, laundry room, and a tiny little added-on half-bath. Upstairs were four bedrooms, two baths, and a large landing where the girls had already put on several puppet shows under the guidance of the nanny, Violette Crespelle. On the third floor was Violette's room, and a large low-ceilinged area used for storage.

Simon's elderly father was in his bedroom, sitting in a chair, looking down at the floor. Part of the reason for the move Paris was that Simon was dissatisfied with the care his father had been receiving at his live-in facility; their apartment on Boulevard des Capucines had been quite spacious, but any apartment is going to feel cramped with two young girls and a parent with dementia. After months of strategic conversation, Simon had finally convinced Camille to allow his father to come live with them, somewhere calm and peaceful, somewhere healthful for the whole family, all of whom suffered from the stress of the big city to various degrees.

"Bonjour, Raphael," said Camille, having not seen her father-in-law yet that morning.

Monsieur Valette did not look up or answer.

Camille sighed and went into her bedroom, which was so neat it looked like a hotel room. An antique vanity stood between two large windows; on top was a straight row of bottles of perfume, then hairbrush and comb, and several lipsticks in classic shades. As she stood in her room, she felt a little kernel of something blooming deep in her chest and beginning to spread through her body. It was a familiar anxiety (mixed with doom), this time triggered because she had no appointment book filled with errands and social duties, and the phone was not ringing since she'd yet to meet a single person in the village. Camille had no idea what to do with herself until with a flash of gratitude and annoyance she remembered all the dust Simon had brought in and went back downstairs to find the vacuum.

She had always had housekeepers, her whole life; until they found one in Castillac, Camille was doing the work herself, which she found exotic and a welcome relief when she didn't know where else to direct her energy.

Meanwhile, Simon had gone back to the ruined building on the side of the property where he had been working slavishly since they arrived the week before. It was unclear exactly what purpose the building used to serve, and equally unclear what use they would find for it in the future; yet Simon was purposefully working to rebuild the walls as though the survival of his family depended on it.

He had not reached the stage of actual masonry but was

patiently dismantling the rubble on top of the walls, making piles of rocks of various sizes. This involved prying off old mortar, sometimes breaking apart rocks that were stuck together, and then wrestling them into a wheelbarrow so they could be carted to the proper pile. It was exhausting and exhilarating work. He took his shirt off and let the warm September sun wash over his body, which he imagined rather indulgently as Adonis-like, now that he was engaged in so much physical labor. As he pushed the wheelbarrow full of stones back to the piles, he kept an eye out for the girls and Violette, but saw no one.

And that was one of the very best things about their new place at the edge of town: everyone in the family had room to stretch out, in private, without bumping into anyone else. A person could pursue whatever interests he or she liked, without someone else looking over their shoulder, and to Simon this prospect was the most delicious thing of all.

༄ 4 ༅

Sunday morning started peacefully enough at La Baraque. The two remaining guests for the week, Darek and Emilia Badowski, had arrived from Poland late Saturday and been installed in the large room in the annex. Everyone was still asleep or at least not stirring, and Molly was enjoying a second cup of coffee and surfing the internet while Ben was out for a run.

One thing she loved about Sundays in Castillac: there was common agreement that it was a day for family and friends, for a big meal in the middle of the day, and that was about it. You could put whatever ambitions you had about pretty much anything aside for that one day. It didn't matter whether you were religious or not, it was a day of rest for the body and soul.

Not so back in Boston, where Molly's Sundays had been spent frantically trying to get ahead on housework and errands before the workweek started up again. As she sat drinking coffee (and wondering how in the world she was out of pastry) she looked back at herself in those days with a bit of sadness. Perhaps Boston was not the problem—it was me, she thought. But whatever, she was in Castillac now, and very grateful for it.

She was so deep into remembering that when someone

25

NELL GODDIN

knocked on the front door, she jumped up as though she'd been caught doing something wrong. Shaking her head, she went to open the door, Bobo at her heels.

"Boris! Bonjour!"

The truck driver from the day before stood on the step, holding a clipboard. "Your contractor, Monsieur Gradin, asked me to finalize this list of materials. Can I have your signature, please?" He held out the clipboard and a pen.

"It's Sunday."

"Yes. Monsieur Gradin intends to begin work tomorrow morning, and in order for that to happen, I'm going to have to get the truck loaded this afternoon so it will be ready to drive over first thing."

"Do you generally work Sundays? I didn't think anyone…" she trailed off, not sure whether it was worth it to argue. "And…I'm not clear on why I am signing for a list of materials. Monsieur Gradin knows what he needs, not me. I have no idea what should be on that list. Shouldn't he be the one signing for it?"

"That would make sense," Boris agreed. "But you are the one paying. So." He held out the clipboard again.

The fact that only seconds earlier Molly had been reveling in the French tradition of relaxing Sundays made this nonsensical intrusion very annoying. "Okay, Boris," she said with a sigh, just wanting to be done with it. She signed and said goodbye. It had been a vexatious couple of days for no reason at all. Maybe she could convince Ben to go to Chez Papa for dinner; she felt like she could use some cheering up, despite nothing having gone very wrong.

Molly had just settled back in the armchair with a gardening magazine, coffee freshened, when she heard shouting. Bobo instantly ran out through the terrace door, barking, followed by Molly.

The Jenkinses ran up from the pigeonnier and looked at Molly with wide eyes.

"Did you hear something?" Molly asked.

"Someone yelling," said Billy Jenkins. Deana nodded.

Molly looked towards the cottage but so no sign of any movement that way. She walked around toward the annex just as the shouting broke out again.

"And I'll thank you to stay out of my room and away from me altogether!"

Molly quickly went inside and into a large room that served as a sitting room for the two annex bedrooms. Arthur was standing in his doorway, his hair wild and standing up sort of comically, while Darek was in front of his wife Emilia, an arm out as though to protect her.

"What is the problem?" asked Molly, in what she hoped was a soothing voice.

"I caught her in my room, that's the problem!" said Arthur, pointing at Emilia.

Emilia shook her head. "Yes, yes, I was in his room, but I was only opening a window so we can get some air." She was tall and lanky, with a prominent nose and a dismissive air.

"You can open your own window if you want air! Don't go into other people's rooms without an invitation. All right?"

"Do not get rough with my wife," Darek said, taking a step towards Arthur, who was half his size.

"Everyone, please," said Molly. "I will have a word with Emilia," she said to Arthur, hoping he would go in his room and close the door, which would hopefully calm the others down.

Instead, Arthur closed and locked his door and turned to Molly. "Do you have a safe? I have some valuables with me and I see now that I cannot take the privacy of my room for granted. I am very upset, Miss Sutton, as you can well understand."

"She told you it was just to get air," said Darek. "Nobody's after any of your crappy 'valuables'."

Oh dear, thought Molly. "Okay. Emilia, would a fan help? It is warmer than usual this week, and I can easily bring a fan over."

Emilia grudgingly nodded.

"Okay good. Badowskis, if you'd like to cool off more, why not take a swim? The pool is on the edge of the meadow as you walk towards the pigeonnier. Arthur, why don't you come with me and we can work out a solution for the safety of your valuables. Come on, Bobo! Hope the rest of your Sunday goes well, Badowskis."

She took Arthur by the arm and led him outside and into her part of the house by the terrace door. "I'm so sorry. Nothing like that has ever happened before. I would like to brush it off and hope that her excuse is legitimate, but to be honest, we don't really know that, do we?"

"No," said Arthur darkly.

"Do you have any reason to think she was in your room for another reason?"

"I have no proof. If I had to guess, I'd say she was snooping. Maybe trying to see if I have anything worth stealing. I don't really care what her reason was—maybe in retrospect it doesn't seem like a big deal, but I'll tell you, when I came back from a short stroll in the meadow to find her in my room like that, it—it shocked me!"

"No, don't worry, I do understand. She had absolutely no business being in there. Now let's see about your valuables. What size are they? I do have a small safe, but anything very large or even medium-sized is not going to fit."

"I have some papers that are very important to me. It would be helpful if I could leave them in your safe while I am out during the day, so that I don't have to carry them with me."

"Certainly, I'd be glad to do that," said Molly, very relieved that at least one small problem had been dealt with neatly.

Arthur thanked Molly and went back to his room.

"Bobo?" said Molly, and Bobo sat and wagged her tail, ears perked up. "Let's go find some rabbits. I have a feeling some other things are going to go wrong and I'd like to be out of the house when they do."

❧

IT WAS such a lovely evening that Molly and Ben decided to walk to Chez Papa for dinner.

"You know how sometimes you can't stand someone the first instant you meet them?"

"I do."

"That was Petit. He's horrible. But I shouldn't complain, at least he's a paying client, and they've been a little thin on the ground lately."

"Well, they always have been, to be honest."

"Why are you laughing?" Seeing Molly laugh made Ben smile for no reason.

"I don't know! Because it's such a gorgeous September night? Because I've been in a bit of a foul mood for two days, even though nothing bad has happened? It feels like a big cloud just lifted, or got swept away by this lovely breeze."

Ben took Molly's hand and squeezed it.

"So," said Molly, "you swear you knew nothing about Maron's leaving?"

"Nothing. Why would I? It's not like the gendarmerie is interested in my opinion about anything. And no, I have no idea who replaced him. Odds are I won't know the person anyway."

They walked in silence past the cemetery, both trying to imagine the new chief and praying they were going to like whoever it was...or failing that, be able to work effectively with whoever ended up in the job.

Ben sighed and pushed that subject from his mind. "Hey Molly, it's been months now. How about we tell everyone about our engagement tonight?"

"No!"

Ben laughed. "A less confident man might get the wrong idea from that."

Molly gave him a light shove. "It's only that it's been so fun having this secret, just between the two of us. Not that it's that big a deal to anyone else, I don't mean that. But…let's keep it only between us a little longer?"

"Whatever you want, chérie. No pressure from over here." This time Molly squeezed Ben's hand.

When the twinkling lights of Chez Papa came into view, she pulled Ben in front of her and kissed him, more than a peck but not so hard that anyone peering out of a window would have been scandalized.

"Bonsoir Molly, bonsoir Ben!" shouted a chorus when they finally made it inside the restaurant. The place was packed with friends—Frances, back from her honeymoon with Nico, who was behind the bar in his old place. Lawrence was perched on his usual stool, Lapin and his newish wife Anne-Marie sat at a table, even Rémy, the organic farmer was there, unusual since he went to bed before it got dark. Molly and Ben made the rounds, kissing cheeks and saying hello, finally ending at the bar next to Lawrence.

"You've been scandalously scarce lately," he said to Molly. "I'm right on the verge of having my feelings hurt."

"Oh, now," said Molly. "You are not. And you are perfectly capable of coming over anytime, and you know it. I have all the ingredients for a Negroni so you can't use that as an excuse, either."

"Well, what in the world have you been doing with yourself? I thought you'd be in here the minute the new chief was announced."

"Wait, there's been an announcement?"

Ben shrugged. "Don't look at me, I resigned over a year ago, remember?"

Lapin got up from the table, unable to resist being the center of attention. "I've met her," he said, expanding his chest and pausing for the reaction.

"*Her?*" said about six people at once.

"Yes, her," said Lapin. "I don't know why you're all in a state, haven't you ever seen a policewoman before? Her name's Charlot, Chantal Charlot I think. Sort of an elegant name for a crime-stopper, if you ask me. Sounds like she ought to be an actress or something, don't you think?"

Molly ignored Lapin and turned to Lawrence. "Did you know about this? Do you know anything about her? Have you met her?"

"I'm afraid not. Yes, I knew she was coming, but that's pretty much it. No details whatsoever."

"Well, what good are you?"

"None at all," Lawrence said cheerfully. "Though I *have* met the Valettes, if that's of any interest."

"Who?"

"The new family in town. They've bought the old manor on the edge of the village. Has a decent parcel of land with it, too. No idea what they're doing in Castillac of all places. He was a big muckety-muck at Byatt Industries. Went to ENA and all that."

"ENA?"

"You're such a provincial darling, you know that? *École Nationale d'Administration* is the elite school in Paris where all the highest achievers go to university. You're more or less guaranteed an excellent career if you make it that far. And to be fair, the education is by all accounts extremely rigorous, so they're not coasting their way through. We don't as a rule see many ENAs down this way," he said, lowering his voice a bit.

"Interesting."

"Indeed. I would guess—escaping from some sort of scandal? Something juicy that would make living anywhere ENAs frequent too horrible to bear."

"Something worse than, say, embezzling."

"Oh certainly. Embezzlers are a dime a dozen, even at that level. Something far nastier, I'd say."

"You're such pessimists!" said Ben, coming back with a kir for

Molly and a glass of beer for himself. "Maybe they just got sick of the rat race, and haven't done anything wrong at all."

"Pollyanna," said Molly.

"What?"

"Nico, what's the French equivalent of Pollyanna?"

"I have no idea what you're talking about." Nico had lived in the States for several years, but although he was perfectly fluent, there were limits to his knowledge of cultural references.

"How do you think I feel?" Frances piped up. "You people jibber jabber in French all the live-long day, and as I believe I have gotten across, I do not happen to speak that particular language."

Nico laughed. "I hate to tell you," he said, in French, "but I happen to know that you understand French quite well."

"I have no idea what you're talking about," said Frances, whipping her straight dark hair out of her face and looking away, but unable to stop a small smile from creeping up.

"They're probably perfectly nice," Ben continued. "You said you've met them? What are they like?"

Lawrence stared at the ceiling, thinking. "Well, I'd say they appear outwardly to be rather...normal. The husband is quite charming and friendly. Not at all arrogant as one might expect."

"And his wife?"

Lawrence shrugged. Suddenly, and somewhat out of character, he did not wish to speak ill of a woman he had only just met. "They have two young daughters. Cute. One, the older, was terribly shy and I could tell having to say polite things to me was killing her. The younger was brash. Skipping about and pretending she had on toe shoes, pirouetting and knocking into her mother. Oh, and I shouldn't forget the nanny."

"Nanny?" said Molly. "How old are these children?"

"I'm not good with that kind of thing at all. Older than toddlers but pre-pubescent, that's the best I can do. The nanny looks, well, like a capable sort. Fresh-faced and all that, like she probably leads the girls out on hikes and other healthful pursuits."

Lawrence said this with an air of disapproval, as though he found the prospect of outdoor exertion extremely distasteful.

"I doubt she's mixing them Negronis for lunch," said Ben, laughing.

"Perhaps she should," said Lawrence with a sniff, and taking a long sip of his drink.

"It does feel like a lot of change," Molly said, "There's a sort of timelessness about Castillac...it feels like how things are is how they will be forever. I know that's not true, but maybe you understand what I mean?"

"It's the old walls, the old stones," said Lapin. "The people pass through quickly, but the cobblestones and old buildings..."

"Maybe we should have the Valettes over for an apéro," Ben said to Molly.

"And invite Chantal Charlot while we're at it?"

"Maybe not right off."

"A little later. Well, much later. Nico, can I have a plate of frites?"

"Thought you'd never ask."

It was a Sunday night in September, everything as ordinary as could be. But everyone at Chez Papa felt something in the air that night—maybe the new family and new chief would turn out to be only everyday changes, and village life would make a few slight adjustments and carry on. Or maybe it was more than that. In the meantime, the friends stayed late at the restaurant that night, eating and drinking more than was perhaps wise, but feeling however vaguely like those moments of friendship and camaraderie were to be cherished, and not hurried away from if at all possible.

5

On Monday morning, Paul-Henri Monsour, junior officer of the Castillac gendarmerie, checked in early at the station —early enough that Chief Charlot would not yet be there. He made sure his desk was neat, though since he never ever left it messy there was little to tidy. He did give the floor a quick sweep, having brought Madame Bonnay's dog Yves back to the station the day before after finding him trotting down rue Picasso as though headed for Pâtisserie Bujold. Paul-Henri did not see the problem with a dog running loose; most of the dog owners of Castillac allowed it, and they all seemed to do just fine. But when Yves got out, Madame Bonnay was not to be consoled until that big Bleu de Gascogne was safely back home.

At any rate, the dog had tracked in sand, and one of the things Paul-Henri could not stand was the sensation of walking on grit. The slippery feeling under his shoes, along with the grinding sound as he pressed on the grains, set his teeth on edge. But once the floor was swept there was nothing else to do, and he was not going to be caught sitting there twiddling his thumbs when the new chief showed up. He left the station and went down rue

Malbec, alert and hoping to stumble upon a situation he could easily solve and thereby impress Chief Charlot.

He saw nothing out of the ordinary as he passed the former mayor's house, which now had a For Sale sign attached to the front door. Down the sidewalk he noticed someone moving slowly, and he hurried to see if he could be of assistance.

"Bonjour, Madame Gervais. How are you this morning?"

"Bonjour, Paul-Henri. I'm as well as can be expected. You do know I'm a hundred and four?"

"Of course, Madame Gervais. Your age is famous throughout the Dordogne, and you give the rest of us hope for a long future ahead!"

"I'm afraid my own future will not be so very long," she said, without a scrap of self-pity.

"Are you not feeling well? I'm very sorry to hear that." Paul-Henri liked old people, especially old ladies, and he did not mind at all listening to long lists of complaints, but actually tried to draw them out on the subject.

"Oh, it's nothing," said Madame Gervais, who found that the less she thought about her aches and pains, the better. "I probably sound a bit morose because fall is upon us, and it's my least favorite season. I much prefer spring, when the earth wakes up and comes alive."

"It hardly feels like fall this year, does it? The air is so warm you'd think it was May."

Paul-Henri and Madame Gervais continued to chat like this for several more minutes until Madame Gervais had had as much of the officer as she could take, and set off to finish her morning errands.

Feeling thirsty, Paul-Henri turned down a side street and headed for the *épicerie*, thinking he would buy a bottle of Perrier. He greeted the girl at the cash register and several customers before disappearing down an aisle of the cramped store to get his water, missing Chief Charlot who was coming up a different aisle on her way out of the store. She was dressed in uniform, a French blue suit with a skirt and a cap, her hair in a braid so tight it pulled the skin on the side of her face. She was small and trim, with a body like a gymnast.

"I came here hoping to find a decent potato," the chief said to Ninette at the register, who was the daughter of the shop owners. "But you're charging a ridiculous amount for what you have. Look —it's practically shriveled."

"Oh!" said Ninette, so taken aback she was at a loss for words. She recognized the new chief because her boyfriend had pointed her out on the street the day before, but they had not been introduced. Ninette wasn't sure whether she should pretend she had no idea who Chief Charlot was, or proceed as though they knew each other. In the confusion, she said nothing but stood with her mouth open, staring.

"Come on now, give me a discount. It's the least you can do. And if you would, pass along my comments about the state of your produce. I'd have purchased lettuce—I hate the idea of lunch with no salad—but every bit of it was so wilted I just could not in good conscience pay money for it."

"Discount?" said Ninette, her voice quavering a bit.

"I'll take thirty percent off. Thank you." Chief Charlot tossed a few euros on the counter, put her groceries in a straw bag she had brought with her, and left.

Paul-Henri had heard every word. When the chief was long gone, he stepped out from the aisle and looked at Ninette.

"What in the world?" he said.

"Oh my God, What a horrible person. There is nothing at all wrong with our potatoes!"

"Or your lettuce," said Paul-Henri. "Doesn't Rémy bring it fresh every morning?"

"Yes! Oh, I can't believe it. It was bad enough when Dufort quit, and we got that moody Maron hanging around all the time. I never liked him, not one bit. But now I want him back!"

Paul-Henri paid for his Perrier and said goodbye, heading in the direction away from the station, thinking Chief Charlot had probably gone there. On the one hand, it pleased him probably more than it should that the new chief was unpopular. And if she continued to argue and be disagreeable to all the shopkeepers, she would soon be hated throughout the village, which couldn't help but raise his own popularity.

On the other hand, he had to work with her. Well, maybe she's just cheap, and that won't affect me so much, he thought. But with a sudden sense of purpose, he headed straight to the station, intending to email some of his colleagues in Paris to ask if they knew anything about Chantal Charlot, either from personal experience or reputation. Much better to know what he's dealing with than go along in blissful ignorance, he thought grimly.

BEN WAS out for a run and Molly was debating whether or not to make another pot of coffee when she heard a gentle knock on the front door.

"Oh, bonjour, Arthur!" she said, ushering the guest inside. "Do you have those papers you want me to put in the safe? I really should ask about valuables when I'm showing guests to their rooms. Some crazy things have happened over the years here at La Baraque, but so far I've been lucky that nothing's been stolen —at least, no one has reported anything. An innkeeper's nightmare, as you might imagine."

Arthur looked a bit stunned by Molly's chatter but nodded and tried to summon a pleasant expression. He had not slept well. The shock of finding Emilia in his room the day before had upset him far more than it should, he thought. It's not as though he was a Resistance fighter and she a Gestapo agent. And she had just been standing there looking around, not rifling through his luggage.

"I'm wondering..." he began, but faltered.

Molly waited. There was no telling what a guest might need or want, and it was always interesting to see what they came up with.

"You see, I am in this part of France trying to research a relative of mine."

Molly nodded encouragingly.

"She is a cousin, on my father's side, and they say she fought with the Resistance. I understand this area was involved heavily in such fighting?"

Molly shrugged. "I'm afraid I'm not the person to ask. I do know that there was some fighting nearby—a terrible massacre in Mussidan, for one thing. I've heard stories of French families being hidden at certain farms, and I'm sure there's much, much more. I'd suggest talking to Madame Gervais, who lives in the village. Would you like me to make an introduction? She was a young woman at the time—not a child—and I believe she knows quite a lot about it. Though I'll admit, she's not necessarily that open about it. In my limited experience, a lot of people who have lived through terrible war do not want to talk about it."

"That would be a disappointment."

"Maybe it's too painful to dig through those memories. Or maybe words just can't express what it was like."

Arthur nodded and said something, but Bobo burst into raucous barking and drowned out whatever he said. A panel truck was turning into the driveway just as the mail-truck pulled up to the mailbox, and Ben could be seen breezing down rue des Chênes on his way back home.

"Heavens, La Baraque is like a three-ring circus these days! I'll take those papers, Arthur? I promise to keep them safe. *Au revoir* —I have to deal with this—"

Molly got the truck headed for the worksite and got a sweaty kiss from Ben.

"I found a new trail, back up behind the Bourgey's place," he said. "Maybe you'll come with me sometime."

"If we walk. I wasn't built for running. Bobo, hush for crying out loud."

Ben reached down to give the dog some attention while Molly checked the mail. "Bills, bills, ads, ads, oh! What in the world?" She held up a square envelope of heavy cream-colored paper, with her and Ben's names and the address written in elegant calligraphy.

"No idea," said Ben.

Molly flipped it over and saw an engraved address on the back flap, but did not recognize it. She tore open the envelope and pulled out a heavy card.

We would be so pleased if you could come to dinner. Friday 19h. RSVP at simonvalette@Valette.fr

"Curious," said Ben.

"I'll say! Have you met them? How did we get on the guest list?"

"No idea."

"You keep saying that. What kind of detective are you?"

Ben swatted her on the rump and Molly let out a shriek and ran for the house. Bobo danced between them, barking.

❦ 6 ❦

The following morning, Ben left right after breakfast to drive to Bergerac and inspect the house of Bernard Petit, while Molly spent the morning digging vines out of the front border—a never-ending, thankless job—and then meeting with Monsieur Gradin to discuss the barn rebuilding. The Jenkinses left to see the cathedral in Périgueux. There was no sign of Arthur or the Badowskis, and the Mertenses seemed perfectly content to sit at the small table outside the cottage, lingering over fresh croissants and watching the activity in the yard at La Baraque.

Ben took the short cut to Bergerac, a series of twisting, narrow roads that wound through forests and farmland, until in short order he was waiting at a stop light on the fringes of the small city. He found Petit's house without any trouble and parked his battered Renault a few blocks away so he could stretch his legs on the way to the meeting.

Despite his dislike of Petit, he was quite pleased to have the job—mostly for the sake of Dufort/Sutton Investigations, but also simply because the case was an interesting enough mystery to pique his curiosity. Who was stealing from the house? Were the thefts done purely for money or was there another motive? And how was he going to catch the thief?

Petit answered the door and mumbled a greeting. "All right then, come in," he said, irritably, as though Ben had appeared at his door to pester him.

Ben smiled. "First I'd like—"

"Come on upstairs, I'll show you the closet where the shoe trees were stolen." Petit began lumbering up a graceful wooden staircase with a patterned carpet running down the center.

Ben did not move. "Before you do that, I would first like to see all the entrances to the house, including basement doors and windows. If you please," he added, with only a faint edge.

The two men stood and looked at each other. Petit broke first, shaking his very large head. "Have it your way," he said gruffly. "Front door, obviously, you just saw."

"How long has that lock been on the door? Do you use that inner deadbolt when you're home?"

"No, I don't. Well, occasionally I might, if I happen to think of it on my way upstairs. You're not suggesting someone is coming in while I'm here? They wouldn't be able to get into the closet in my bedroom if that were the case!" Petit glared at Ben.

"I'm asking routine questions, Monsieur Petit, calm down. The point of routine questions is to fill in the big picture, so I have a good idea of your habits regarding security."

Petit shrugged and looked away. "The lock's been there quite a while. Never had any problems with it, never needed to change it."

"Who else has a key?"

"My children, I suppose, but as I say, they are in school and haven't been home in months. We don't get on all that well. Not every family is a happy, joyous group, you know."

"Right," said Ben. "And you're sure they haven't been back, maybe came to Bergerac to see friends, something like that?"

"I can't say it's categorically impossible," said Petit, raising his voice. "But my children did not steal the shoe trees!"

Ben sighed. "I am not suggesting they did. I am only trying to understand who might have been going in and out of the house in the last few months, that is all. If you don't mind my saying so, you're quite...unsettled, Monsieur Petit. Is something bothering you, I mean apart from the thefts?"

"Did I hire you to be my psychiatrist or private investigator? I'll thank you to limit your investigation to the job as I have described it. Allow me to state the situation again in case you missed it: over the course of several months, someone has been coming into my house and stealing my things. Nothing exceptionally valuable, thank God. I have found no broken windows or other evidence of a break-in. I have fired my housekeeper and hired a new one. Yet the thefts have continued."

Ben kept his expression unperturbed, though he couldn't spend five minutes in Petit's company without wanting to punch him in the nose. "Would you list the stolen items, please?" He pulled out a small pad and had a pen at the ready.

"All right," said Petit, seeming a bit mollified. "The shoes trees, as I believe I have mentioned. Pillowcases, at least six or eight. All the umbrellas from the umbrella stand." He tapped his sausage-sized finger against his chin, thinking.

"All somewhat utilitarian items, then."

"What do you mean? That they're useful? Well, anything is useful one way or another, or it wouldn't exist."

Ben shrugged. "So three different items at three different times?"

"Yes. I feel like there's something I'm forgetting, but that's what I remember for now."

"Are you often forgetful?"

"Dammit, Dufort! For the last time, you are not investigating the inside of my head! The shoe trees, please!"

Hiding a smile, Ben went upstairs followed by Petit. He rather thought that every investigation, no matter what it was about on the surface, was about the insides of people's heads. And even though he thought Petit to be a dreadful person and disliked him intensely, it was also true that the inside of Petit's head held some mysteries Ben was not incurious about.

Did someone want to torment the man? If so, the plan appeared to be working. Was someone only trying to steal things that might not be missed...no, that couldn't be right, anyone's going to notice when the pillowcases all disappear right off the pillows. Why was Petit so exceptionally grouchy, and why did his children not get along with him?

Ben did his best to remember all the questions flooding his mind as Petit showed him around the house. He took notes from time to time and did not see anything at this first inspection that gave him any hint about why Petit's household stuff was disappearing. Which was a little nerve-wracking, because Petit did not seem to be the kind of client whose middle name was Patience. He wanted answers, and it was obvious that if he didn't get them soon, things were going to turn even more testy.

7

Raphael Valette suddenly stood up from his chair and went to the window. The sky was nearly black, with clouds roiling up behind the line of trees, a stiff breeze whipping the branches. He put his palms against the glass, listening.

He heard his son in the corridor outside his door—his mind was not clear on many things, but he knew the sound of his son's footsteps as well as those of the other members of the household. Raphael spent most of his time in his room, listening with a troubled intensity to everything that went on beyond his door, and it had not taken long in the new house before he was used to the sound of the creak on the third step, the way Chloë skipped whenever she went down the long stretch of the corridor, how Violette barely made any sound at all.

He felt lifted up by the approaching storm, welcoming its violence.

Seeing an unfamiliar car in the drive, he grimaced. There were strangers in the house. He didn't want them there. With a flash of comprehension, he saw that all he had to do was descend the stairs and tell the people to leave. And if they did not listen, he would take more forceful action. He would get rid of them easily enough.

❧

SIMON VALETTE WAS STANDING in the bedroom with his shirt off, covered in stone dust. "Camille, if you had only asked me..."

"Asked you? If I had asked you, you'd have said no. You know you would have. And I just...I know it was impulsive, but it will come off all right. I'm not exactly a beginner who's never thrown a party before."

"That's not what I meant. It's only that the stress..."

"Oh, I'm absolutely sick to death of that word! If you try to make everything free of stress you end up with nothing! No existence at all that anyone would want! And I'd be stuck here with you and your father, and that Violette, and—"

Simon cocked his head and narrowed his eyes just a bit, but Camille was ever-alert to any disapproval on the part of her husband. Or anyone at all. Switching tactics, her voice softened. "I didn't mean anything by it, Simon."

"Violette is lovely with the children and we're lucky to have her. Not everyone would put up with being in a household with my father—and darling, I know it's hardly a perfect solution, but what is? I couldn't leave him in that antiseptic, uncaring place. Even on days when he didn't recognize me, I swear he was staring at me with a kind of fury because I had put him there."

"He had a bad spell this morning."

"How so?"

"Snarled at me. Told me to stop stealing his scissors. That he absolutely knew I had them and I had better put them back or else."

"That's not good."

"No, it's not. He may turn out to be more than we can handle by ourselves."

"Not yet, Camille. It's not as though he actually hurts anyone, it's just meaningless bluster."

"Paranoid bluster. It reminds me of...you know, the people in the hospital."

Simon nodded but did not want his wife going down that road. "What time are the guests coming? And how in the world did you come up with a guest list?"

"Well, I...you're going to think I'm ridiculous."

Simon went to the armoire in the hallway to get a towel. "I'm sure I won't. Just tell me. You haven't met anyone yet, have you?"

"Last week, when you went to the school, to talk to the principal? I strolled into the village by myself."

"Was that wise?"

"It doesn't matter whether it was wise!" Camille snapped. "I did it! I'm not an invalid, so don't talk to me that way! I have ears and eyes, Simon, sometimes I think you forget that. I'm not *broken*."

"Sorry, you know I'm only trying to look out for you. All right, so how did you get any names and addresses? I assume you sent invitations and didn't call people up out of the blue?"

"As I was saying, while you were at the school, I went into the village and had a coffee at the little café right on the Place, across from that statue. It was an odd time, between breakfast and lunch, so the restaurant was empty except for me. The waiter there—he's very sweet. I told him I was new to the village and asked if he could tell me about some of the people who live here."

"And then you just invited them all to dinner?" This was so out of Simon's experience that he could not quite believe his wife had done such a thing. "We've got a random assortment of people coming to dinner tonight, all friends of the waiter, people you have not actually even met?"

"You're not...that wasn't sarcasm, was it?"

"Never, my darling," Simon said, laughing and stripping off his clothes. "I'm only surprised, since back in Paris you were so

47

careful about your guest lists. I expected that you would be searching out the more prominent members of the community."

"Are you calling me a social climber?"

"If the shoe fits," said Simon, grinning. "No, darling, only joking with you. I look forward to it, honestly I do. I'm going to clean up and then see how I can help. Is the woman you hired to do the cooking working out all right?"

"Well, I saw her car pull up, so I know she arrived on time. She's been in the kitchen with her daughter helping for several hours now. The main thing is, we can't judge that until we taste the food," said Camille. "Obviously," she said under her breath.

If he had his way, she thought bitterly, I would stay in the bedroom with the door closed, and he would be free to do anything at all, as though he were single again with no responsibilities. She had known Simon since she was a young girl—their parents had been close friends, and the families had even vacationed together when they were teenagers. Their romance had been all but inevitable. After Simon had distinguished himself at school and then at ENA, they had, to the great satisfaction of both their parents, been married and quickly had two girls.

That success notwithstanding, Simon and Camille both sometimes admitted (only to themselves) that happiness had been elusive. They had done everything that was expected of them—studied hard, married and had children, been successful at business and socially—and found that, somehow, all of that accomplishment added up to very little.

Camille dressed three times and each time rejected the look; a pile of dresses lay in a heap on the end of the bed. It felt impossible to hit the right note when she had no idea what sort of people were going to arrive on her doorstep. They had all RSVP'd to say yes: fourteen, including her and Simon. Perhaps she should have started with something less ambitious? But it was helpful to have enough people so that one could get a little lost in the crowd, so that the group had enough energy to run on its own without her. She could slip away, if need be, for a few moments alone without her absence being noticed.

She settled on a pair of beautifully tailored slacks of a wool so light it barely felt as though she had anything on. A cream-colored silk blouse, heels because she was on the short side. She knew it was time to check on the kitchen but she stayed a long time sitting at the vanity, looking at herself in the mirror, ostensibly trying to decide which earrings to wear, and whether to put on the onyx necklace Simon had given her for her thirtieth birthday, which now seemed a lifetime ago though it was only a few years.

Before Simon got out of the shower—and he always indulged himself with a household's worth of hot water, staying in so long his fingers pruned—Camille went downstairs to check on the dining room and see how the cook was getting on. She left the girls to Violette.

The table was dressed simply and elegantly, with white candles in silver candlesticks in a row down the center, and a silver bowl of light pink roses. Thick linen napkins embroidered with a capital V so large it bordered on egocentric, heavy silver place settings, the mahogany table polished to a high shine. She worried it looked too Parisian, and her guests would think she was putting on airs. But it was too late to change now; they were due in half an hour.

Quickly Camille stepped to the sideboard where the wine was decanted, poured herself a glass, and downed it in one gulp. Her doctor in Paris had warned her that alcohol was contraindicated with her prescriptions, but surely he did not mean that she could not allow herself a minor fortification before hosting a dinner party of strangers?

In the kitchen, all was bedlam.

Camille stood in the doorway, eyes wide, watching Merla, who had been recommended by Pascal, whirl from stove to sink to table, her hair flying up in a cloud around her head from the steam of something cooking at a rapid boil. Merla had brought

her daughter to serve and act as sous-chef, and the girl was chop-
ping onions with a ferocity that made Camille feel a little queasy.

"Merla? How is everything? I do appreciate your hard work.
May I—"

"Everything under control madame, no time to chat. First
course will be ready in fifty minutes on the nose."

"Good. It smells wonderful. I'm very—"

"Yes, madame. Ophélie, that's enough! You don't need to chop
the onions all the way to mush, it will ruin the texture of the dish.
Go have a drink, madame. I'll have Ophélie come out with a tray
of tidbits once enough of the guests have gotten here. I hope no
one's put off by the storm."

"Storm?" It had not occurred to Camille to check the weather.
An unpleasant surge of adrenaline shot through her body.

Merla opened the oven and Camille could feel the heat all the
way across the room. "Take a look," the cook said, jerking her
head at the window.

The sky was dark and foreboding. In September, it stayed
light until eight-thirty, but it looked as though night was falling
before seven. "Oh no," said Camille, leaving the kitchen and
heading directly to the sideboard for another small
reinforcement.

There was some sort of hubbub under the dining room table.
Piping voices, and then a loud smack.

"Chloë! You are horrible!"

"Come along now, girls," said Violette, crawling out from
under the table. "Oh! *Bonsoir*, Madame Valette."

"*Bonsoir*, Violette," said Camille, so frostily that even in the
middle of their fight the girls noticed. "My guests will be arriving
any minute. Are the girls clean and dressed? No?" She did not
offer any criticism besides her expression, which was plenty.

Violette tugged on Chloë's hand. "I said, come along," she
pleaded.

"I want to sit under here during the dinner," the girl said. "We can poke the grownup's legs and tickle them!" she said with glee, thrilled with her idea.

"You tickle too hard," said Giselle, the older girl, coming out from under the table. She gave Violette a sympathetic look, knowing her little sister was not easy to manage. "Come on!" she said excitedly. "First one to our room wins a prize!"

Chloë shot out from under the table and got ahead of her big sister on the way upstairs, Violette following gratefully. Once upstairs, she told the girls to wash their faces while she took their dresses out of the armoire.

"Now, listen to me," she said when the girls were back in their bedroom, faces glowing. "It's important that your behavior be a step above the usual tonight, do you understand? Your family wants to make a good impression, after all. It would be best if they didn't go back to their friends and report that the Valette children are a pack of wild beasts who don't know how to behave."

Chloë stuck out her tongue, put her fingers in her ears and up her nose, and said, "Bah-de-beee, bah-de-doo."

Giselle rolled her eyes.

"All right then, here are your dresses. I'll be back in a few minutes to give you a last once-over." Violette stepped out into the corridor, about to go up to her room for a precious few moments to herself. Just as she was closing the door behind her, Simon came out of his bedroom. He was dressed in a sport-coat and a crisp shirt with an open collar, his thick hair swept back from his deeply tanned face.

They stood for a long moment, looking at each other.

"Bonsoir, Violette," Simon finally said softly.

"Bonsoir, monsieur," answered Violette, edging past him on the way to the stairs to the third floor and holding his gaze the whole way.

❧ 8 ❧

"It *is* odd, but since when have we ever minded odd?" Molly was saying to Ben as she tried on dresses and discarded them, one after the other. "I guess if you're new in town and want to meet people, you could do worse than just going ahead and inviting a random group over for dinner. And please, the next time I breathe a word about *Pâtisserie* Bujold, divert my attention to something else, for heaven's sake. I can't find a single thing to wear that fits!"

"You look incredible," said Ben slipping an arm around her waist, which was thicker than it used to be, no question about that, but he meant every word of the compliment.

"You say all the right things," said Molly. "I do like that about you. So, have you picked up anything about the Valettes around the village? Is Pascal really the only person who's met them?"

"As far as I could tell. The wife—Camille, I think her name is —dropped by the café a few days ago. I talked to Pascal but he didn't have much to say. Could barely give me a decent description. Too bad really—a guy in his position at the café could be an A plus valuable informant, but Pascal just doesn't fly that way."

"He thinks the best of people. But we know better."

"Do you think our work makes us pessimistic about humanity?"

Molly considered, turning one way and another while looking at herself in the mirror. "Not really. Actually, it's made me more sympathetic, in a weird way. Like, I'm sorry that people are so wounded, so desperate, that they feel they have to kill someone."

"I'm not quite as generous as you."

"But at least you fit into your trousers."

They managed to finish dressing, say goodbye to Bobo, and get into Ben's car before the rain started.

"Looks like it's going to be a whopper," said Ben, looking up at the clouds, which seemed to be almost boiling.

"'It was a dark and stormy night...'" intoned Molly.

Just as they turned into the Valette's driveway, the skies opened. Ben had an umbrella, but despite his most gallant efforts, the wind was blowing so hard that they arrived on the Valette's doorstep like a pair of drowned rats.

Camille opened the door and quickly ushered them in. Introductions all around, and Simon went to a small table in the foyer and poured them glasses of champagne.

"So!" said Camille with forced brightness.

"It's a dark and stormy night," said Simon.

"Just what we were saying," said Ben.

The foursome struggled through some small talk, but for whatever reason it did not flow easily, and all four were relieved to hear the doorbell ring.

Simon opened the door, and in came Lawrence, and then Pascal, with his arm protectively around Marie-Claire Levy, who was currently head at *L'Insitut* Degas, the art school just down the road from the Valette's.

"Bonsoir!" cried Molly, thrilled to see so many friends at once.

"Ghastly night," said Lawrence, shivering as he peeled off his wet overcoat. "Though I am always glad for an excuse to wear this trench. Burberry, 1972."

"Where in the world do you find this stuff?" said Molly. "Do you have a vintage clothing supplier tucked away somewhere?"

"It's no good telling all one's secrets," said Lawrence as he kissed both her cheeks. "Everyone would ignore me if every last bit of the mystery was gone."

"Hardly," said Molly with a laugh.

Simon was pouring glasses for everyone, the doorbell kept ringing and more drenched guests poured in amid exclamations and some shrieking, until all twelve guests were present, accounted for, and sipping excellent champagne from antique flutes. Pascal saw with some surprise that Camille had invited all the people he had suggested, and every single one had come.

Edmond Nugent, the *pâtissier* at Pâtisserie Bujold. Dr. Vernay, the village doctor. Lapin and his wife, Anne-Marie. Rex Ford, a longtime teacher at Degas. Molly's best friend Frances, with her husband Nico, who tended bar in the village.

"It's been so warm, but with this crazy storm raging, I lit a fire in the library—why doesn't everyone come this way, if you'd like?" Simon said, raising his voice to be heard.

"Pretty nice place," Frances whispered to her pal Molly, as she gazed at the art on the foyer walls.

Molly nodded, checking to see whether the hostess was close enough to overhear.

"I wonder where the money came from," said Frances, a little too loudly.

"Hush," said Molly. "Do try not to insult them before we've even sat down to dinner."

"I am horribly affronted at your suggestion," answered Frances, giving her friend a dig in the ribs.

"The champagne is quite good," murmured Nico, as the group filed through the dining room and into the cozy library. "Wish I'd gotten a look at the vintage."

"The table looks lovely," Molly said to Camille, who seemed on edge.

"Thank you," said Camille. The two women looked at each other for a moment, but once again, the conversational thread wasn't strong enough to pull them along, and Molly and Frances continued on their way to the library.

Simon was standing in front of the fire, but he stepped aside so that some of the damper guests could dry off in front of the blaze.

"I don't remember ever seeing the sky look like it did on the way over," said Edmond. "A deep dark gray, with streaks of black. And this kind of humidity is not kind to dough, I will tell you that much. I'm going to have to make all manner of adjustments tomorrow if I don't want to be flooded with complaints."

"Oh, come on, you don't get complaints, do you?" said Molly.

"You'd be surprised," sniffed Edmond. "People adore complaining. With some in the village, it's practically an Olympic sport. And if they think it will get them a discount or a freebie, they will go on and on to the point where you want to strangle them."

"Oh dear," said Camille, looking stricken.

"Baba-loo, baba-leeeee!" shouted Chloë as she ran through the library waving her hands in the air. She wore a pretty dress with a wide blue sash but no shoes.

Marie-Claire Levy smiled. "Sometimes I wish I were still six," she said to Pascal, who kissed her forehead and tightened his arm around her waist.

"Where is Violette?" said Camille, plaintively. "I'm so sorry," she said to Molly. "The nanny is supposed to be looking after the girls, and I can't imagine where she has disappeared to. Chloë!" she called, but the girl was long gone.

"Oh, please don't apologize, she is adorable," said Molly, who often wished she were still six, too.

Holding her hand to her brow, Camille went quickly back through the dining room; Molly hoped she didn't find the nanny too quickly so the girl could prolong her freedom.

The library was not a big room and the guests were packed rather tight. Lawrence began talking to Rex Ford about an exhibit of modern art he had seen in Paris a month earlier. Dr. Vernay stepped away from the fire to give Pascal a chance to dry the legs of his trousers. And Frances marveled at the fresco on the ceiling.

"How old *is* this place?" she asked Nico. "I thought frescoes were like, really old, like Michelangelo-old. Isn't this house younger than that?"

"Considerably," said Nico. "But you know how people are— they get enthusiasms. One of the owners somewhere along the way must've gotten interested in frescoes, and wanted to have one, and the long-suffering spouse went along with it, knowing that it would be easier than trying to get in the way."

"What a weird thing to get obsessed with."

"You're not a fan of cherubs?"

"I have never considered that question before," said Frances, pretending to think very deeply. Her jet-black hair had gotten long, well past her shoulders, and her skin was luminous and pale as it always was, no matter how much time she spent outdoors.

There was a murmur of appreciation as the cook's daughter, Ophélie, appeared with a tray of crabmeat wrapped in puff pastry. Edmond took one and peered at it, inspecting the puff pastry to see if was homemade. Molly popped one in her mouth and grinned at Ben. Conversations were starting to take off; the room was getting noisy.

"Wait," Molly said to Ophélie, "I need to see if that was as good as I think it was." Ophélie winked and Molly took another. "Where did Camille go?" she said in a low voice to Ben.

Ben shrugged. "There's not really enough room in here for everyone. Maybe she went to find the nanny?"

"Isn't that girl too old for a nanny? Or is there a baby as well?" Molly was ever curious about children, her secret wish to have some of her own never having come true.

"Castillac is not much of a village for nannies," said Ben. "In fact, I'm not sure we've ever had any. Possibly the Fleurays, up at Château Marainte? Anyway, I'm not going to be much help about any of that."

Violette appeared just then, scanning the crowd, and then bending down to look, but the room was too crowded for her to see whether Chloë was hiding somewhere or had moved on.

"Have you misplaced something, Mademoiselle Crespelle?" Simon asked, teasing her.

Violette smiled. "Your youngest is going to be the death of me!" she said, craning her neck to see into the corners of the room.

"'Crespelle,' such a delicious surname you have," said Dr. Vernay. "I remember a trip to Rome once, when my wife and I ate crespelles by the wagonload." He looked misty-eyed, thinking back on it.

Violette nodded patiently, having had that particular conversation a thousand times. "Well, off I go to see where the little monkeys have got to!"

Lawrence managed to squeeze through to get next to Molly. "Those little crab doo-dads were extremely good," he said. "Portends well for dinner, don't you think?"

Molly was just about to answer when a sudden movement in the doorway startled her. An older man stood there, brandishing a fire extinguisher. He was dressed in a bathrobe—a rather nice one, she couldn't help noticing.

"Is something on fire?" she asked politely.

"Who *are* all these people?" Raphael said. Then louder, "Get *out!* Get out of my house! No one wants you here!"

The crowd fell back, stunned and a little frightened. Simon sprang to his father's side. "We're just having a few people for dinner," he said, reaching for the extinguisher.

"I don't want all of this!" shouted Raphael. "I don't want strangers in my house!" He lifted the fire extinguisher over his head and jerked it, as though about to hurl it into the crowd.

Simon put his hands on the heavy extinguisher and forced his father to lower it. "Come on now, come with me, Father," he said, his voice soothing.

Raphael looked startled himself, as though unsure how he had found himself in the library with a fire extinguisher.

"Come on," said his son. "We're having a very good dinner tonight, and I'll bring a tray up to your room. Are you hungry? Would you like a glass of champagne?"

Molly thought maybe giving the man alcohol wasn't the best idea, but figured Simon knew what he was doing. Her own father had suffered with Alzheimer's but had been lucky enough not to linger long.

After a short pause, the guests began talking as though there had been no interruption. Out of the corner of her eye, Molly saw another young girl, older than the first, also dressed up and wearing cute patent leather flats, sidle into the library. Molly went toward her.

"Bonsoir," she said, holding out her hand. "I'm Molly Sutton. I'm guessing you are a Valette?"

"Yes, madame. I'm Gisele. Have you seen my little sister?"

"She ran through a little while ago, but not since. I hope she didn't go outside, because it is absolutely ridiculous out there!"

Gisele laughed. "It's my little sister who's ridiculous. Anyway, thanks." She moved through the guests without attracting any attention as Molly watched.

Lightning flashed across the sky and a crack of thunder was so loud the guests gasped. Molly thought the storm was a happy bit of luck for the hostess—it made the night exciting and unusual, and gave everyone something to talk about. She could already imagine years in the future, sitting on a stool at Chez Papa, and saying, "Remember that crazy storm the night we went to the Valette's for the first time?"

And the room did feel electric, or at least as electric as things got in Castillac. Every drop of the champagne was guzzled down,

NELL GODDIN

and every tidbit of crab gobbled up. The group shared gossip and jokes, and for once, no one had any bad news.

"All right," said Camille, with careful consideration to timing with the kitchen. "Shall we be seated?"

At each place was a small card with a name written in an elegant script. The guests moved around, looking for the spots, all smiling from the champagne and anticipation of a delightful dinner. The gourmands among them noted the gilt-rimmed bread and butter plates, three forks, the two wine glasses at each place, and smiled to themselves at the luxurious promise of it all.

Simon returned before everyone was seated. "As you all might have guessed, my father has not been himself of late. Ah, what would life be without a bit of drama?" he asked from the head of the table. Molly was charmed, glad that he did not seem ashamed of his father. But as she glanced to the other end of the table to the hostess, she saw to her surprise that Camille was staring at her husband with an expression of unalloyed hatred.

It was only a split-second, but Molly was sure that was what she saw.

❧ 9 ❧

"In Paris, it would never do to have a dinner so unbalanced between men and women," Camille was saying as she slid into her chair, held out for her by Lawrence. "But you know, Pascal was so kind to make my guest list, and hopefully Castillac is a bit more forgiving about those old rules than some of my friends at home."

"This is home now," said Simon lightly from the other end of the table.

"Oh yes. I didn't mean..." Camille trailed off, her cheeks reddening.

"I feel so special, making it to your list," Lapin said to Pascal with a smirk.

"I asked him to invite all the most interesting people," said Camille. "And the best doctor, because of course the girls need looking after."

Dr. Vernay bowed gallantly and lifted his glass.

"Of course, Castillac is not nearly as exciting as Paris," Lawrence said. "But I think you will find we don't die of boredom, one way or another."

"It's a big adjustment, for sure," Frances said, in English. After living in the village for nearly two years, she could understand French quite well, but tried to get away with speaking in English whenever she could; she guessed correctly that the Valettes were fluent, and so from that point the conversation swerved back and forth between the two languages, depending on who was talking to whom.

Ophélie came in with an enormous tray, which she placed on a sideboard.

"I skipped lunch," Marie-Claire whispered to Ben. "I have a feeling this is going to be a magnificent dinner."

"You've eaten Merla's cooking before?"

"Only once. It was unforgettable."

Molly was on the same side of the table as Ben, but she leaned forward to say something to him and saw Marie-Claire whispering in his ear. Well, that's just rude, she thought, remembering that Marie-Claire had been Ben's girlfriend when she first met him, and then chastising herself for feeling like a jealous teenager.

As Ophélie began to move around the long table serving small plates of salmon rillettes on a bed of endive, Violette came to the doorway and paused, then leaned down to Camille. "I'm so sorry to intrude on the party," she said in a low voice, "but I cannot find the girls anywhere. I'm not worried, I'm sure they're just hiding someplace, but wanted to let you know."

"You don't need to bother Camille with that," said Simon from the other end of the table, guessing what Violette was saying. "I'm sure they're off playing somewhere out of the rain."

Another flash followed by a loud crack of thunder, and the guests looked out of the window to see the sky lit up again and again as the storm rolled through. As Molly's eyes came back to the table, she noticed Lapin looking at Violette in something of his old, lascivious manner. She watched him lick his lips as though the nanny herself might be on the menu. Not wanting Lapin's new wife to feel wounded by this display, she stretched her leg out to give Lapin a swift kick from across the table, but kicked something much closer. A small yelp, and Molly realized that at least one of the Valette daughters was under the table. Lapin was still staring so Molly gave it another try, this time connecting with his ankle. He startled and looked away from Violette but did not meet Molly's eye.

The nanny was no beauty, but attractive enough, Molly thought, watching the young woman go back to the foyer. I wonder how that plays out in a marriage, with a third adult—young and unattached—in the household. Must take a lot of confidence on the wife's part, she pondered, looking back at Camille and doubting she had it. Pretending to drop her napkin, she peeked under the table and saw the two girls huddled against a central support. Chloë held a finger to her lips and Molly nodded with a grin.

"It is wonderful how you used smoked and fresh salmon in this dish," Edmond said to Camille. "It makes the texture so much more interesting."

"I can't take any credit," said Camille. "Merla deserves it all. Though I did put together the menu—what a struggle that was! You never know what the weather's going to be in September, do you? And so many other considerations. I didn't want to serve the standard dishes of the region, which you've all had a million times. Or something so fancy you'd think I was—" she stopped in mid-sentence, realizing she was saying things better kept to herself. "Anyway," she said, trying to recover, but could think of nowhere to turn the conversation.

"Would it be terribly impertinent for me to ask what the main course will be?" asked Lawrence, trying to come to her rescue.

"Lamb," Camille said, but was too off-balance to say anything further. She gulped a bit of the lovely Château Latour Ophélie had poured and busied herself spreading rillettes on a toast.

"I adore lamb above all things," said Dr. Vernay from down the table. "I do wish my wife had been able to come—she is a great lover of lamb as well. But she did not want to pass along her head cold to the children. And a nasty cold it is."

"Marie-Claire, not to talk shop, but have you finalized the schedule yet? Classes start next week, for God's sake."

"Really, Rex, we don't need to talk about that right now. If you have anything to offer besides wanting to rush me, you may call me at home tomorrow."

Rex shrugged. "Only want to do the best for our talented students," he said, with a notable edge of sarcasm.

It wasn't the most successful dinner party ever, that was true —the conversation ambled here and there, sometimes diverting but never captivating. There was laughter, but not very much. The guests outdid themselves in eating, however, enjoying the seven-hour roast leg of lamb and all the vegetables that came with it, infused by the meat drippings and herbs. The wine was of very high quality and Ophélie generous in refilling glasses, and towards the end it seemed as though just maybe, the party was going to reach that state of contentment and conviviality where the jokes start coming faster and everyone starts to feel a great deal of warmth for the others in the group.

It almost got there.

Ophélie was just coming into the dining room with an impressive looking pair of mocha dacquoise cakes when a crack sounded even louder than the others, a series of flashes ripped across the sky, and the lights in the house went out.

There was a quiet pause, no more than a fraction of a second, as people tried to assimilate this new fact, that the dining room was lit only by three candles. The other guests' faces seemed to flicker for a moment, as though they were images in a film and not actual people, and then a gust of wind coming from the direction of the foyer blew out the candles and they were all in darkness.

The fourteen people at the party could literally not see their hands in front of their faces.

Or tell who was screaming.

❧ 10 ❧

Lightning flashed again but it was over too quickly for people to get their bearings. Chairs scraped as some guests pushed away from the table and got up. The screaming tailed off and then stopped; all at once, everyone began talking.

"Please, everyone, stay calm. It's probably just a blown fuse. Electrical system is old," said Simon, again using the calm voice he had used with his father.

Loud laughter from the Molly and Lawrence end of the table.

"Molly?" said Ben.

"I'm here. I'm just hoping that cake survived, I had a quick glimpse and it looked amazing."

More laughter, more scraping of chairs. Giggling from under the table followed by "Ssshhhh!"

"I think I'll go up to the landing on the stairs by the window, chérie. I want to see if any trees are down," Anne-Marie said. No answer from Lapin.

"Camille?" asked Ben. He was out of his chair, feeling his way towards the door, thinking he might be able to give Simon a hand with the fuse box. No answer from Camille.

"Get *out!*" a voice thundered from upstairs.

"That must be Monsieur Valette," said Anne-Marie, about to leave the room but changing her mind, having no desire to run into Simon's father and his fire extinguisher.

"Everyone's all right? I'm going to find Simon and see if I can help," said Ben.

"No, I am not all right!" shouted Edmond. "I don't like this, I don't like it at all. The darkness is...is suffocating us all!"

"Good heavens, just breathe," said Frances. "See? You're not suffocating. Maybe you're hoping that cake tips over so we won't be comparing it to yours?"

Chuckling from somewhere.

"Pascal?" said Marie-Claire, though not from the direction she had been seated. No answer from Pascal.

"Does anyone have matches?" asked Nico. "We could just relight the candles on the table. Can somebody on the window side of the room make sure the windows are all the way closed, so they don't get blown out again?"

They were in the kind of darkness you don't experience except in the less populated areas of the world. No stars or moon could be seen thanks to the cloud-covered sky, and no light from the village. They could see no better than with their eyes closed—no shapes, no contour, no shadow. Just absolute pitch black in every direction.

"This is getting a little ridiculous," said Rex Ford. "I have half a mind to go home."

"Lapin?" said Anne-Marie, listening out to see if the coast was clear of the senior Monsieur Valette. No answer from Lapin.

And then, without warning, the lights came back on, brighter than before since the switches had all been turned on by people flipping them to see if they worked. Everyone squinted, making exclamations of "Finally!" along with laughter.

Another pause while they adjusted to seeing again.

Rex Ford was standing in the doorway to the library. Edmond was sweating profusely and nearly panting, having never realized before that he was profoundly afraid of the dark, or at least the dark in the Valette's dining room.

"Where is everybody?" said Molly. She looked under the table but the girls were gone. The only guests still at the table were she, Lawrence, Frances, and Nico.

"How many dinner guests does it take to change a light bulb?" said Frances, and then howled at her own joke.

Molly got up and went into the foyer, where she found Camille standing by the small table from which the champagne had been served.

"It's ruined now, isn't it. Monsieur Ford just ran out—he left with barely a word." Her shoulders slumped down and she turned away.

Molly was normally full of sympathy, but something about Camille struck her as self-pitying, which didn't go down particularly well even after that incredible lamb.

No, she thought, it's not self-pitying, exactly—it's that I haven't once seen her say a single word to either of her children. Well, maybe she's just preoccupied, having a dinner party with a pile of strangers. I suppose anyone would be rattled.

Marie-Claire Levy came downstairs, her heels tapping a brisk rhythm. "I just took a look out that big window on the landing," she said. "It looks as though the storm is not letting up one bit."

"Get out!" shouted Monsieur Valette, loud enough that Molly stepped back even though she was all the way downstairs and not close to him.

"The storm must be very upsetting for him," said Molly to Camille, but Camille didn't seem to hear, and she went off to the kitchen without another word.

At one end of the foyer, under the stairs, was a door to the basement through which Pascal suddenly appeared. "Well, I got it straightened out," he said to Marie-Claire. "Very thankful that the previous owner had left a packet of fuses right on top of the fuse box. And for the mini-flashlight I keep on my key-ring."

"Flashlight on your key-ring! I had no idea you were such a Boy Scout!" cried Molly.

"Boy Scout?" said Pascal.

Molly laughed. "Oh, it's—just that you are so prepared, is all I mean. Is Simon still in the basement?"

Pascal looked confused. "Simon was never in the basement."

Molly stared. "He wasn't with you, fixing the fuse?"

Pascal shrugged. "I haven't seen him. So...what happens now? Are people just going home?"

"I would rather like to, if it's all right," said Marie-Claire, and Pascal nodded.

Molly drifted back to the dining room, where Nico and Frances were digging into the mocha dacquoise.

"Franny!"

"Well, it's not like we just wandered in off the street. We were supposed to get a slice, right? Is it so terrible that we helped ourselves?"

Nico just grinned and licked icing off his lips.

Simon came trotting downstairs. "Thank you to whoever worked the miracle with the lights!"

"It was no problem," said Pascal.

"I felt I should attend to Father first. Very much appreciated. Now, has anyone seen Violette and my daughters?"

Marie-Claire and Pascal shook their heads. They wanted to leave, but now that Simon was back it felt awkward, so they stood in the foyer waiting to find out what next.

"I'll look for them," said Molly. She had been enjoying her time at the Valette's but thought it was rather sad the way no one seemed to pay any attention to the girls at all. Where had Camille disappeared to?

In the interest of being thorough, Molly checked the basement first, then stuck her head in the kitchen. Merla and Ophélie were sitting down, having a glass of wine before beginning to clean up. No sign of the girls.

Some of the remaining guests were in the dining room eating slices of mocha dacquoise cake under blazing lights. No one had bothered to re-light the candles and the uplifted mood of the dinner had of course evaporated, but they were all pleased nonetheless because the cake was indeed magnificent: a layer of almond meringue, buttercream frosting, and a topping of rum-spiked whipped cream, bits of which were seen on the cheeks of various guests as they dug in with fervor.

"Anyone seen Lapin?" Anne-Marie asked.

"Nope. Have some cake!" said Frances, pointing to the massacred remains with her fork.

Anne-Marie shook her head, feeling worried. She left the dining room and went into the library.

And then she screamed.

Molly leapt up from the table, followed quickly by Ben and Nico. All of them had a sick feeling in their stomachs, feeling pretty sure that Anne-Marie's scream was not just melodrama or overstimulation due to the storm.

They were not wrong.

11

Molly was first to the library. Anne-Marie stood with her hand over her mouth, looking down at Violette, who was stretched out behind a wing chair next to the fireplace. She was face-up, eyes closed. Her dress was not hitched up, her hands lay at her sides; it was almost as though the young woman had decided to lie down next to the fire for a nap, yet Anne-Marie and Molly both felt the situation was not so innocent.

"Violette?" said Anne-Marie, squatting down next to her, and putting her hand on the young woman's arm. Violette did not move.

"Dr. Vernay!" cried Molly. The doctor hustled in immediately and bent down beside the nanny.

Molly shot Ben a look and shook her head slowly. Ben nodded, then pulled out his cell and called Paul-Henri at the station. He was about to call Florian Nagrand, the coroner, but did not want to rush things.

Meanwhile, the doctor had put his fingers on Violette's neck to feel for a pulse, then put his head against her chest.

He sat back on his heels. "I'm afraid...there's nothing to be done," he said, shaking his head.

"What happened?" said Molly. "Can you tell how...how she died?"

Ben went ahead and texted the coroner, Florian Nagrand, then looked around at the guests in the dining room. "Frances," he said. "Would you go find Simon and Camille? There's been a... well, to speak plainly, the nanny is dead."

Frances's eyes flew wide open. "The *what?*"

"Just go find them," said Ben. Returning to the library, he waved at Molly, Vernay, and Anne-Marie standing by the body. "All right, all of you need to come this way. Don't touch anything on your way out."

"Are you...are you saying this is a crime scene?" asked Molly, though of course she had been thinking along those lines herself.

"We don't know yet, right, Gérard?" said Ben. "But it's good practice to take precautions, just in case."

Dr. Vernay shrugged. He and Anne-Marie passed through and Ben pulled the pocket doors of the library closed, then realized he should secure the door leading into the library from the kitchen as well.

"Stay in front of the door, chérie," he said to Molly in a low voice. "I'll be right back."

No sign of Simon or Camille. Dr. Vernay had taken a seat at the dining room table and was answering questions from the others.

"You can't tell how she died? Was it...was it natural?" asked Anne-Marie. Her face was pale.

"I can't say without a thorough examination. I didn't notice anything out of order—she certainly wasn't shot or stabbed, in any case. Of course, my expertise is with the living." He passed a hand through his sparse hair. "It's true that it's not unheard-of, someone this young dying of a heart attack. Though it would be quite unusual. Terrible thing," he added, shaking his head.

"Anne-Marie, if you can—could you try to find Chloë and Giselle? This is going to be an awful shock for them. Ben has parked me right here guarding the library or I'd come with you. And where is Lapin?"

"I just want to go home," said Marie-Claire. She had not had any cake but sat with her coat on, looking anxious. Pascal jerked his head toward the door and nodded, and the two of them left by the front door. A burst of wind whipped through but the rain had finally abated.

Molly stood with her back against the pocket doors, thinking quickly. Ben almost certainly believes Violette was murdered, she thought. Right in the next room, with such a crowd here! It seemed impossible. How long were the lights out, anyway? And if she had been murdered, how? Molly longed to get back in the library and have a look around, but she knew Ben would disapprove. And she had no desire to get on the wrong side of the new chief of gendarmes, who must be on her way that very second.

"What in the world?" said Simon, striding into the dining room followed by Frances, who went straight to Nico and wrapped her arms around him.

"I'm sorry, it's obviously your house, but Ben told me not to let anyone in. Potential crime scene," said Molly with a grimace.

"Crime scene? What are you talking about? If something is wrong with Violette, I want to see her!"

"She's dead, Simon," Molly said quietly. "Here, I'll slide the door open so you can see for yourself."

Molly pulled the doors apart about ten centimeters, and Simon stuck his head in. She thought she heard a quick intake of breath.

"Has someone called an ambulance?" he said, his voice rising.

Molly shook her head. She could see him slowly taking in the situation.

"Are you telling me that Violette has been murdered in our house, right in the middle of a dinner party?" He was incredulous. "How is that even possible?"

No one answered, since there was no answer to give.

"So what now?" he asked Molly. "Is Ben—have the gendarmes been called?"

"Ben used to be the chief, so he has things in hand. Perhaps you want to go to your wife and children?"

Simon looked at her distractedly, then blinked several times. "Yes, of course," he said, and left the dining room, his expression stony.

"I guess we should all go home," said Frances. "I'm feeling like a kind of grisly spectator, watching this whole thing play out. That poor young woman. I'm about to throw up my cake."

"Do you and Ben need us?" asked Nico, and when Molly shook her head, the couple left, Dr. Vernay following them out.

Way too many people to keep track of, Molly thought, still standing against the door, trying to fix in her mind all the comings and goings she could remember over the course of the night.

And where was Lapin?

❦

THE WHITE VAN of Florian Nagrand pulled up while Molly was still standing guard at the library door.

"I'm very glad to see you!" she said, as the big man bustled through the dining room, smelling of tobacco and smoke, his black bag in hand.

"Always on the scene, eh?" he said, making a sly smile as he opened the pocket doors and stepped through.

Ben came into the dining room and put his arm around Molly's shoulders. "Once Paul-Henri gets here, we should probably leave," he said quietly. "Just to give the new chief some room. But in the meantime, see what you can overhear. Still no sign of Camille?"

Molly shook her head and then went to have a look around as discreetly as possible. She was worried about the girls, not having heard or seen them since just after the lights went out. It was strange, the way Camille had disappeared. The house was roomy, but not so large that multiple people could get lost in it and not be overheard at all. She must have heard the commotion down-stairs. And would a woman of her background just vanish in the middle of her own dinner party?

Molly considered for a moment, and decided to see if anyone was still in the kitchen. For sure, the gendarmes would not appre-ciate her talking to the cook before they did, but the opportunity was too good to waste.

Merla was at the sink, washing a pot, while her daughter unloaded the dishwasher.

"Bonsoir," said Molly, and introduced herself. "Though I suppose it's not a very good evening at all, is it. Did Monsieur Dufort tell you what has happened?"

Merla nodded, her expression dark. Ophélie brushed a tear away and kept stacking plates. They did not speak.

Molly had been hoping at least one of them would be chatty. She took a deep breath. "I want to tell you how much I was enjoying the meal before the lights went out. The lamb was abso-lutely superb! I know you must have some secret ingredients in there somewhere—I could identify some of the herbs but there was an elusive flavor, something extraordinary I couldn't quite out my finger on…"

Merla smiled faintly. She started to say something but only got out a half-syllable before stopping herself.

Dang it, thought Molly, what does she want to tell me? And why does she feel like she can't say it?

"Are you still hungry?" asked Ophélie. "I could heat up a few of those crab hors d'oeuvres you liked."

"I'm stuffed, really I am…but maybe just one, if you'll join me?"

Ophélie got a tray from the refrigerator and peeled back the plastic wrap.

"I don't know why you want to go messing everything up again," said her mother.

"I'm not. Just warming up a few of these. I'll put some in for you, too."

Merla looked somewhat mollified, but turned back to the sink with her lips firmly pressed together.

"What did you do when the lights went out?" Molly asked. "That was a little scary."

"At least we had the pilot light on the stove," said Ophélie. "So it was dark, but not like the rest of the house. Plus we're sort of used to it, because the power at our house goes out all the time. I think we've got some mice in the basement who keep chewing on the wires or something."

"Ophélie!" said Merla.

"It's not a big deal, Mother. Not like Molly's going to be running all over the village telling people about how our electrical system needs updating. For one thing, that's boring. And for another, you've heard of Molly Sutton, right? She listens more than she talks."

Molly was momentarily flustered by the unexpected compliment and could think of nothing to say except thank you.

Merla faced her, crossing her arms. "I haven't been in this house long. Madame hired me for this dinner, and I hoped it might lead to something more permanent, you understand? So I came one day to talk about the menu, and then early this morning to start cooking. That is the only time I have been here."

Molly nodded, having the sense not to interrupt.

"I am a plain speaker, Madame Sutton. And I will tell you this: that nanny was the best person in this house. Well, apart from the children." She turned back around and scrubbed the pot with vigor.

"Are the kids okay?" asked Ophélie.

"Honestly, I don't know. I haven't seen them since the lights went out."

Ophélie took the pan of heated hors d'oeuvres from the oven, and the three women picked them up, lightly burning their fingers, and ate. Molly had many more questions to ask, but decided it was more important to tread lightly so that they would trust her, rather than hit them with rapid-fire questions at such a sensitive moment.

She ate six more of the crab doo-dads, as Lawrence called them.

And where the hell had Lawrence gone? Was there a secret pit somewhere, swallowing people up left and right?

"I'm sorry if I sound nosy," Molly said. "But I can't help wondering—had Violette seemed ill at all? Fragile?"

Merla grunted. "If you think that girl died all on her own, with no assistance? Then I don't know if you're such a great detective after all."

Molly would have laughed if the subject weren't so somber. "So you think it was murder," she said softly.

"Violette has been running after those two young girls all day. In and out, past the kitchen window, riding bicycles, what have you. She was *not* ill."

"Thank you," said Molly. "I appreciate hearing your observations very much. If it's all right," she added, on her way out, "could I drop by sometime for a chat? Or maybe you'd like to come to La Baraque? I'm not at all your equal in the kitchen, but you won't starve!"

Merla shrugged but Ophélie looked thrilled. "I'll give you a call," said Molly, and went back through the swinging door to the foyer, set on finding the young Valettes and making sure they were safe. The poor things would undoubtedly be very upset, given the horrible turn the night had taken.

What was going on in this house? She looked around at the details of the decoration, as if the wallpaper or silver teapot could have something to tell her. Eventually she heard young voices and headed in their direction.

12

Florian was an old hand, and he set about this latest case by going through his usual careful procedures, step by painstaking step, taking notes as he went along. He was pleased to be the first on the scene and hoped the gendarmes took their time and did not arrive too quickly.

Ben had been a colleague for many years, back when he was a gendarme. He knew Florian well, and they had always had a mutually agreeable relationship, occasionally cutting the odd bureaucratic corner when it was sensible to do so. Now that he was a civilian, Ben had enough decorum to stay out of the library, though he watched the coroner work from the dining room. Molly was leaning so far into the library she was about to fall onto the rug.

"Can't you ask him *anything?*" she whispered to Ben.

He shook his head.

"Just whether it was a natural death or a murder? Just that one tiny question?"

"Patience, Molly! We'll find out soon enough."

"I'm a bit surprised Gérard didn't catch it," said Florian to Molly and Ben, speaking of Dr. Vernay and sounding quite pleased with himself. "It's true that it's an exceptionally neat affair, lacking many of the most-often seen attributes. Also true that the ligature was high up, hidden under the chin as it were, instead of lower down the neck where it would easily be noticed. But of course, the effect is the same."

"Ligature?" said Molly, unable to help herself.

Grunting, Florian struggled to his feet. "As usual, I will have more to say after I've given her a good once-over at the morgue. But yes, I did say 'ligature.' I don't see the cord anywhere near the body, but that's the gendarmes' job, anyway. As for manner of death: she was asphyxiated, strangled. By a thin cord or string."

"But we were all right in the next room!"

"Yes, well, apparently so. Perhaps everyone was distracted by their dinner and heard no disturbance."

"Can you say how much noise it would have made? I didn't see any sign of struggle—no furniture overturned at least. She was lying by the fire rather peacefully."

"I'm glad, for her sake," said Florian, "because I don't need to point out that strangulation is generally not a very pleasant way to meet one's end. My guess—though again, I'll be able to give a more complete picture later on—is that she died quickly. Perhaps she was surprised, the killer was strong, and it was over in a matter of seconds. Pressure to the carotid artery could have caused her to black out, which might explain no noise or visual indications of a struggle."

Molly shivered. "So it was simply that ...the lights went out, and the killer seized his chance."

"Bonsoir, Ben and Molly," said Paul-Henri Monsour, coming through the dining room with a grave expression.

"Not for the nanny," said Molly. "Florian says she was strangled."

Florian sighed, wishing that for once he be allowed to speak for himself.

"Is she local?" Paul-Henri asked Ben.

"Is this your idea of securing a crime scene?" said a stern voice from the direction of the foyer.

Ben, Molly, and Paul-Henri turned to see Chantal Charlot, the new chief, standing with her hands on her narrow hips, glaring at all of them and taking control without hesitation. "Officer Monsour, get out the tape and mark off both of these rooms. I don't know who you people are, but get out. We've got work to do and your interference is not welcome."

Ben and Molly both started to speak but the chief's tone warned them off. They said *au revoir* and went to the foyer, looking around for the Valettes, but couldn't see or hear anyone at all.

"I GUESS there's a new sheriff in town," said Molly.

"This is not good," said Ben, shaking his head.

"No. And the weirdest thing..." Molly said as they walked to the car. "Where did everyone disappear to? Lapin, Lawrence, the Valettes...one minute, the party felt so crowded! We were all packed in that library like sardines. And the next minute I couldn't find anyone."

Ben shook his head again as they got in the car. "I'm not even focused on the murder right now. I'm wondering how we're going to make any progress on any case if Chief Charlot is this...this..."

"This much of a jerk?"

"Yeah. Of course she is completely within her rights to keep us away from the investigation. It's just that Maron spoiled us."

"And we haven't been hired, so we don't even have that going for us."

"Right."

They drove back to La Baraque, the picture of gloom, and did not raise a smile when Bobo barreled over to greet them with muddy paws and ecstatic licks.

"Did you get the feeling that something wasn't right in that family?" Molly asked, as they flopped on the sofa together.

"Definitely. In about ten different directions, actually. Simon's father is in a bad way."

"Yes. I went through that with my father, as I think I've told you? Terrible disease for everyone, obviously. But…I wasn't talking about that though. More about…the undercurrents between Camille and Simon. I had the feeling things weren't going that great between them."

"Moving is stressful. Having a bunch of strangers for dinner? Very stressful. So what you saw might just be a normal response to a momentarily difficult situation."

"Could be," she said doubtfully.

"What's tomorrow look like? Do you have any changeover? Is Constance coming?"

With a groan, Molly got up to check the schedule on her computer. "Yes, Constance is coming, but only to do a light once-over. The Badowskis are leaving, thank God, because there's bad blood between them and Arthur, and they're all staying in the annex. Everyone else is staying a second week."

"Are you throwing them a party?"

"I was going to. But with this murder…"

"Maybe you could do something for the guests next week? I've got to go see that blasted Bernard Petit tomorrow. But since changeover's easy this week, maybe you could get a decent start. How about you go to the market in the morning and do some preliminary legwork?"

"Even though no one has hired us?"

"Maybe if we have some worthwhile information, someone will *want* to hire us. We need to know where Lawrence and Lapin went, for starters."

"You're not thinking—?"

"No, of course not. But we have to follow the protocol, Molly.

Determine where everyone was, and as far as we're able, what they were doing at the time the murder occurred."

"Which is not going to be easy, given that we were sitting in pitch dark."

"Luckily, I happen to know you never shy away from a challenge," he said, leaning in to kiss her neck. Molly closed her eyes and smiled, grateful to have Ben in her life, and also grateful for another murder to solve.

Though she felt a little guilty about that last one.

﹩ 13 ﹩

Ａll the dinner party guests were of course long gone, as well as Merla and Ophélie, the coroner, and the gendarmes. But the Valette household, as might be imagined, was hardly a place of calm or relaxation that Saturday morning after the storm. Chloë was intermittently gripped by wild sobbing to the point of hysteria. Raphael kept shouting for someone to bring him a baguette with butter and ham, or a drink of Perrier, or his scissors. Camille was a zombie—no expression, no emotion, utterly shut down.

Simon was left to run from one to the other, trying to soothe and placate. He sorely missed the staff they had had in Paris but thought they wouldn't need in Castillac; someone to tidy up would be a big help. Someone to cook and look after the girls. Someone to make this new horrible problem go away.

"Can I bring you anything, darling?" he asked Camille, who was sitting up in bed, wearing a quilted jacket though the day was warm, pretending to read a magazine.

Camille shook her head but said nothing.

Simon left the bedroom and stood for a moment in the corridor. He remembered standing there just the day before with

Violette. Remembered the burning look she had given him, and the intense temptation that had flooded him.

And since Simon was the unusual sort of fellow who was honest with himself even when that meant seeing himself in a bad light, he acknowledged that he would have, eventually, given in to that temptation. It was only a matter of time. She had not been beautiful, but she had been young, smart, and a talented artist. His wife was...frequently indisposed. He closed his eyes for a moment, fantasizing...until he snapped back to the present moment, feeling terrible that he had briefly forgotten that the object of his daydream was dead.

"*Ahhhh,*" groaned Raphael from his room, and Simon knocked on the door and went in. "Father," he said. "Is there anything I can get you? I know yesterday was trying, but things are back to normal now," he lied, hoping to calm him.

Raphael's eyes were wide and he looked terrified. Flecks of spittle were scattered on his lip and cheek, and his hair stuck up in every direction.

"Maybe if you comb you hair, you'll feel better," Simon said wryly, picking up a comb from his father's dresser and handing it over. "Did...did you happen to see anything last night?" he asked nonchalantly. "Or hear anything? The lights were out for quite some time. And there...there was a kind of accident, and I was just wondering if you happened to know anything about it?"

Raphael turned his face to the window.

"Were you in your room until the lights came back on?"

"Give me back my scissors," growled Raphael. "And you've taken all my string. I need it, give it back."

Simon bowed his head for a moment, and then left his father's room. It was no secret where the girls were—Chloë was sobbing again, with occasional keening that hurt his ears. He went to the dining room and found his daughters under the table, wrapped in blankets.

Gisele looked sadly at her father. "I can't get her to stop."

Simon sat down, bumping his head on the table. "Dearest girl," he said to Chloë, patting her shoulder. "It *is* awful. There's no use pretending it isn't. And I know—you are young to have to learn this lesson, which is that in fact, terrible things do happen sometimes. It is part of life."

Chloë howled all the louder.

"Are we going to get a new nanny?" asked Gisele.

Simon sat up, bumping his head again. Somehow he hadn't thought of that. And what a very excellent idea it was. The household desperately needed someone new, someone young, someone who had nothing at all to do with any of the awful things the Valettes had been through, in Paris and now Castillac. "Well, I don't see why not. Would the two of you like to help conduct the interviews?"

"Yes!" shrieked Chloë, and Gisele nodded.

"She can't be mean," said Chloë. "Or ugly."

"I would like to have another artist," said Gisele. "Violette taught us so much about drawing."

Chloë unleashed another torrent of tears.

"All right then," said Simon. He patted them each on the back and crawled out from under the table, thinking that if he didn't get himself to someplace quiet he was going to lose his mind. Never in a million years did he think he would miss his old corporate job, where the pressure of conformity in all things had been so oppressive. But as he went into the kitchen to make his father's baguette, he reminisced fondly about sitting down at his large desk, wearing a fashionable suit and a crisp shirt, the events of the day more or less predictable if not terribly interesting.

There's just nowhere to hide, he thought crossly. Either life is utterly dull or the drama will put you in an early grave.

He made the sandwich and took it to Raphael, who grabbed it and began eating without a word of thanks. Simon trotted downstairs and outside into the damp day. As he walked quickly to the ruin and his careful piles of rocks, he stripped off his shirt and felt the sun on his skin, trying to push everything else away.

❧

MOLLY DIDN'T LINGER over coffee, though she wanted to. The weather was perfect for sitting on the terrace and staring into space, deliciously wasting time, or lounging by the natural pool, watching dragonflies flit about. But there was legwork to be legged, as Ben had pointed out, so after only one cup and nothing to eat, she hopped on her trusty scooter and zipped into the village and the market. It was not quite as crowded as it had been in August, when almost the entire country goes on vacation, but there was still a good crowd and Molly had to wait in line to talk to her friend Manette, who ran a thriving vegetable stand.

They bonjour'd and kissed cheeks, happy to see each other. "Still feeling good?" Molly asked, looking at Manette's big belly.

"Yep. Only have to make it to early December. Oh God, when I put it that way, it seems like I'll be pregnant forever."

Molly just smiled and pointed haphazardly at eggplant and lettuce, barely registering what she was choosing, as she went through the list of questions she wanted answered that day.

"So Manette, have you seen Lawrence this morning?"

"Oh yes, he was here at eight on the dot, as he always is. Bought a lot of tomatoes. Might be making sauce or some such."

"I've had that sauce. It is *amazing*. And um, how about Lapin?"

"Nope, haven't seen him." Manette narrowed her eyes at her friend. "Why do I feel like I'm being interrogated? Is this about last night?"

"Last night?" said Molly, with no idea why she was playing dumb, since of course news of the murder was all over the village by now. "Well, okay, it *is* about last night. I'd like to catch up with Lawrence and Lapin to ask them a few questions—we were all there when it happened."

"How awful! But—it's not been explained when anyone has told me the story, and so far I've heard it from six, no seven people—how did someone manage to get murdered in the middle of a dinner party? It's like some kind of terrible magic trick!"

"Not really," said Molly. "Big storm, right? The power went out. And you know how it is—no cities nearby to brighten the sky at night. The Valettes live far enough away from the village that there were no streetlights. It was *dark*."

"So how did the murderer see what he was doing?"

"That's a very good question," said Molly. Assuming it was a 'he,' which she was not ready to do.

"It was a crazy storm, for sure. But *we* didn't lose power. I haven't heard of anyone who did, actually."

"Huh," said Molly, thinking that over. "It was more rain, thunder, and lighting than wind. No trees down, no fallen branches to knock out power lines?"

Manette shrugged. "You'd have to ask Gaetan about that. He takes care of anything having to do with wires at our house."

Molly felt a bit envious at the idea of having a husband who was handy, but swept that away to get back to business. "One last question," she said, taking the bag of vegetables and rummaging in her purse for exact change. "Have you met the Valettes? Seen them in the market yet?"

"Not yet. I figured they were neck-deep in boxes at this point. With a house that big, it will take them ages to unpack."

"No, they seemed all set, actually. Which now that you mention it—that *was* fast, wasn't it? Didn't they just get here...less than two weeks ago?"

"Eh, some people are fanatics about that stuff. They've gotta have everything just so or they go crazy. Au revoir, Molly!" Manette turned to the next customer and Molly moved off, walking towards Pâtisserie Bujold without realizing it.

Curious that no other houses lost power last night.

Curious that the murderer could do the deed in total darkness.

She was thinking so hard about the case that she walked right past the bakery. Edmond saw her go by and rushed out to the sidewalk, calling her.

"Is something wrong, Molly? How you wound me, watching you stroll past without a care, as though I was a stranger and you had started getting your pastries at Fillon!"

"Oh, Edmond, you do get dramatic. I was just distracted." She took his arm and they walked into the shop, Molly inhaling deeply through her nose as she always did, fully enjoying the bliss of vanilla and butter. "What have you got that's interesting today? I'll get the usual half dozen almond croissants, and a dozen regular croissants for my guests. But I could use a pick-me-up right now, something a little...different?"

"Because we are old friends, I will talk to you as such and not as merely a customer, a stranger. It is about something I have learned over the years," Edmond said seriously. "Often we think we want something new, when in fact, what our soul yearns for is something familiar, something from our past. I do not say this to dissuade you if you are sure, and of course you are welcome to look on the left side of the display case if indeed you are certain novelty is what you are after. But I *see* you, Molly Sutton, I take you in completely this morning. And in my judgment, it is flan. Flan is what you need."

"Flan?"

"Flan. Perhaps your grandmother made it for you, when you were a girl?"

Molly laughed. "My grandmothers were both dead by the time I came along. So your fortune-telling is a little off."

She sighed and looked at the display case. On the left were a series of fanciful pastries with icing in patterns, even little parasols stuck in some of them. On the other side were the old standbys, and Molly peered at the lowly flan and considered.

"Well, it wasn't exactly the same because there was never any caramel sauce. But my mother did use to make an egg custard with nutmeg when I was a little girl," Molly said. It was the first time Edmond had ever heard her sound wistful and he was completely charmed.

She ended up sitting at the tiny table in the corner of the shop with an espresso and the flan, and she had to admit, the experience was sublime.

Not so sublime that she was distracted from the nanny's case, however. She got out a little pad and took some notes, trying again to remember who had been talking in the dining room when the lights went out, and who seemed to be missing during the crucial time of the murder. The exercise was not made any easier for involving many of her closest friends.

The bell on the bakery door tinkled, and in came Madame Gervais. Molly was glad to see the hundred-and-four-year-old moving better than the last time she'd seen her, when she had been going slowly up rue Picasso with a walker.

"Bonjour, Madame Gervais," said Molly. "How are you?"

"I will be much better once I've had a bit of chocolate. What do you think, Edmond? Is this the day for a *pain au chocolat*, or should I go for a cup of pudding?"

Edmond considered. Molly had never realized that he regularly performed the service of intuiting which of his products a customer should buy that day; she found it amusing and wonderfully ridiculous.

"The pudding. Definitely."

"He's got me eating flan. I admit I'm enjoying it immensely."

Edmond nodded and smirked at her.

"I am sorry to hear about last night," the old woman said. "Terrible business. And a family new to the village! I daresay they'll pick up and move within the month."

"Hm, I hadn't even thought of that," said Molly. "But you might be right. I think *I* would, wouldn't you? Even if you're not superstitious, it would be hard not to see a murder during your first dinner party as a sign you'd made a wrong turn somewhere along the way."

"Well, somebody *did* make a wrong turn, I think we can safely say that's indisputable."

The question is, what kind was it? thought Molly, scraping the last of her flan out of its cup. And who made it, and when?

14

Chief Charlot got up from her desk and forcefully yanked the hem of her jacket down so as to disallow any wrinkling. Her brown hair was in a short braid on her back, and her heavy eyebrows, unplucked, were pulled down as she glowered. Paul-Henri could hear her walking to her office door; he inwardly cringed.

"Is this how former Chief Maron instructed you to do your paperwork? Because if so, he was sadly in error. You can't simply leave out portions whenever you feel like it, Officer Monsour. Did you sleep through Officer's School? Perhaps your Papa pulled some strings to get you through, something like that?"

Paul-Henri was used to condescending nags; he had one for a mother. But familiarity with the type did not make being in the same room with Chief Charlot, much less being her subordinate officer, any easier. In fact, he thought, as he made sure to keep his expression noncommittal, it is worse, because every time Chief Charlot starts in on me, I'm hearing my mother in a kind of chorus. These days life in the station is like being in the third circle of hell.

"You've lived in Castillac for how long?" she asked.

"One year, almost exactly. I know it's a small village, but it's impossible to get to know every single person. And the Valettes, as you know, just arrived. Haven't been here two weeks, I don't think."

"Exactly right, you don't *think*," the chief spat at him.

Paul-Henri turned away and pretended to look for something in his desk drawer so she would not see his angry face. How soon would his transfer come through? He tried to think back about Maron, trying to remember how many years he had been posted in Castillac before being moved on.

By all rights, *I* should have been the next chief, he said to himself, but though he had the thought often, he did not really believe it.

"—and Officer Monsour, as I was saying, I can commend you on the state of your uniform, weak sauce, to be sure. I suppose you did manage to have all the DNA samples taken from those present at the Valettes, so you're not one hundred percent incompetent. It's just that we have a murder investigation on our hands and we need to hit the ground running, do you understand?"

"Actually, we've had several—"

"I've read the files. I've seen the embarrassing...it appears that the gendarmerie can take credit for catching none of these murderers, correct? I was hoping my eyes deceived me but I'm afraid they did not. This Molly Sutton...she is the person doing all the work, is that right? Someone with no connection to the gendarmerie, a civilian, and not even French?"

Paul-Henri allowed himself a moment of enjoyment, seeing how bothered Charlot was by Molly. "Well, I wouldn't say *all* the work. Or no connection. She and Maron were friends, and her boyfriend, Ben Dufort, was the chief for some years. Quite well respected, by most accounts, though if you wanted to really dig into it, it seems that his personality was quite genial but his investigative techniques somewhat spotty. All before I got here, of course. But—"

"Oh *mon Dieu*, stop your prattling. Murder, Officer Monsour. That's what we have to focus on *today*. I am going to the Valette's. While we wait for the coroner's and forensics reports, I'm going to take statements from everyone in that family."

"Didn't we—"

"Yes, I began the process yesterday. But I got nothing in writing. And just as a basic point: when a family shows up, new in town, nobody knows them at all...and then, when the boxes have barely been unpacked, there's a dead body in the library? That, Officer Monsour, is a decent indication that something is not right in that house. I don't know what it is, not yet, but we will get to the bottom of it. I've put requests in to the Paris bureau and expect to hear back from them promptly. If there was any funny business at their former residence, we should soon know about it."

Paul-Henri found himself relieved that none of the villagers seemed to be on Charlot's suspect list. He had few friends and no particularly warm feelings for anyone there, but felt protective about them nonetheless.

And he had a few ideas about what he might do to further the investigation. "I could—" he began.

"I want you to track down the guest who disappeared the night of the murder..." Charlot took out a notepad and consulted it. "...somebody named Lapin? I want to know if he's still in the village or if he's fled, which would at least give us a prospect with a guilty conscience."

Paul-Henri liked the sound of that. Despite only a few seconds ago being glad the chief was focused on the Valettes, Paul-Henri was no fan of Lapin, having suffered a few insults from him that had stung. Quickly he pulled his equipment together and followed the chief out of the station, feeling better about his job than he had in the weeks since Charlot's arrival.

&.

CHIEF CHARLOT WALKED to the Valette's, wanting to stretch her legs. She had stayed up late the night before, unable to sleep after spending hours at the crime scene trying to herd cats. Never had she seen a forensics team more lackadaisical, or a junior officer more inept. It was no wonder at all that the village of Castillac had suffered so many murders in the last few years—the gendarmes in charge were woefully, painfully inadequate. It was a criminal's playground, this seemingly sleepy little village tucked in among the farms and estates of the Dordogne.

With a satisfied smile, she thought about how she was going to change all that. Adherence to regulations, follow-through, attention to detail—these were the mundane steps that brought results. Not friendship, she thought with contempt, thinking of the way Maron had apparently palled around with Sutton and Dufort, embarrassing the gendarmerie in the process. Things were going to be very, very different now that she was in charge, Charlot said to herself. And what better way to prove it than to solve this murder quickly, before the private investigators find a way to sink their teeth into the case?

Charlot turned into the Valette's drive, putting her thoughts aside and paying attention to her surroundings. An expensive house, certainly, though not at the highest end of what was available; she would check how much they had paid when the office of the *notaire* opened on Monday morning. She made a note to find out how much land they had bought with it, and what its boundaries were. One car, a Mercedes. The yard was well taken care of —was there a gardener or was the family doing the work themselves?

She saw a workman pushing a wheelbarrow over by a ruin and ignored him, going up the front steps and rapping hard with the knocker.

"Bonjour, chief!" called the workman, walking over. It was only when he got closer that Charlot realized he was Simon Valette. She hid her surprise.

"Bonjour, Monsieur Valette. I am here to interview each of you formally. I hope this is a convenient time." She spoke in such a way as to make plain that Simon's convenience was not her concern at all.

"I...well, of course, anything we can do to help. Would it be all right if you spoke to my wife first, while I do a quick wash-up? It's sweaty work, stone walls."

Charlot squinted at him. She liked that he was sweaty and shirtless, thinking that it gave her a bit of an advantage; a fancy big shot from Paris would be far more comfortable in his native clothing, freshly showered. "This shouldn't take long," she said. "Is there someplace we can sit down?"

Simon shrugged and led her inside, through a small sitting room on the other side of the foyer from the dining room, and through a door to a terrace.

"Would you like coffee? Or anything to drink?"

"This is not a social call, Monsieur Valette," said Charlot, taking a seat and pulling out a notepad. "Now, I know I asked some of these questions last night, but I am going to ask them again. Sometimes in the heat of a crisis, the proper detail gets left out."

Simon nodded. He swatted a bug from his arm but maintained eye contact.

"Mademoiselle Crespelle, Violette Crespelle, that is the name of the deceased?"

"Yes."

"How long had she been in your employ?"

"Six months? Possibly less? I can look it up if you need an exact date."

"Yes, do that. You may call later on to give it to me. Were you pleased with Mademoiselle Crespelle's acquittal of her duties?"

"Yes, quite."

"The children liked her?"

"Very much."

"How about your wife? Would you say that Madame Valette also approved of the nanny?"

"You'll have to ask her."

"Neatly done, Monsieur, but I am asking for your assessment of your wife's opinion."

Simon drew in a breath. He did not seem at all discomfited by his sweaty, shirtless appearance, and gave the question some calm thought before answering. "The situation, you see, is like this: my wife has some health problems which make it impossible for her to give the children the attention they need. That is why we hired Violette in the first place—obviously the girls are old enough that they don't need someone looking out for them every minute. But the...their mother needs a great deal of rest, and so we thought hiring a nanny to be a good solution for everyone. For the most part, I handled it—the hiring, paying of salary, and overseeing her. Camille, as I said, needs rest. She has not interacted all that much with Violette...*did* not interact, I suppose I should say..." Simon's voice trailed off, and he looked away from the chief for the first time.

Charlot did not write this down but she made a mental note of it.

"And your relationship with Mademoiselle Crespelle. Would you say it was businesslike? Cordial? Warm?"

"Are those my only choices?" he said with a laugh. "Violette and I got along just fine. It isn't easy bringing a third adult into a household, as you can imagine. But she accepted the duties that Camille and I outlined for her and did not stray beyond that. In other words, she was not a bossy, controlling sort of person, interested in instructing us how to raise our children. She followed our directions cheerfully and was responsible and attentive to Chloë and Gisele. So we got along well with her, as I've said. And the children adored her. This whole thing is very, very hard on them."

"Do you plan for them to receive any counseling?"

"I've thought of it, but it's...it was only yesterday. I haven't done anything yet. Perhaps you can direct me to some resources?"

"I'll have Monsour, the junior officer, get in touch. I'm afraid I haven't been in Castillac much longer than you have, Monsieur Valette."

"Ah, the blind leading the blind," he said with a laugh.

Chief Charlot squinted at him again, not hiding her distaste for him.

They sat on the terrace for close to an hour while she asked him every question she could think of in order to elicit the clearest possible picture of the nanny's life in the Valette household, and the relationships of all the family members to her. Finally, when Simon was on the verge of losing his patience at her repeated questions, she asked to see Madame Valette, and after directing the chief upstairs, he went back to his pile of rocks.

❧ 15 ❧

S unday morning at La Baraque. Ben and Molly were enjoying a hearty breakfast on the terrace when someone rapped on the door and Bobo began barking wildly.

They exchanged glances, neither of them expecting anyone.

"Bonjour, Monsieur Valette!" said Ben, opening the door wide and allowing himself the faintest hope that the man had come to hire them to solve the nanny's murder.

"Please, call me Simon," he said.

"Bonjour, Simon," said Molly. "Please excuse the house, we've been a bit slothy of late."

Simon waved her excuse away. "I'm the one who's sorry, for barging in on a Sunday morning when people should be allowed a civilized breakfast in peace. I've come to talk to you about something of importance, something that would require your immediate attention, if you are so inclined."

Molly allowed her flicker of hope to turn into a solid flame. "Of course, come on in. Would you like coffee?"

Simon said he would and Molly went to make a fresh pot, keeping her hands out of sight so that no one could see she had her fingers crossed.

"Let me get right to it," Simon said to Ben. "This horrible business of the other night...as you might imagine, it's wreaking havoc on my family, and to be perfectly honest, we do not need this right now. As you doubtless realized, my father suffers from dementia and this sort of thing is extremely difficult for him to process. And my wife...this is just terrible for her...she's...well, she's not quite as stable, emotionally, as one would wish, if you see what I mean? It's terribly upsetting for her.

"I understand how it sounds, as if I am making my wife's feelings count more than the life of Violette. I don't mean it that way at all. I feel absolutely devastated for the poor girl. But right now I have to stay focused on the present and do what I can for my family."

Molly stood behind the counter, absorbing every word. She poured the coffee and brought Simon his cup, which he accepted gratefully. Then remembering there were leftover croissants, she went back and got them, putting them on an antique plate decorated with bluebirds.

"How can we help?" asked Ben.

"Getting straight to the point, as I said...I understand the two of you run an investigation business—you spoke of it briefly during dinner. I would like to hire you to find out who killed Violette. Obviously I know the gendarmes are working the case, but I..." he wasn't sure how to say what he thought of Chief Charlot without possibly insulting the two locals, so he didn't finish the sentence.

"We'd be happy to take the case," Molly said quickly.

Ben nodded his agreement. "Of course, since we were right in the next room when it happened, we've taken a particular interest," he said. "But I'm curious—are you hiring us because for some reason you do not have faith in the local gendarmes to do the job?"

Simon looked out of the window for a long moment. "And I

should say, I'm willing to pay your top rate, if indeed you have some sort of scale. I don't want financial considerations to impede the investigation in any way."

Molly and Ben almost exchanged a glance at Simon's dodging of the question, but they didn't have to; they knew what the other was thinking.

"I'm sorry, I do understand that I need to be forthright with you if you are to do your job successfully. It's just that there's a rather long habit of...of not revealing..." he said, clearly struggling. "You see, as I was saying, my wife is not well. We went to doctor after doctor in Paris, and finally, one suggested we leave the city and settle someplace calm, someplace peaceful."

Molly nearly said, "Ha!" but managed to choke it back at the last second. She couldn't help remembering that when she moved to Castillac she had been looking for the exact same thing. Castillac had turned out to be many things, but calm and peaceful it was not.

Simon continued, "Chief Charlot came out to the house this morning and talked to me and then Camille. It was something between an interrogation and an interview. She seems...*ardent*, if I may put it that way. Quite intent on catching the killer. Which is just as it should be. But here is my worry: in her desire to prove herself in her new post and get a quick conviction, she may try to pin the murder on my wife. Charlot could claim she is erratic, mercurial at times. That she was jealous of Violette's talents and affection from the girls. That is why I want the two of you involved: to prevent a miscarriage of justice as well as the ruin of my family if Charlot accomplishes what I think she has in mind. I know I may be jumping the gun and I shouldn't infer too much from one conversation, but that is the way it looked to me yesterday after she was gone. I had half a mind to pack the family up and drive away—that's how much I feared this chief gendarme of yours."

"Did she say anything specific that led you to believe she suspects your wife?"

Simon smiled ruefully. "Well, she made it quite plain she dislikes us. I suppose in an exceptionally professional detective, dislike and guilt would not be connected. But as I found in my business life, few people in any job are actually exceptional. Do you agree?"

Ben shrugged, agreeing more or less but for some reason not wanting to tell Simon that.

"Camille was not in the dining room when the murder took place," said Molly, matter-of-factly.

"I know," Simon said simply. "For that matter, neither was I. It was bedlam, wasn't it? The loud cracks of thunder, the rain pounding on the roof..."

"The darkness."

"I will admit that having spent most of my life in Paris, the darkness was quite something. I have never experienced anything like it."

"You have been in Castillac almost two weeks. Are you saying you've not found yourself in the dark in all that time?" asked Ben.

Simon laughed. "Maybe I am a creature of urban habits. When dusk comes, I turn on lights. As I'm sure you realize, most of Paris is well lit after dark, and so bright we can barely make out any stars. But I can see now that using all that electricity is a mistake, or at least a missed opportunity. I will go out in the yard tonight after dark, with no flashlight. Hard to believe that this experience is new to me, at my age, but there it is."

Is he rambling to distract us, or because he's that kind of talker? Molly wondered.

"I understand the desire for privacy, but you will need to give us more detail about your wife's condition. Are you prepared to do that?" asked Ben. "I don't mean to sound brusque. I just want all the cards on the table before we begin."

Simon nodded. "Understood. As I said, it's a habit, keeping all that to ourselves. But this situation calls for a change, and I am prepared to proceed with that."

"Molly!" someone called from outside.

Molly jumped up. "Excuse me, be right back," she said, and left through the terrace door.

"All right, I'll get started with a personal question," said Ben. "Perhaps it will be easier to answer with Molly out of the room. Having a nanny...that often puts quite a lot of strain on a marriage, does it not? Having a vibrant, young, single woman suddenly joining the household?"

Simon looked evenly at Ben but said nothing.

"I'm asking if there were tensions of that sort," Ben said. He was careful not to look Simon in the eye, which Ben knew could make answering easier.

Simon shrugged. "I would be a cad to fool around when my wife isn't well," he answered.

"Many men behave like cads but give themselves a dispensation for one reason or another. Or they accept that they are cads, and do what they do regardless."

Simon took a deep breath. "True enough. I won't deny that it crossed my mind. But nothing happened, Dufort. This murder is not about that, I can swear to it."

The two men talked for much longer while Molly attended to Elise Mertens who had eaten a bad cream puff and become violently ill. Molly was gracious and helpful, making sure Elise was comfortable and her husband had the number of Dr. Vernay in case she took a turn for the worse.

Once that situation was managed, Molly trotted back to the house. Valette had left, and Ben spent the next hour relating every word of their conversation. More than once, with Molly often pressing Ben on whether he had believed the man or not.

Was there any other job in which your client's guilt or innocence was so often at issue?

They were pleased to be hired—more than pleased, close to

elated. Perhaps they were both ants instead of grasshoppers, but it gave them both a happy feeling of security to have a solid job as they went into fall and cooler weather. Happy, of course, except for the fact that once again, someone in the village had felt it necessary to kill a neighbor in cold blood.

❧ 16 ❧

Chief Charlot was not young; although she had joined the gendarmerie as a young woman, her career had not been a smooth rise to the top by any means. But she had, over the years, gotten to know many others in the service—not to call them friends, exactly, because Chantal Charlot was not very good at making those—and when she needed some help with the background checks for the Crespelle case, she knew someone to call who could make it happen.

"See, it's all who you know," the chief said to Paul-Henri, who had likely said similar things himself, though hearing it from Charlot made him want to throw something. "Marco Abedin, I went to the Officers' School with him. I can't say we keep up, but I can get in touch when something like this comes up." She smiled at her computer screen and leaned back in her chair, letting Paul-Henri stand in front of her desk in total ignorance of what she was talking about.

"I've got hold of some new information. Can't decide whether it changes anything or not. Lapin still missing?"

"Yes. As far as I know. I drove past his place this morning and his car is still gone. I spoke to Anne-Marie yesterday. Hadn't heard from him."

Chantal nodded and steepled her fingers together, which Paul-Henri thought the height of pretension when someone else did it.

"Aren't you curious?" she said.

"Of course I'm curious," said Paul-Henri, exerting great will not to clench his fists.

"It's about Madame Valette...Camille. From what I've heard, she's something of a caged bird. Her husband seems to want her shut up in her room all the time, though to my eye she seemed perfectly capable of being up and about. Some men are like that, you know," she said, throwing him a glance that he interpreted to mean that she thought he might be among them.

"But now I see that the actual situation is different from how it looks. Often the case," she said, and Paul-Henri allowed himself slowly to curve his fingers into his palm and squeeze, though of course there was no question of being able to avail himself of the release of actually throwing a punch in the chief's direction.

"She has spent time in the hospital," said Charlot, dragging the news out interminably. Just when Paul-Henri was about to lose it, she added, "A *psych* hospital."

"Ah," said Paul-Henri.

"*Ah* indeed."

"What was the diagnosis?"

"My friend was not able to get the actual treatment file. Only her name on the list of patients."

"Well, that would matter quite a bit, wouldn't it? If she was suicidal or homicidal, just for starters."

"I'm not sure I like your tone, Officer Monsour. I suggest you stop hanging around my office like a bored teenager and go out and find some evidence. Go on, go!"

He did not need to be told twice. Oh, how he despised her! After a quick trip to the bathroom to check his uniform in the mirror, Paul-Henri left the station.

Chief Charlot stayed in her chair, leaning way back and looking up at the ceiling. It would be so neat, so easy, if the murderer was Lapin, she thought. He has no prior convictions but he has spent time in jail, back when Dufort was chief. He had fled the scene and failed to get in touch with his new wife to let her know where he was. He was, to any person playing the odds, acting guilty, whereas all the other people present at the dinner had gone about their business after the murder as though nothing was any different. At least, as far as she had been able to determine.

But this latest bit of information about Camille threatened to upset Charlot's assessment of the suspect list. She knew little about psychiatry but surely one could safely say most murderers were a little crazy? She would need to think more about it while she pressured her friend for more details on Camille's stay. It wouldn't do to run after a local man when someone in the same household of newcomers had documented mental illness.

Suicidal or homicidal, Charlot wondered, irritated that Monsour had posed the question. Or more likely—neither one, she thought with some satisfaction. Lapin was still at the top of her list of suspects...and still at large.

MOLLY AND BEN had intended to go to Chez Papa for dinner that Sunday, wanting to see friends, unwind, and hear the latest village gossip. But the unexpected appearance of Simon Valette along with Elise Mertens's illness had thrown off the rhythm of the day, and they found themselves still on the phone taking care of various business when it was past eight o'clock.

Bernard Petit called to make it clear what he thought of Ben's "non-investigation" of the repeated burglaries of his house. Ben stayed on the phone with him, spinning something of a yarn about all the things he was doing to catch the thief, which, to be honest, were at that point intentions rather than actions. It crossed his mind that Petit could be making it all up, just for attention or to garner sympathy. He suffered through the conversation with a lighter heart, now that he and Molly had the Crespelle case.

Molly, meanwhile, had been talking to Deana Jenkins in the front yard. Deana was a fanatic on the subject of medieval and early-Renaissance architecture, and apparently had worn out her husband on the subject and wanted a fresh listener. Molly found Deana interesting, and on a normal night would have enjoyed hearing about the cathedral in Périgueux and how it was modeled on a Greek cross just like St. Mark's in Venice. But on that Sunday, all she could think about was Violette Crespelle, and she was fidgety and distracted.

They were finally free and ready to leave for the village when Molly's cell buzzed.

"It's Anne-Marie," she said to Ben, who was standing by the door putting on a jacket. "I guess I should take it."

Ben nodded, putting the jacket back on a hook on the hat rack and going back to the living room.

"I'm so sorry to call now, late on a Sunday when I'm sure you and Ben have better things to do," said Anne-Marie, her voice betraying how upset she was. "It's Lapin. He's still not home. I haven't seen him since...since before the lights went out."

Molly stood still. Like everyone who had been at the Valette's dinner, Lapin was on the list she had started the instant Simon left, noting all the people in the house at the time of the murder, with their whereabouts before, during, and after the murder listed next to their names. The night had been confusing and plenty of details were left to be nailed down, but it had never occurred to her that anyone might still be missing.

"So okay, after the lights came on," Molly said slowly, "if my memory is right, everyone was accounted for eventually except for Lapin and Lawrence. I just assumed they went home early, though I did think it a little strange that either of them would willingly pass up a mocha dacquoise cake," said Molly. "I know Lapin travels a fair amount for his shop, doesn't he? Could he have run off to an auction or special sale somewhere, and forgotten to tell you?"

"Does that sound at all reasonable?" asked Anne-Marie.

"I guess not. Unless he's been flaky like that before?"

"Never."

The two women stayed quietly on the phone for some time, thinking their own thoughts. Molly was remembering how Lapin had looked at Violette like he wanted to have her for dessert, but she had no idea if that meant anything, and didn't see how telling Anne-Marie about it would be helpful.

"Well," Molly finally said. "I'll let you know if I hear anything or see him. One thing—and I know it might be hard to say, since it was dark—do you have any sense of when he took off from the Valette's? Was it right after the lights went out, or later on?"

"I don't know, Molly. I mean, I was calling for him right after, but have no idea whether he was already gone or just in the next room or something. But he's a grown man, you know? I wasn't worried about him—I was thinking of those girls and how scared they might have been, especially having grown up in Paris where they probably weren't used to power outages and that kind of total darkness. I was looking for them, not Lapin."

"Right, I was thinking about the girls too. I wish I could be more help."

"I love the man, but oh, he can be maddening!" Anne-Marie tried to laugh off her worry and Molly laughed with her, but it was false humor on both sides. They said goodbye and Molly turned to Ben. "It's so late, why don't we skip Chez Papa? Half the people will be gone by now anyway. And according to Anne-Marie, Lapin won't have been there at all—he's been missing since Friday night."

"Missing? Since when?"

"Since the lights went out."

Ben scowled. He had known Lapin since they were young and been looking out for his sometimes hapless friend all the way along. "Without a word to Anne-Marie?"

"That's what she says."

"I thought their marriage was going well."

"Same. And I didn't get the idea from Anne-Marie that anything was wrong between them. She seems totally baffled about where he might have gone."

"Did you get the impression he knew Violette, or had any connection to her?"

"Nope. Not that I saw. Violette came through looking for the girls at some point, but I don't know that any of the guests talked to her at all. But," she added fretfully, "I'm afraid I wasn't paying close attention, you know?"

"Yes. I've been beating myself up as well, for not having clearer memories about the evening. It almost feels like the night was cloudy, and the events are sinking back into the darkness, out of reach of memory."

"Sounds like a horror movie, if a rather poetic one," said Molly. "But I do know what you mean. It's...we were right there, Ben! It happened right under our noses!"

"I know," he said, putting a hand on her shoulder. The pleasure they had felt at Simon's offering them the job was dulled when they thought of the dinner party, the darkness, and the fact that they had most likely been sitting at the table with a murderer and been unable to lift a finger to stop him.

❦ 17 ❦

Monday morning dawned cool and cloudy. Ben took a shorter run than usual and headed off to Bergerac to meet with Petit, wanting to clear the decks at least for a few days so he could concentrate on the Crespelle case. Molly had a quick cup of coffee and a croissant, quite stale, and went to check on Elise Mertens.

"Oh, bonjour Molly," said Todor, opening the door of the cottage and ushering her inside. He looked a little frazzled, his hair sticking out; his clothes did not look fresh.

"Just wanted to see how Elise is doing this morning, and if I can get anything for either of you when I go into the village in a few minutes."

"Much better," said a weak voice from the bedroom.

Molly smiled. "Glad to hear it!" she called, not wanting to intrude by going to the doorway.

"She would like some tea, if it wouldn't be too much trouble. Something with mint, and perhaps ginger? To settle the stomach."

"Of course. Anything I can get you?"

"No, no. Well..." he said, with a guilty smile. "Perhaps a pastry

NELL GODDIN

from that excellent Pâtisserie Bujold. Poor Elise wouldn't be laid up like this if we hadn't gotten that cream puff from Fillon."

Molly laughed. "I can't begin to tell you how happy Monsieur Nugent, proprietor of Pâtisserie Bujold, will be to hear that! And please—I know it's very hard to be ill when you're not at home. If there's anything I can do for either of you, do not hesitate to tell me."

She said her goodbyes, remembered to refill the water bowl for Bobo and the orange cat to share, and sped on her way to L'Institut Degas, the art school where Marie-Claire was the director.

Monday was usually a sleepy day in Castillac, and this one appeared no different. An old woman was sweeping the sidewalk in front of her house on rue Picasso, dressed in a frayed blue housecoat. A couple of cats dozed in the sunshine on top of a stone wall. At Café de la Place, a few people were having breakfast, but nothing compared to the crowds on market day. Molly bumped along the cobblestone streets until she hit a paved section on the far side of the village where she could speed up, trying to organize her thoughts so she would be prepared when she questioned Marie-Claire.

When Molly first met Ben, almost exactly two years ago, he had been dating Marie-Claire. Molly had learned from past experience that digging around in other people's romantic history pretty much inevitably led to disaster, so she had never asked him about Marie-Claire or why they had broken up. But that didn't mean she wasn't curious.

L'Institut Degas was a fixture in Castillac. Though the school was not large, it brought talented students to the village from all over the world, and the artistic education they received had an excellent reputation. Marie-Claire had taken over after a small hiccup involving some funny business with the accounts, and since then, the school had gotten a little bigger and its reputation only more burnished.

Molly parked the scooter and walked into the courtyard, surrounded by two old buildings and one modern one that had an unusual outer covering that made the building look like it had been swallowed by a jellyfish. Students were lounging around outside, some chatting and others sketching. She found the administration building by looking at a small map posted in the pathway, and went inside.

"Bonjour, madame," Molly said to a white-haired woman sitting at a desk, looking at a computer screen. "I'm looking for Madame Levy? I called earlier, I think she's expecting me."

The white-haired woman smiled and gestured to a closed door. "Go right on in," she said.

Molly opened the door, and she smiled too because Marie-Claire's office was such a pleasant place to enter. Blooming orchids lined one windowsill, and the furniture and the pale blue color of the walls made the place feel soothing.

"What a night, eh?" said Marie-Claire, coming around from her desk and sitting on a small sofa. "Would you like a coffee?"

Molly was almost never able to resist coffee, so she nodded and Marie-Claire called to her assistant to bring two cups.

"Yes, it was a crazy night. On the way over there, Ben and I had been joking about the dark and stormy night, but of course we never..." Molly stopped, suddenly self-conscious about having mentioned Ben, worrying that it might seem a little pointed, given their history.

But Marie-Claire did not seem to notice, and Molly remembered that Pascal, the movie-actor-handsome waiter at Café de la Place, had seemed very smitten with her at the Valette's, which would be more than compensation for most women. The assistant arrived with two tiny cups of espresso, and Molly forced herself not to throw it back in one gulp.

"All right, so...thank you for meeting with me. First order of business, as you might imagine, is to hear everyone's recollections of that night, both before and after the lights went out. Let's start with just trying to figure out who was where, if you can do that for me." Molly pulled out her notepad and showed Marie-Claire a drawing of the seating arrangement. "Does this look right to you?"

"Yes. That's what I remember too."

"Was everyone in their seats when the lights went out, if you can recall?"

"I think so. I'm pretty sure, yes."

"And what about after? I mean, when the lights came back on?"

"Definitely not. The party was in complete disarray—the dining room had practically emptied. I remember you were still at the table, and me. Nico and Frances were eating the cake, or maybe that was later..." she stopped, looking up at the ceiling while she tried to recreate the scene in her mind. "Rex Ford was coming back into the dining room from the library, I just realized that now."

"Yes! I had forgotten that as well. Talk to me for a minute about him. What sort of teacher is he? Do the students like him?"

"Oh, he's a giant sourpuss and not well-liked by anyone. Always has something to complain about. But...in spite of that, he's an excellent teacher, and the students manage to put aside their personal feelings about him and are genuinely glad to take his courses. He's always fully booked."

"By any chance did he mention any connection to Violette Crespelle?"

Marie-Claire shook her head slowly. "Not to me. Have you asked him what he was doing in the library?"

"You're the first person I've talked to. We're just beginning, and have a long way to go yet."

Molly continued through her list of questions, taking notes from time to time while sipping her espresso. The beginning of an

investigation was exciting, for sure, and this one was no exception. But there were so many people to interview and so many
angles to cover that it was difficult, on a gray Monday morning,
not to feel at least a little daunted.

❧

PAUL-HENRI WAS FIRST to the station, as he usually was. He went
through his unvarying routine of vigorous sweeping, polishing the
windows, and inspecting his uniform in the mirror, making sure
there was not the tiniest thing off that would give Chief Charlot
an excuse to chastise him. So far though, in the few days Charlot
had been there, she had not been burdened by the need for an
excuse, but rather fired off criticism with both barrels anytime
she felt like it, without bothering about niceties such as having
reasonable cause.

He would have expected to be pleased by the new chief's
attention to detail and her strict adherence to the myriad rules
and regulations of the gendarmerie, since that was the direction
in which his own inclinations lay. Maron, the former chief, had
been far too loose in Paul-Henri's estimation, willing to throw
nearly any rule by the wayside if it served him in the moment.
That was no way to run a station, Paul-Henri thought, adjusting
his posture to ramrod straight even though he was sitting alone at
his desk.

And yet, as the days working under the new chief piled up, he
found himself bristling at her finickyness, and wishing she would
loosen her grip on protocol just enough to take in the bigger
picture.

Well, what he really wished was that she would stop insulting
him. It seemed as though he could not put a foot right, and when
he tried to adjust, the adjustment did not suit her either. He was
well acquainted with women who were difficult to please, and had

thought himself something of a master at handling them; but so far, Chief Charlot had him stymied. He was so distracted by dodging her thunderbolts that he had not been able to give the Crespelle case the attention it deserved. He had driven out to Lapin's place, but not found him there. Checked his junk shop over on rue Baudelaire, not there either. Paul-Henri knew that the next step would be to swing by some of the village gathering places such as Café de la Place and Chez Papa, but he just hadn't felt up to it. Instead, he walked the streets thinking about how much he disliked Chief Charlot.

The dislike was unchanged Monday morning, and sat in his chest like a heavy lump. He put his hand on the phone, considering. Then, without thinking of it as a step in the direction of blackmail, he called up a classmate of his from the Academy, a man who was posted in Paris. Probably not the exact precinct where Charlot had been before coming to Castillac, but hopefully close enough to have heard any gossip, if there was any to hear. The friend got back to him immediately, saying that yes, there was definitely some dirt there, but he didn't have the details. He gave Paul-Henri the number of a friend of his who might know more.

He wasn't expecting to strike gold, or even to have something awful he could hold over the chief's head. It was more—so he told himself—that when you have an enemy, it is prudent to find out all you can about her.

He left a message on the friend of a friend's service, and took out a snowy white tablet of paper and made some notes about the Crespelle case with an ink pen. His handwriting was elegant and flowing, and he enjoyed the sensation of the pen nib scratching across the paper.

If only he could be the one to solve this case, he thought. Paul-Henri enjoyed police work well enough, though admittedly he had gone to the Officer's School party because it had irritated his mother so much. He liked going around the streets of the village, seeing if there was a way to make himself helpful. If he could choose to work in a suburb of Paris, where the houses were stately and the cars late model and shiny, it would suit him very well.

He was just about to drive by Lapin's house and shop again when the chief arrived.

"Make me a coffee," she said, breezing past his desk without so much as a bonjour.

Paul-Henri set his mouth in a fake smile, and jumped up from his desk. Oh, how he loathed her.

When the coffee was ready, he set the cup on the corner of Charlot's desk. She did not look up. Her dark hair was in a tight, short braid in the back, and she furrowed her thick eyebrows while staring her computer screen.

Paul-Henri waited. Finally she said, "What about this Lapin? Did you find him? Funny name for a grown man."

"I have not. Not yet. I've checked his house and shop several times." The lie fell out of Paul-Henri's mouth without a pause, and he wondered at it, not being in the habit of lying except to his mother.

Charlot leaned back in her chair. "I spoke to Simon and Camille Valette at some length yesterday. I found them to be forthcoming, and while of course at this stage of an investigation it is unlikely that any possible suspect can be cleared of the crime, I believe we should focus our attention, and woefully limited resources, in another direction."

The junior officer was surprised. "What about the hospital-ization?"

"Surely you're not going to try to tell me that mental illness, by itself, makes one a murderer? You're not that much of an imbe-cile. I hope."

Paul-Henri opened his mouth but no words came out.

"What demonstrates guilt more than absconding?" continued the chief. "I will answer that one for you: nothing. I am going to put aside the long list of tasks I had for myself, and look for Lapin as well. From what I hear, he has been in jail before, and is perhaps involved in some shady dealings of some kind or another. If he killed once, we must stop him from doing it again. Some of these criminals get a taste for it, you know. So come on, Monsour, shake a leg. There's not a moment to be lost."

❧ 18 ❧

M olly could not get to Chez Papa fast enough. It had been a long, productive day; she had interviewed Anne-Marie after finishing up with Marie-Claire, and felt she had gleaned a few promising nuggets in those conversations. Work on the ruined barn was due to start in earnest the following morning, and that was definitely something to look forward to. Molly wanted to share her good mood and spend a convivial evening with her friends that would hopefully not end on the same kind of dark note as it had the last time she had seen them.

Ben was busy in Bergerac until late, so he would meet her at the bistro. She spent about fifteen seconds on her appearance and flew into the village on her scooter, driving a little faster than was strictly prudent. Seeing the little strand of twinkling lights in the scraggly tree outside Chez Papa gladdened her heart, and she happily slipped inside.

"Molly!" cried Lawrence, from his stool.

"Bonsoir, my dearest," she said, as they kissed on both cheeks. "Let me get a drink, and then I have about a hundred questions to ask you."

"The usual?" asked Nico from behind the bar.

"Hmm, I'm feeling like something a little different tonight. No, Lawrence, I've had Negronis loads of times. How about...do you have any grapefruit? I'm having a sudden craving."

With a grin, Nico reached under the bar and pulled out a grapefruit in each hand. "You must be a mind reader. I just picked these up today, thinking of making up a new cocktail."

"Perfect!" said Molly, grinning back.

And from that bright moment on, the evening deteriorated quickly.

"Hey Molls, before I make your drink, step into the back with me for just a sec, will you?" said Nico. The two friends went into the empty backroom, Molly feeling some unease. "I just heard something this afternoon, you know how it is with bartenders, people will just talk and talk, it's like I'm a substitute priest or psychiatrist or something. Generally I keep my mouth shut, but in this case...anyway, I thought you should know."

Molly had no idea where Nico was going with this.

"There's talk around town that Simon Valette shouldn't have hired you to work the case of the murdered nanny."

Molly's eyebrows flew up. "What? How come?"

"They're saying...they're saying that you were there, at the dinner, at the crime scene. You and Ben were in the dark just like everyone else. And so by rights, you should be on the suspect list yourselves, instead of looking into everyone else's business while you get away scot-free."

Molly's mouth dropped open.

"I'm giving you pretty much the exact words I was hearing. I figure you'd want the whole enchilada, right, not just the summary?"

Molly nodded slowly. "Of course. Who was saying this?"

Nico looked uncomfortable. "Aw, Molly, I don't like to be a snitch."

"Nico!"

"Yeah, yeah. Look, it was just some chumps sitting at the bar getting drunk in the middle of the afternoon. They obviously don't know you and were just jawboning for something to do. I wouldn't sweat it too much. I just...if people are talking smack about me behind my back? I want to know. So I thought you and Ben would want to know too."

"Thank you. Yes, I definitely do. For one thing, that kind of talk can be a sign of guilt. I'm not talking myself up here, it's not about me and Ben, I'm just talking about any effort to impede or stop an investigation, no matter who's doing it."

"But those guys weren't at the Valettes'. Couldn't have been any of them. Like I say, they were just a bunch of bored gossips when you get right down to it."

She stood thinking, tapping her fingers on her thighs. "But you know, the troubling thing about this isn't that some villagers were talking about me behind my back. I mean, let's be honest, we *all* do that sometimes. It's that—they're not wrong. Ben and I *were* there, in the dark, when the girl was murdered. Looking at it objectively...we *should* be on the suspect list."

"You didn't even know the girl—that makes no sense at all!"

"You know how many murders are committed by people who don't know their victims?"

"No."

"Me neither. But it's more than one, I think we can agree. The villagers aren't wrong. And hey, for all we know, the new chief has Ben and me at the top of her list."

Molly laughed but Nico looked skeptical. "If you say so. Okay, come on, I'll make you a grapefruit cocktail and you can put the case aside for a little while, and enjoy the evening."

Molly thought to herself that other people—non-detective people—just don't understand how it is when you're on a case. You never stop thinking about it. Even when you're doing something else, even thinking about something else or having fun with friends, the case is always there, and part of your brain is picking over it, making lists, going over and over what someone said or how someone looked or what was on the table in the library, on and on and on, endlessly until the criminal is pinned down by the evidence and cannot escape.

She and Nico went back to the main room. Ben had arrived, looking glad to be there, and so had Frances.

"Get anything?" Ben whispered in her ear when he kissed her.

"Not anything big," she whispered back. "Tell you later."

Ben raised his voice to ask if anyone had seen Lapin.

"Since when?" said Lawrence. "I gave him a ride home from the Valettes' the other night."

"Wait, what? How did I not know this?" said Molly.

"You didn't ask," said Lawrence drily.

"When did you leave? I was intending to come see you tomorrow, I've got a load of questions I'm asking everyone. All I know is that when the lights came back on, you and Lapin were gone."

"Did you suspect me?" he said, looking hopeful. "I'm always sitting on the sidelines during these things. I wish just one time I could be in the spotlight."

People down the bar laughed.

"Sorry to disappoint," said Molly. "But seriously, I wouldn't make light of it, at least not publicly. You can see how disappearing into the dark could look a bit shady. Especially if no one sees you for some time after."

"Here I am! Yesterday I cleaned up my yard—the storm had made a mess of it and I picked up sticks for what seemed like an eternity. I read in front of a fire even though it wasn't really cold. And I made myself a superb mushroom sauce to go with some fresh pasta I whipped up. That was my day."

"No witnesses?"

"None. Except the cat, and she dislikes me, so I wouldn't trust anything she says."

Molly smirked and then looked serious. "And Lapin...you dropped him off at home? Do you remember what time? As far as I know, you must be the last person to have seen him. Anne-

Marie called, worried about him. And I don't have to tell you," she said, more quietly, "that running off without a word after a murder has been committed is pretty much the worst thing a person can do."

Lawrence nodded. "I hope he turns up soon. Though I can't believe anyone would try to pin it on Lapin—he had nothing to do with that family. It's got to be an inside job, don't you think?"

"Quite possibly," said Molly. "The victim was in their house, after all, and part of their household. The murderer could have nipped down to the cellar and pulled out the fuse himself. The storm would be the perfect cover."

"Well, I've got a story about a new person, if anyone happens to be interested," said Frances loudly, pouting a little because everyone was talking to everyone else.

"Tell us in French," said Nico, mischievously.

"Oh, Lord," said Frances under her breath. "You're a *slave driver*, you know that?"

"Are you talking about the Valettes?" asked Molly.

Frances took a deep breath and put her hair behind her ears. "No Valettes," she said in French. "It is big police."

Molly scrunched up her face. "Huh?"

"Nico!" said Frances, pleading.

"You're doing fine, chérie. They'll get it. Just keep going!"

"I hear big police in grocery store. Is...she has desire to pay... Nico!...Okay, okay. Item cost two euros, she want pay one. Only one!" Frances finished with a look of triumph.

Molly and Ben stared at her. "Wait, you're saying...that the new chief was trying to bargain at the grocery store? At the épicerie? Tried not to pay the price on the sticker?"

"Yes!" shouted Frances, and she got up from her stool and did a quick hip-hop routine in the middle of the room, among the tables. "They understood me! I'm practically fluent!"

"Some people think they are being cheated if they pay full price," said Ben.

"Sure, in some places. But the village épicerie? That family is hardly known for wallowing in vast sums of profit! It's ridiculous!"

Molly felt a great deal of affection for the various shopkeepers in Castillac, all of whom had been very gentle with her when she was first learning French, not to mention getting to know the customs of the village. It appalled her that anyone would try to cheat them.

"Frances, do you know if this was a one-time thing, or something Chief Charlot is doing all over the place?"

"*Partout!*" said Frances, glowing, and amazed that the right word had just appeared in her mouth, just like that, without her having to search for it.

THE TRUCK CAME through the front yard of La Baraque at exactly six in the morning, waking Bobo, then Molly and the Mertenses, as well as Arthur Malreaux, who had been sound asleep in his room in the annex after staying up late reading. Ben had the talent of deep sleep no matter what, and snoozed through the din.

"What on earth," mumbled Molly crossly, as she flung on some clothes and went to talk to the driver. It was never a good idea to have pre-caffeine conversations first thing in the morning, but she pulled on her boots and stomped across the meadow to the old ruined barn, where the truck was now parked.

"Boris!" she said, seeing him sitting in the cab.

"Bonjour, Madame Sutton," he said, as insolent as the first day she met him, when his reckless driving had put Constance in a ditch.

"The next time you come, please use the short driveway right over here," she said pointing. "There is no need to drive through my yard, waking my guests!"

Boris shrugged. "Gradin said he needed this stuff first thing."

"Yes, fine, wonderful. Bring Monsieur Gradin everything he

needs and do it when he says. Just don't drive the truck through my yard anymore. Do you understand?"

He nodded, but Molly saw that he'd wanted to get a rise out of her, and was pleased with how his morning had begun. If she had anyone to bet with, she'd put a hundred euros on his doing it again. And again.

She was hoping to have a word with Monsieur Gradin that morning anyway, so after Boris drove off, she decided to wait a bit to see if she could catch him, and take a look at how things had been coming along. It was a big project, so she was happy to see how much progress had already been made. The plan was to turn the ruined barn into three gîtes, giving her a total of seven additional beds. The building had started out nearly entirely covered in vines, with a collapsed roof and only two-and-a-half good walls. The mason needed to build one wall from scratch, stabilize and rebuilt another, as well as make doorframes, window-frames, and chimneys. Once he was done, another man was slated to build the interior walls, put in kitchens and bathrooms, and do the rest of the finishing work.

Monsieur Gradin had only been at work for a short time, but the site was already practically unrecognizable. The vines were gone, and Molly could see he had built a fire and burned most of them. The loose stones had been piled to one side and he had begun removing the debris of the collapsed roof. All in all, Molly was very pleased. She would be spending almost the last of her windfall on this project; it was going to cost a fortune, but she hoped the new spaces would make La Baraque so much more profitable that she would be able to relax when those low-tourist winter months came.

What good is money, just sitting in a bank? She wanted to use it for something. And as far as Molly was concerned, La Baraque deserved every penny.

But there were more interviews to do, and Molly was impatient to get going; she headed back to the house, had a quick cup of coffee with a sleepy Ben, and took off for the Valettes'. She thought about the last time she had gone to their house, only a few days earlier. How she and Ben had looked forward to the odd dinner party—a group of friends and acquaintants, invited by a family of complete strangers.

Were the Valettes hiding some kind of secret, and the murder somehow the result of that? Why would a successful man like Simon give up an important and lucrative job and move his family to Castillac, of all places? How were the girls doing, after the shock of losing their nanny so unexpectedly?

So many questions. There was never any end to them.

She turned into the Valettes' driveway with a vague sense of foreboding. She didn't see anyone outside. Parking her scooter out of the way of the car, Molly stood still for a moment, looking around, taking in the house and the grounds as though it was her first time seeing it. A flash of white on an upper floor caught her eye, but when she looked up at the window, it was gone. Slowly she walked toward the house, her footsteps crunching loud on the gravel.

Then shrieks, a door slam, and Chloë came flying out to a terrace on the side of the house. Nimbly she vaulted the wall and jumped down to the ground, letting out a dramatic "*Uhh*" when she landed. Molly smiled as the girl disappeared around the side of the house.

"Bonjour, madame," said a young voice, as Molly started up the steps to the front door. Gisele was standing just inside, and she opened the door, her expression serious.

"Bonjour, Gisele," said Molly. "You are not joining your sister on her obstacle course?"

"What is an obstacle course?"

"I probably have the word wrong. It's a thing we do in America, sort of a race where you have to jump over things, climb things, maybe go through water, swing...it's quite fun actually. If you're in the mood."

Gisele seemed to be thinking this over, but did not say anything.

"I just wanted to say...I was looking for the two of you the other night. It was a harrowing night, obviously, and I wanted to make sure you were all right. I mean, as all right as you could be, under the circumstances."

Gisele looked into Molly's eyes but still said nothing. Molly had the urge to smooth the girl's blonde hair back from her face, but restrained herself.

"I know we barely know each other. But I'd like you to know that I live at La Baraque, on the other side of the village, just a little ways down the road. Anyone can direct you there. So if you ever have any reason to want to...I don't know, take a little break, come for a visit? You are always welcome at my house. And you can bring Chloë too. Not that I'm encouraging you to run away from home," she added, with a laugh. "I only mean...just come, if you like."

The girl nodded and Molly thought she saw a fleeting warmth in her eyes.

"Do you want to talk to my parents? I heard that my father hired you."

"He did. I'd like to talk to your mother today, if I could. Is she feeling okay, do you know?"

"Well enough to—" the girl looked away and cut herself off.

"...to what?"

"Nothing. She's upstairs. I'll run up and tell her you're here."

What was that about? Molly wondered. In the girl's absence, Molly looked around the foyer, again remembering the other night when Simon had been so gracious, pouring everyone glasses of a good vintage champagne. He had not been a stingy pourer.

Chloë appeared, breathless, and stared at Molly.

"Bonjour, Chloë," said Molly. "You look as though you're enjoying country life more than anyone."

The girl tossed her head. Then she looked goggle-eyed at

Molly and stuck her fingers in her ears. "Boo!" she shrieked, and ran through the front door and out of sight around the side of the house.

"Come on up, Madame Sutton," said Gisele, having trotted partway down the stairs. "My mother is supposed to rest, so she'd like to talk in her bedroom, if you don't mind."

"Not a bit," said Molly, glad of the chance to see the Valettes' bedroom, both for investigative purposes and out of plain curiosity. The door was thick and old, with many layers of paint and an ancient brass lock. The room was in a corner of the house; tall windows on both sides would have let in a lot of light, but Camille had pulled the gray silk curtains halfway closed, so that the light was soft and diffused. It made Molly feel a little sleepy.

"Bonjour, Camille," said Molly, reaching to shake her hand.

"Bonjour, Molly. I want to thank you so much for taking the job. I was very pleased when Simon told me you and Ben had agreed to help. I just don't know what...I know it's been days, but I just can't quite believe it happened."

"I understand," said Molly, dropping down on a pouf next to the bed. "It is always difficult to process violence. And it changes us, when we've been exposed to it."

"No doubt."

"Are the girls doing all right? It must have been a terrible shock for them."

Camille shrugged. "As well as one could expect."

Molly waited but the other woman did not elaborate. "All right, let me begin by asking a few questions. How long had Violette worked for your family?"

"Six months, something like that."

"You were happy with her?"

"Yes. She was quite accomplished."

"Did she get along with everyone in the family?"

"Quite."

"How about Monsieur Valette, Simon's father?"

"What is your question? Did Violette get along with Raphael? As far as I know. I don't believe they had much to do with each other. He stays in his room most of the time."

"All right. Excuse me for jumping right in with what will sound like a rude question—did Raphael or your husband ever show any interest in Violette sexually?"

"You don't beat around the bush, do you?" Camille smiled, but her eyes were flat. "No, they didn't. Neither one of them. All we wanted to do was leave the hectic life we had in Paris, and replace it with something calm and peaceful. It was going to be good for all of us. And now this had to happen. I'm sure everyone in the village has probably decided we're a pack of murdering crazies and will have nothing to do with us."

Molly noticed tension around Camille's mouth, and saw several patches of raw skin on her lips.

"I think you'll find that the villagers aren't quite so quick to judge," Molly said.

They talked for another half hour, at which point Camille said that she was terribly fatigued and would Molly mind finishing their chat another day?

Molly agreed, feeling she had no choice, and left on her scooter, seeing no one on her way out.

When the sound of the scooter could no longer be heard, Simon appeared in the doorway to the bedroom. "What did she want to know?" he asked his wife.

"I don't know why you hired that woman," said Camille. "You really think it's a wonderful idea to have not only the bumbling gendarmes but that woman poking her nose into all our affairs? Whatever possessed you, Simon?"

"What better way to deflect guilt than to add more investigators?"

"I'll take that as an admission," she said, her eyes blazing.

"It's nothing of the sort," he said, changing his tone from exasperated to patient. "Only that...look, how do you think it will go for a bunch of strangers to show up and immediately one of the household gets murdered? They're going to think it's one of us, Camille, don't you see? And it's a fairly sensible conclusion. Why would some random person from the village that you happened to invite to dinner kill her? It lacks reason!"

Camille fell back on the pillows, both hands picking at her lips, an old habit that Simon knew was a bad sign. But there was nothing he could do for her at the moment, so he went back outside and continued with the laborious sorting of rocks at the stone wall.

❧ 19 ❧

Ben made Molly a kir and joined her in the living room. "I do have one question," he said, handing over the drink. "You remember you agreed to marry me, right?"

"Haha!" said Molly. "Oh wait, that came out wrong. Of *course* I remember, and I think about it every day with great joy."

"Well?"

"Is it bothering you that we aren't making plans? You're not in any hurry?"

"I'm not in a rush to have the ceremony, Molly. And I know we just talked about this. But something about what happened at the Valettes…I'd like to tell people. Stop keeping the secret."

Molly sipped her drink. For the first time in her life, everything relationship-wise was going so well that she felt a little superstitious about rocking the boat. "You know, I just realized I've been acting just like Frances."

"That's a little scary."

Molly laughed again. "I know. Like I said, I've been enjoying having our little secret, you know? But I think I've probably done that long enough. I'm ready to tell if you are."

Ben grinned. "All right, chérie, same here." He leaned over and gave her a lingering kiss on the side of her neck.

Molly sighed, not quite believing how content she was.

"Now that that's out of the way," said Ben, "let's sit down and put our heads together on the case. We need a timeline with everyone's movements on it. I think at this point we have most of that nailed down, don't we?"

"Well, if you include the disappeared and unaccounted for, yes, I think so."

"Here's what I have," said Ben, looking at his notes and writing a master list on a big pad. "It looks like everyone except for the cook and her daughter were seated at the table when the lights went out. So the only notation after a person's name is where they were when the lights came back on."

"Got it."

"Nico, Frances, Edmond, Anne-Marie, and the two of us: at table. Lapin and Lawrence: missing. Marie-Claire, Camille, and Dr. Vernay: in foyer. Pascal: coming up stairs to foyer from basement. Rex Ford: coming into dining room from library. Simon: missing, then coming downstairs to foyer."

Molly got up and looked over Ben's shoulder at the list.

"Anything jump out at you?"

"I'd feel a lot better if we knew where Lapin was now. It's exactly the kind of thing Charlot might jump on."

"Seems like it's Rex Ford who should be getting our attention."

"I know he was in the wrong place, but at least in my talk with him, I didn't see anything to pursue. Do you think Simon was upstairs checking on his father?"

"Seems likely, or at least plausible. How long do you think the lights were out? Long enough to strangle Violette, leave the library through the kitchen or dining room, and hurry upstairs before Pascal got the new fuse in?"

"How long does it take to strangle someone?" Molly asked quietly.

"Not long. Two minutes or less, if the person knows what they're doing."

Molly took a deep breath and exhaled it. A young life, snuffed out for what had to be selfish reasons of one kind or another. Which of the twelve had done it?

"But why?" she said plaintively to Ben.

"I know how you feel. And I don't know. But we'll figure it out, Molly. We will."

NOT LONG AFTER MOLLY LEFT, Chief Charlot pulled up in the Valettes' driveway. She walked over to where Simon was working, and held her hand up as a visor to the strong sun.

"Looks like you've got yourself quite a job," she said, seeing the sweat on his naked chest.

"Oh bonjour, Chief," said Simon. "I know it's early, but do you have any news?"

Charlot glared at him. "No, I don't have news. Are you under the mistaken impression that I'm going to be sharing the information I gather with you?"

"I...no, I'm not," said Simon, wanting to say something sarcastic but getting control of himself in time.

"We're still waiting on lab results," she said. "I'd like to have a talk with your wife. She is home, I hope?"

"Yes. She's resting upstairs. I do hope...I hope you will take into account what I told you the other day about the state of her health. Not surprisingly, this whole affair has set her back considerably."

"Oh boo hoo," said Charlot, and set off for the house.

Simon stared at her. He couldn't believe a public servant

would say such a thing. Knowing he shouldn't do it, he trotted to catch up with her. "Chief?" he said.

Charlot stopped and looked at him defiantly, hands on hips. Simon, who had vanquished many powerful men in the halls of international business, suddenly could not think of a single appropriate thing to say. Her behavior was appalling, but the last thing he needed to do was get on her bad side. "Try to be gentle with her," he said.

Charlot's lip curled into a victorious smile. "We'll see," she said, and walked on.

She found Camille still in bed, still wearing the quilted Chanel bed-jacket, sitting up and staring into space.

"Bonjour, Madame Valette," said the chief. "I'm sure this is all very trying but I have a killer to track down, so you'll excuse me if I skip over the usual pleasantries."

Camille went back to picking at her lip. "When did you come to Castillac?" she asked. "I heard you are a newcomer as well."

"Apologies—not relevant. Now, can you explain to me how you arrived at the guest list for your party on Saturday night?"

Camille looked at her feet. "You're going to think I'm silly."

"Probably. Just explain, please."

"Well, I very much wanted to meet some people in our new village. I know that it takes time to make friendships, and I thought I might try to hurry the process along a little bit. One of the first mornings here, I went to the Café de la Place for breakfast—if you haven't been, I recommend it highly. Good, strong cup of coffee, and the—"

"Yes, yes, you may skip the restaurant reviews."

Camille paused, and swallowed. "Anyway, I met a waiter there who was particularly friendly, especially once I told him I had just moved to Castillac. And somehow, one way or another, he helped me make out the guest list."

"So you had a waiter you had never met make a guest list for a dinner party?"

"Yes." More lip picking.

"Do you see that it looks a little strange?"

Camille shrugged, unable to think of anything else to say about it.

"Were you jealous of Violette Crespelle, Madame Valette?"

"What?"

"She was young, talented, and lively, from what people are telling me. While you are, excuse me, some sort of invalid?"

Camille's mouth opened and then shut. "I don't want you here insulting me. Simon!" she called, but the windows were closed and she knew he would not hear her if he was out on his rock pile.

But to her relief, he opened the door to the bedroom almost right away. "Darling?" he said. "Is anything the matter?"

"I'll be going," said Chief Charlot, with a satisfied smirk. She didn't like these Valettes; she thought them arrogant and self-absorbed.

It would please her to hang a murder on one of them.

Problem was, she didn't really think either one of them was guilty.

20

"I think it's so interesting that you moved here out of the blue and ended up a private investigator! Well, I suppose anyone who's a big mystery reader would get excited about the turn your life has taken," said Elise Mertens. She and her husband, Todor, were sitting on the terrace with Molly, Ben, and Arthur Malreaux, having a drink at dusk. The Jenkinses were off touring yet another cathedral somewhere.

"'Out of the blue' describes it pretty well," said Molly with a laugh. "Although once I met Ben, maybe it was fate," she added, and he threw an arm across her shoulders and kissed the side of her head.

"So when are you going to marry her?" Elise asked Ben. "I can say things like that because I'm seventy-two. Once you pass seventy, you're allowed to say whatever you bloody well like."

"Oh, Elise," said Todor, but he was smiling.

"Actually," said Molly slowly. "We *are* getting married. And that's the first time I've said it out loud."

"Congratulations," said Arthur Malreaux.

"That's lovely!" said Elise. "Where will you have the ceremony?"

"We…we haven't figured out the details yet," said Molly. "So, Arthur, have you had any luck tracking down your relatives?"

Arthur looked down. "Well," he said, switching his gaze to the woods, which were darkening as the sun dropped. "When you start looking into something, sometimes you discover things you do not expect."

"I'll say," said Ben.

They all waited, but Arthur did not continue.

"Another drink, anyone?" asked Ben, reaching for the bottle of cassis.

"I'm at my limit," said Todor. "And since Elise has already warned you that people of our age can say whatever we like, I'll go ahead and ask you, Arthur. What did you find out that surprised you?"

Arthur ran his hand through his thick, wavy, hair. He stood up from the table suddenly. "If you must know, I had believed my second cousin twice removed to have been involved with the Resistance. For various reasons I won't go into, it would mean very much to have a relative who had behaved with honor during such a frightening and dangerous time."

He paused. The others were on the edge of their seats, wondering what he had found out. Molly noticed how exciting it was, anticipating bad news.

"Turns out my original information couldn't have been more wrong. He was a collaborator of the worst kind, responsible for the deaths of Resistance fighters throughout the Dordogne, all because he was lining his own pockets."

"Oh dear," said Elise. Todor shook his head and downed the rest of his wine.

"Of course, *you* didn't do those things," said Molly. "It doesn't reflect badly on you because you had nothing to do with it."

Arthur shrugged, looking as though the weight on his shoulders was very heavy indeed.

"How did you find out the real story?" asked Ben.

"Madame Gervais. I do want to thank you for introducing me to her, Molly. She was very happy to talk with me, and we spent quite a few hours together. I've found that a lot of people don't want to talk about that time. She was a real exception."

"I'm sorry she didn't tell you what you wanted to hear," said Molly. "And...this is going to sound, I don't know, very American, I guess...but if heroism is really important to you—if it matters so much that you were willing to spend your vacation tracking down the history of your second cousin twice removed—then find some way to be a hero yourself. It's not like there aren't a million ways to do it these days."

"It's true, the Americans are far more interested in self-improvement than the rest of us," said Elise with a chuckle.

"Hard to say which is better," said Ben. "Unbridled optimism about what we can accomplish, or a steady pessimism that makes any accomplishment a lovely surprise."

Everyone laughed.

"I suppose the vast majority of people during the war just tried to keep their heads down and hope none of their loved ones were killed," said Todor. "A few were courageous and valiant, and a few were craven. I don't imagine it's possible to know what factors determine which group a person ends up in."

"Todor reads about psychology all the time," said Elise. "I can't tell you how many conditions he's diagnosed us both with." The others chuckled.

"A collaborator is likely to be a narcissist," said Todor, undeterred by his wife's joking. "Someone who thinks the world revolves around him, who thinks he deserves the best of what's available—and he won't care a whit about anyone else."

"That's just it," said Arthur. "If it was just a matter of my cousin's enriching herself, that wouldn't be nearly as bad. But she was stockpiling food to make a bigger profit, and letting people starve."

"Classic, I'm sad to say."

"What makes a person like that?" asked Arthur.

"I don't think anyone knows," said Todor. "Early life experiences, biology, genetics...the brain and how personalities are formed are almost entirely uncharted waters, though you'll find plenty of people willing to give opinions. Not much that is backed up by actual science, I'm afraid."

Arthur ate an olive while concluding that what he had found out had only increased the mystery, not solved it.

Molly was completely distracted, thinking about what Todor had said and how it related to the Crespelle case. Were almost all murderers narcissists, she wondered. By definition, you're making the decision that your own needs, whatever they are, are worth more than another person's life.

And looked at through that lens, one person at the dinner party stood out among the rest. She couldn't wait for the guests to wander back to their lodgings so she could talk it over with Ben.

❦ 21 ❦

Merla was in the kitchen, just beginning the Valettes' dinner, when the moaning started. Dropping an eggplant into the sink, she froze, a feeling of dread passing through her. She did not know whether she should see if someone needed help or flee the house as quickly as possible.

Chloë and Gisele were under the small table in the foyer. Gisele had found a tablecloth that nearly reached the floor, and the two girls had brought stuffed animals and cookies with them, planning to bivouac indefinitely. When they heard the noise coming from upstairs, Gisele pulled Chloë close and put her hands over her sister's ears.

Simon had put a small chair on the balcony of their bedroom, and Camille sat there watching swallows dive after insects in the early evening, having put her book aside. When she heard the moans, she closed the door behind her and the sound was somewhat muffled.

Simon was at the rock pile, his shirt dark with sweat although the air was cooling. He stopped when he heard the first moan, hoping he was mistaken about the cause. Another one came, louder and more ragged. He sighed. Putting the crowbar down,

Simon made his way into the house and upstairs to his father's room.

"Father," he said gently.

Raphael did not look in Simon's direction but bellowed again, a mournful drawn-out sound that came from deep in his chest. The sound would be heartbreaking for anyone to hear, and for Simon to hear it coming from his father filled him with sorrow and frustration.

"I wish there was something I could say that would calm you," he said, reaching out to put a hand on Raphael's arm.

Raphael twitched and shook his son off. His eyes were wide, and Simon had the clear feeling that his father was seeing things he himself did not. "Would you like something to drink? Are you hungry? Cold?" He had asked these questions every time his father had this kind of spell; they had never led to any understanding of what the trouble was, but he kept asking because he had no idea what else to do.

With a sudden lurch, Raphael was out of his chair. He was a bigger man than his son, his body far healthier than his mind. "*Where are my scissors?*" he bawled.

"Are you fond of eggplant? I can't remember. I know Mother used to make that ratatouille when we were in Provence in the summer. Remember how she would cook it for a long time so that the vegetables—"

"My *scissors!*"

"Please, calm yourself, Father. After you stabbed the sofa cushions, I thought it best to take the scissors. Go ahead, vent your outrage all you like, make the entire house as miserable as you are!"

Raphael moaned, his anguish bare. His son bowed his head, wishing, not entirely selfishly, that his father would die.

22

Ben was very tired of dealing with Bernard Petit, but hopeful he would soon solve the man's problem. He had ordered a set of motion detectors with video, which he planned to set up at various locations in and around the Petit house. It had been an expensive outlay, but Ben figured that if Petit balked at paying for the cameras, he would find plenty of uses for the equipment in the future.

After spending the entire morning dragging ladders around in order to install the cameras, Ben, like any Frenchman, was ready for a good, long lunch. He drove back to Castillac and settled on the terrace of the Café de la Place, dreaming about Pascal's mother's pâté and a big bowl of cassoulet, in the mood for hearty fare since the day had turned colder.

"Sorry, but it's been so warm lately, cassoulet isn't on the menu," said Pascal to a massively disappointed Ben.

"Agh, I could practically taste it," said Ben, letting his irritation at Petit spill over into lunch.

"Maybe the beef stew?" asked Pascal, with a twinkle in his eye, knowing that his mother's stew was a favorite of everyone in the village.

Ben ordered it gratefully, along with a glass of Médoc.

"Terrible thing, the other night," said Pascal. Ben thought he looked a little pale.

"Yes. I'll want to talk to you at some point, maybe if you have some time after this lunch?"

Pascal nodded. "Hard to predict how busy we'll be. And I don't think I'll be any help. But happy to talk, of course." He moved off to the kitchen, gracefully dodging another waiter and a woman looking for the bathroom.

Ben put his jacket back on and stared into space, thinking about Violette Crespelle and her relationships with the other members of the Valette household. Was Camille jealous of the attention and affection her daughters gave the nanny? Or was something going on between Violette and Simon? Or even, implausible as it might seem, Raphael?

Out of the corner of his eye he glimpsed a gendarme's uniform, spotless and perfectly creased, and turned to see Paul-Henri heading straight for him.

"May I?" asked the junior officer, pointing to the seat across from Ben.

"Certainly," Ben answered, quickly trying to figure out a way to entice Paul-Henri into telling him about any progress the gendarmes might have made in the case.

Pascal arrived as though by telepathy and put down another place setting without a word. "I'll have the stew," said Paul-Henri, and Pascal winked at Ben and disappeared inside the kitchen.

"I'd like to talk you in confidence," Paul-Henri said, his voice so soft Ben could barely hear what he was saying.

"Of course," said Ben.

Paul-Henri ran his teeth along his bottom lip, thinking hard. "Will you swear not to say a word about what I'm about to tell you? Well, you can tell Molly, since you're partners and I know you would anyway. But no one else."

Ben was loathe to make any such promise, but his gut told him that whatever Paul-Henri had up his sleeve, it was going to be worth it.

"All right," said Ben. "As long as you're not asking me to break the law."

Paul-Henri let out a nervous guffaw. "Hardly! The whole idea is to help catch criminals, not propagate them."

Pascal appeared with the pâté. "Give my regards to your mother," said Ben. Paul-Henri usually relished the dish but was too consumed by his thoughts to have any at first.

"So?" said Ben, digging a knife into the crock and spreading a thick layer of pâté on a piece of toasted baguette.

"I'm...I'm not feeling a great deal of confidence in the new chief," said Paul-Henri slowly.

Interesting, thought Ben.

"She's quite by-the-book, which I would have guessed would suit me quite well, but in the event...all right, let me get to the point. I am very serious about my job, Monsieur Dufort. The idea that a murderer is loose, running amok in the village—it's intolerable, frankly, and I believe you understand perfectly well where I am coming from."

Ben nodded, chewing.

"I am no different from many other Castillaçois; I have a great deal of respect for what you and Madame Sutton have accomplished over the past few years. It was my pleasure, when Maron was chief, to work with you both, and I can say with all modesty that I think we worked well together and ensured a safer village for us all."

Oh, how he does drone on, thought Ben, taking a sip of his wine.

"In short," said Paul-Henri, lowering his voice even more, so that Ben had to lean halfway across the table to hear him. "In short, I am so worried about the competence of the new chief that I propose—completely against protocol, I am sorely aware—I propose sharing such information with you as is pertinent to the investigation. I believe Maron did as much, am I correct? And which sharing, against protocol or no, has proven to have excellent results, thus far a hundred per cent arrest rate if my arithmetic is correct."

Ben felt like leaping out of his chair and doing a victory dance, but he had long experience in controlling his emotions and gave no hint to Paul-Henri. "We would appreciate that," he said mildly, and grinned with anticipation as Pascal came out holding a tray with two steaming bowls on it.

After they had eaten several mouthfuls of the rich and flavorful stew, spiked with rosemary, thyme, and some other spice that remained Pascal's mother's deep secret, Ben waited to see if Paul-Henri would volunteer anything without prompting.

"We've got Lapin in our sights," Paul-Henri said, after swallowing and wiping his mouth with a napkin. "You know that on the night of the murder, he disappeared right when the lights went out and hasn't been seen since?"

Ben sighed. "I was afraid Charlot would draw the wrong conclusion about that. But you know Lapin, Paul-Henri, at least a little? Do you really think he's a murderer? And why in the world would he kill someone who had just arrived in town, a total stranger?"

"Number one, it's your belief that Lapin and Crespelle didn't know each other, but you haven't seen him to ask him, have you?"

Ben shook his head.

"I thought so. As you know better than anyone, only painstakingly accurate legwork will determine who had any connection to the nanny. Number two, who am I to judge what people I know are capable of? Every day, people are known to run off the rails, Monsieur Dufort. And number three, how do you account for his sudden flight without telling a soul? His new wife doesn't even know where he is. You must admit, his behavior..."

Ben sighed again, longer and louder this time. "Running off wasn't the best decision, there's no denying that. But it's *Lapin*, Paul-Henri. He has never been known for making great decisions. I've known him since we were in *primaire* together—"

"With all due respect, I don't think his early school days are relevant to the case. Perhaps if he is innocent, you will find him and he can come back and clear his name. But in the meantime, Chief Charlot and I—"

"I thought you had no confidence in Charlot?"

"Well, I...I'm not saying that I never agree with her on anything. Or that it is even my job to agree or disagree," he said. "In short, I am not even arguing with you about Lapin or not Lapin. I have no horse in that race, you understand? I only want the killer brought to justice, same as you do. If Lapin is innocent, I trust you—and he—will be able to demonstrate that."

Ben wiped the last of the sauce from his bowl with a torn-off hunk of baguette. "Oh, that was a good meal. I was planning to go for a run this afternoon but now I'm not so sure."

"Do you not keep the usual work hours?" Paul-Henri looked horrified at the idea of such irregularity.

Ben shrugged, enjoying the other man's discomfort. "Sometimes we work really late, sometimes very early in the morning. So taking a very long lunch, maybe a nap or some exercise—it all works out in the end."

He had given up hope that Paul-Henri had anything useful to say when the officer leaned forward and said in a low voice, "One more thing. It's about Camille Valette. Before moving to Castillac —and I believe not very long before—she spent some time in a psychiatric hospital."

"Hm," said Ben, noncommittal.

"You're not interested? You don't think that's possibly meaningful?"

"To the investigation? Maybe, maybe not. Do you know what the diagnosis was?"

"That's exactly the question I asked. Charlot doesn't know any details, only that Valette was there for nearly a month. Someplace just outside Paris, in one of the suburbs. Probably someplace swank, like a high-end hotel," he added, giving in to his imagination.

"All right. Anything else?"

"Like I said, we don't have any details yet. I'll get back in touch when I get them."

"Much appreciated, Paul-Henri," said Ben, though he did not seem as grateful as Paul-Henri would have wished.

Overall, he was rather disappointed in Ben. He didn't seem impressed by the risk Paul-Henri was taking in order to pass him information that absolutely should not be transmitted to anyone outside the gendarmerie. And he also did not seem to have the same clear image of Camille in the nuthouse that Paul-Henri did: wandering the halls wearing a thin cotton nightgown and a vacant expression, a bloody knife raised in her fist...just as an example.

All right, perhaps he was veering a little toward an operatic scenario, Paul-Henri admitted to himself. But it *could* be true.

They ordered coffee. Ben was intentionally not making a fuss over Paul-Henri's offer, thinking that his nonchalance might draw him out more successfully than enthusiasm would. But instead of becoming talkative, Paul-Henri became sullen. He was thinking about the long list of slights and insults he had suffered at the hands of Chief Charlot, and not about the Crespelle case at all.

WHILE BEN WAS HAVING lunch with Paul-Henri, Molly had zipped into the village on her scooter to pay a visit to Merla and Ophélie. Molly found the place without any trouble, a small, unremarkable house on rue Saterne, only three houses away from the decrepit, falling-down house of Madame Luthier, whom Molly had still never met.

Merla ushered her in seconds after Molly knocked, and offered her coffee, which, Molly being Molly, she accepted with a smile.

"I don't think I'm going to have a single thing to tell you," said Merla. "You know I've only worked for the Valettes for a matter of days. And honestly, I am not in the habit of gossiping about my employers. As you might imagine, discretion is an important part of my job."

"Of course!" said Molly. "If a young woman hadn't been murdered in their library, I would not be asking you a single question about the family. However, I hope you'll agree that circumstances require...well, being more open about certain things than you would be otherwise?"

Merla gave a short nod—very short—as Ophélie served coffee and some small pastries.

Molly thanked her. She saw that Merla was skittish, and didn't want to overwhelm her or give her a reason to clam up. "All right, let's get started," she said, in what she hoped was a reassuring tone. "How did the Valettes find you?"

"Pascal. I guess Madame Valette had breakfast at the Café de la Place a few days after they moved in. She got to talking with Pascal, as almost everyone does, and said she was looking for a part-time cook. I've filled in at the Café from time to time—when they needed extra help catering special events and such. So Pascal thought of me."

"He's a good friend," said Molly, and the two women nodded but said nothing further.

"And do you like the Valettes? As employers?"

"No problems. I have dealt with Monsieur Valette exclusively. Monsieur came to the house and offered me the job, and paid me. Promptly, just as we agreed, which I thought was good of him, considering what they were all going through."

"And what about personally?"

Merla was taken aback. "My personal feelings are not part of the job. Monsieur talks to me about the menu, I do the shopping, I cook. They have only had people over the one time, and as you remember, Ophélie came to help serve and assist me in the kitchen."

"So you don't especially like them," said Molly, with a small smile.

Merla allowed herself a whisper of a smile. "I had a difficult marriage," she said quietly. "I don't tell you this because it gives me any pleasure to talk about it, but my ex-husband was a cheat like you wouldn't believe. I'm not sure there was a woman in the entire Dordogne that he didn't proposition. And plenty of them said yes. Sorry to say that about your father, Ophélie."

Ophélie waved away her mother's apology. She was very interested to hear what her mother really thought about the Valettes, because she herself had been unable to pry out a single word, and hoped Molly would manage better.

"And so..." Merla ran her hand through her short hair. "So it's no surprise, is it, that I don't exactly love working in a house where I suspect that kind of thing was going on."

At first Molly didn't get what the cook was saying. Then Molly said, "Oh! Which kind of thing?" she asked, wanting to make sure.

"Monsieur and the nanny. I can't swear to it, I never saw them do anything, so don't go getting any ideas about making me testify because I won't do it. But I can sense these things. I've got experience with it, as I said. I would bet anything you can name that Monsieur Valette and Violette were up to something together."

Molly took a few breaths. "Just to be absolutely clear—when you say 'up to something,' you mean something...sexual?"

Merla nodded, this time emphatically, as though Molly were a bit dim. "Like I say, I'm uncomfortable talking like this. I want to keep the job! But also...that poor girl...."

For another fifteen minutes, Molly asked other questions of them both, mostly about the night of the murder. But it was

Merla's insistence on something happening between Simon and Violette that was most interesting by far, not least because it fit quite neatly into the way Molly had already seen the case shaping up.

Quite neatly, indeed.

23

Though Simon thought the girls should be excused for a week of school given the circumstances, Camille prevailed, and they got a mere three days off. In this case, however, it was better for the girls to be in school, where every day was more or less the same, where all they had to do was complete their assignments—a relief, given everything happening at home.

When the school day was over, Gisele found Chloë on the playground trying to climb up the side of a wall by stepping on some small decorative protrusions in the stone. A boy was cheering her on but it was unclear whether he was being genuine or trying to encourage her to go higher so she would fall.

"Come on," Gisele called up to her. "It's time to go home." She shielded her eyes from the sun and looked up at her sister, who was gripping onto the lintel while searching for a foothold. Once Chloë got her teeth into something, it could be nearly impossible to pry her away. Gisele glanced at the boy, but Chloë was moving too slowly and he had lost interest; with a whoop he ran into a group of boys at the other end of the playground and disappeared.

"Chloë!" said Gisele. "You're going to get in trouble!"

The younger girl could find nothing higher to stand on, and her audience has abandoned her, so with a dramatic sigh she let go of the lintel and dropped to the ground, scraping her knee.

Chloë sprang up, not crying though her knee stung mightily. "Can we at least go by the épicerie and get some candy?"

Gisele grinned. She might be the older, more responsible sister, but she liked candy as much as any kid. The sisters held hands and left the playground, a trickle of blood slowly moving down Chloë's leg.

"I'm getting sour Haribo. The little apple ones. Oh, I hope they have them. The sours are the absolute best, don't you think so? Gisele! Hey, Gisele!"

Her sister was staring ahead at a group of villagers, where she had spied Molly Sutton.

Chloë slammed her elbow into Gisele's side and took off for the épicerie, which was half a block away.

Gisele did not hurry after her. She held her schoolbooks to her chest, drumming her fingertips on them, wondering...should she talk to Madame Sutton? She seemed so friendly. But that didn't mean she would take anything Gisele had to say seriously.

Grownups can be so stupid, she thought, walking past the group of villagers quickly, not wanting to be noticed. They don't realize that children have eyes and ears, just as much as they do. They think we don't see, don't pay any attention.

But some of us do.

She slipped into the épicerie in time to talk Chloë out of putting seven bags of Haribo on the counter. "I only have money for one each," said Gisele, eyeing a chocolate bar with raisins and almonds that was a little too expensive. There was no one else in the store and they made their purchase and headed home.

"I know," said Gisele. "How about we drop off our bags without saying anything to anyone, and take our candy out into the woods. We can pretend to be explorers or something."

"Papa will see us. He's always playing with those rocks beside the driveway."

"We can circle around, where he can't see us. Put our books by the back door and run for freedom!"

Chloë grinned at that, as Gisele knew she would.

24

It was too late for lunch and too early for dinner, which was precisely why Molly had asked Simon Valette to meet her at Chez Papa at five. She wanted a degree of privacy, along with a location where he might be more likely to speak freely than he would at home. And it never hurt to talk over drinks.

"So how's the case going?" Nico asked her as he wiped down the bar.

"Eh," said Molly, not wanting to oversell her theory even to herself.

"I'll give you my unasked-for two cents. Something's a little funny when a guy like Simon Valette quits his job in Paris and moves to a place like Castillac."

"What exactly does 'a little funny' mean?"

"It means it needs explaining. I haven't gotten to know the dude, but he went to the *École Nationale d'Administration*, right? A guy like that, ENA grads, the world is their oyster. The best jobs, great apartments, important contacts in business and government. He was up at the very top of the heap, the tippity-top, right? Why give all that up?"

Molly considered. "Make me a kir, will you? And keep the questions coming, that's a good one."

Nico reached for the cassis and got to work while Molly tried to come up with reasons why Simon would turn his back on all that success. She came up empty.

"I didn't talk to the nanny the other night. Did you?" asked Nico.

"Not much, I'm afraid. She seemed energetic and lively enough. The children had disappeared and she was trying to find them. I got the feeling this was not unusual."

"Do you think Simon would be interested in someone who, um, wasn't that good-looking?"

"It's a good question, Nico. Well—she wasn't beautiful, okay. But I would definitely say she was attractive. At my age, youth all by itself starts looking pretty damn good."

"At your age?" Nico cracked up laughing. "Right up there with Madame Gervais?"

"I'm turning forty in an alarmingly small number of days," Molly said in a low voice, as though protecting a state secret.

"Is that so? Having a party?"

"I don't think it's cause for celebration." It wasn't that Molly was vain, or especially worried about getting older in general. It was only that at this point, every year that went by made the possibility of having a child shrink further, and that fact was hard to face.

The door opened and Simon Valette swept in, wearing a very expensive-looking sport coat, a starched button-down shirt with stripes, and a scarf artfully tied around his neck.

"Bonjour, Simon," said Molly. "I'm afraid you need to go home and change. We don't go in for such fashionable clothing around here and you're going to make all the other men look bad."

Simon's eyes widened.

"Joking!" said Molly with a merry grin. "Get a drink and let's talk in the back room."

Nico poured Simon a glass of a local red that wasn't very good, and he and Molly went to the back and sat in a booth across from each other.

"Have you got news?" he said hopefully.

"Oh, not yet. It takes quite a while just to get the information organized, Simon. Especially with a group this large. Just mapping out the comings and goings..."

"Oh yes, of course. Well, anything I can do to speed things along...."

"Much appreciated. I wanted to ask you a couple of specific questions, though. All routine. Violette—she'd been with you around six months?"

"That's right." He took a sip of his wine and grimaced slightly, though he made no comment.

"How did Camille get on with her?"

"Fine. She's—Camille, I mean—not a very...she hasn't been well, as I explained. I think she was relieved to have someone else taking care of our daughters. Not that Violette replaced Camille, I'm not saying that at all. But you know—Violette braided their hair, made sure their clothes looked nice, played games with them —things that Camille couldn't keep up with, day after day. And if you saw me braid hair, well...." He gave Molly a brilliant smile, and she couldn't help noticing how magnetic he was when he turned all his attention on you.

"So the girls liked Violette? Would you say they liked her quite a bit?"

"I would, yes. The drawing lessons, for one thing, were a big hit with both of my daughters."

"And Camille...it would be totally understandable, but was she jealous of your daughters' attention going to Violette?"

"I don't believe so, no. She never said anything to me about it. As I said, I think relief was the main thing Camille felt. Gratitude that the girls had someone so dependable. We all counted on Violette, Camille included."

Simon let go of his glass and brought his fingertips first to his chin and then his cheek. He ran his finger along his face several times, stroking pensively.

"And how about you, Simon?" Molly continued. "Of course I'm aware that you hired us, and it's quite awkward to bring things like this up. But I'm sure you understand that all lines of questioning must be pursued nonetheless."

Simon waved a hand as though to brush away her discomfort. "Of course, of course," he said. "Yes, we've got some things in the family closet that would be...somewhat embarrassing if they became public knowledge. Like all families, I suppose. But ask away, Molly, none of it is of any real consequence."

"All right," said Molly, taking a sip of her kir and then arranging her notebook to prolong the moment. "Tell me," she said finally, "was there anything between you and Violette that Ben and I should know about?"

Simon made a quick intake of breath. He sipped his wine with the same small grimace. "Nothing whatsoever happened between me and Violette," he said. "She did a good job and I was grateful to have her on the household staff. I cannot for the life of me discover even an inkling of why anyone wanted her dead. Certainly not me or Camille, I can swear to that."

"All right. I hear you are a graduate of ENA? I suppose that's like Harvard to an American, and you know I was Boston-raised so I have a soft spot in my heart for the place."

Simon smiled and nodded. "Yes, I suppose they could be considered on a par."

"In terms of prestige, I'm saying."

"Yes."

"I'm wondering why, with that kind of impressive qualification —and your job was just what one would expect, also very important and consequential. And lucrative," she added. "Why walk away from all that? Why come to Castillac, of all places?"

Simon leaned back in the banquette and shrugged, that particular Gallic shrug that is far more expressive than mere words. "Oh, a combination of things, Molly. Camille's health. The stress of the city is invigorating, but not necessarily always the best thing for everyone, you understand? And perhaps...perhaps there was a dash of mid-life crisis as well."

"Ha! You're too young for a midlife crisis!"

"I've always been precocious," he said, deadpan.

Molly laughed, completely sucked in by his charm, though she at least observed the sucking-in as it happened.

She had thought up a few other random questions to ask so that her interest in the potential goings-on between Simon and Violette did not appear to be the only reason for asking for a meeting. Molly observed him carefully. He did not seem anxious or tense. He answered the rest of her questions with deliberation and good humor, and after about a half an hour, she thanked him for his time and said goodbye.

"Get what you needed?" asked Nico.

"Eh," said Molly.

Just because Simon hadn't admitted to anything between him and Violette, didn't mean she had to believe him. His wife was ill, and he was clearly a man who loved paying attention to women *and* getting attention from them. Molly put herself in Camille's place: she imagined being taken out of a stunning Paris apartment and dropped in Castillac with a difficult father-in-law, then being shut up in the bedroom much of the time while my charismatic husband and a lively nanny (that my children adored) ran the household...it made Molly burn with jealousy just thinking about it. She had no idea what the statistics were on jealousy being the motive for murder, but she was ready to push Simon out of a window just after imagining the situation for a moment.

And the point was, it didn't actually matter whether Simon was cheating on his wife or not, Molly mused, riding home on her scooter. If Camille thought he was having an affair, or even that he *might*—she could have seized the opportunity of the sudden darkness covering a dinner party full of people to put an end to what for her was an existential threat.

Sometimes the most likely suspect is actually the murderer, she thought. Simply connect the dots between means, motive, and opportunity, and any detective with any talent at all will end up knocking on the bedroom door of Camille Valette, and no one else.

❦

WHEN MOLLY GOT BACK to La Baraque, Ben was in the kitchen and the house smelled incredibly good. "Oh, I am starving!" Molly exclaimed, wading through Bobo and the orange cat to get to him for a kiss. "And can I just say that coming home to find you behind the counter whipping up dinner is pretty much the best sight ever!"

Ben just smiled and stirred the carrots, which were bathing in an ungodly amount of butter and slowly caramelizing.

"Is that a chicken roasting I smell?"

Ben smiled and nodded. "How did the meeting with Simon go?"

"Eh," she said, but then grinned. "It was terrifically awkward at some points, actually, which only solidifies my thinking."

"Yes?"

"Let me lay it out. Obviously we have to wait for the DNA reports from Florian, and it would help to find the cord that was used as a garrote, but at this point I just don't see this case as any big mystery. Sometimes the most obvious answer is the correct one, you know?"

"Umm...well, about that last bit, sure, sometimes the obvious thing is correct. Though I'm not at all sure what that is in this case."

"Seriously? You haven't been thinking it's probably Camille right from the get-go?"

"*Camille?* No. Not in the least. Not for a moment."

Ben and Molly stood looking at each other with mixed expressions of horror and disbelief.

"How could you—" they both said at once.

"Let me go first," said Molly, pulling herself together a bit. She pulled a leftover container of her favorite lemony mustard dressing out of the refrigerator and stirred it before pouring some on the salad. "Okay. Step by step. We've got a murder in a houseful of people, which at first seems like a whole host of suspects, right? But unless one of our friends is a secret homicidal maniac who prefers to do in total strangers, by far the more likely scenario is that the murderer is one of the people who actually knew the victim, correct?"

"Correct," said Ben, somewhat reluctantly.

"That leaves Simon, Camille, and Raphael. I think we can agree the daughters aren't in the running?"

"Correct," said Ben, more willingly.

"Any of the three had opportunity. The house was pitch dark and you can get to the library through the kitchen. I spoke to Merla and Ophélie, and they both say that they could have been in the pantry just before the murder, which would allow anyone to slip through the kitchen unobserved. They also said that both Simon and Camille came through the kitchen multiple times during the party. They were of course focused on the cooking and cannot remember who came through when."

"But they did not mention Raphael coming through?"

"They weren't standing guard, Ben. He could have come through while they were taking something out of the oven, before the lights went out. Or they could've been in the pantry. Look, any of the rest of us could have gotten to the library through the dining room. But in addition, all the Valettes could have taken the back way. That's what the evidence shows."

"Okay," said Ben. "So that narrows it to three. I'm still not seeing why you choose Camille over the others."

"You're in agreement that they all had opportunity to get to Violette in the library?"

"Yes, all right. Opportunity points among the three are even. I'll also give you means, since a cord to do the job would not be hard for anyone to find, though I'm honestly not at all convinced that Raphael has the mental capacity to pull off something so neat."

"I would agree," said Molly, "thank you for bolstering my conclusion. And that leaves us with motive. And that, my dearest, is where all signs point to Camille."

Ben shook his head slowly.

Molly's eyes widened. "Why do you disagree? I do like Simon, but it's nothing at all to do with that. And—I'm well aware that he's our client and that he hired us expressly to avoid the conclusion I'm reaching—which, to be honest, is a bit suspicious all by itself, isn't it? Why was he so afraid that his wife might get nailed for a murder, unless he guessed—or knew—that she had committed it? At any rate, to get to the bit of information I haven't told you...Merla accuses him of having an affair with Violette."

"Do you have any evidence that she's right? Does he admit to it?"

"Of course he doesn't. But the thing is, Ben—it doesn't matter whether he was or not. Only that Camille thought he was. Or worried about it. And if Merla thought something was going on, wouldn't his wife have been feeling suspicious too?"

Ben took the chicken out of the oven and did not answer at first. "Let's get the food on the table, pour some of that good Médoc, and talk some more," he said finally. They bustled about, Ben slicing the chicken into parts, each with a crispy covering of herbed skin, and Molly opening the wine and scraping the carrots into a serving dish.

"I have something to tell you," he said, after swallowing a few mouthfuls of the comforting food. "Paul-Henri is dissatisfied with

Chantal Charlot. So much so that he is willing to feed us information from time to time. He believes Charlot is pursuing the wrong suspect...but I think his motive is more about embarrassing Charlot than some huge fear that the killer will go free."

"Interesting," said Molly, breaking off the end of a baguette and smearing it with butter. "I wonder what's she's done to make him that upset. He's such a rule-follower, it's a little shocking that he's willing to go against protocol like that."

Ben nodded. "So, what he passed on today, with virtually no explanatory detail, is that Camille Valette has spent some time in a psychiatric hospital."

They looked at each other. Ben waited.

Molly took a long drink of her wine, savoring the woodsy flavor, and then a bit of chicken. "Did he give any details at all? Like what were the circumstances, what was the diagnosis?"

"Nothing else. I don't think Paul-Henri was holding out on me, he just didn't know."

"Well, without more information, I don't think we can do much with it."

"I'm glad to hear you say so."

"It would be ridiculous to think that having mental illness means you're automatically violent and murderous."

"My thought exactly."

"Not automatically...but possibly," said Molly stubbornly. "Okay, I've given the case my best shot. Now let's hear your side," said Molly, managing a smile that was only slightly phony.

25

G lad for a reason to be out of the station while the chief was in, Paul-Henri made his way over to Dr. Vernay's office, working his way down the list of guests at the Valettes' dinner. He stopped briefly on the doorstep to check his uniform, brushed a bit of lint off his sleeve, and knocked on the door.

Robinette Vernay, rosy-cheeked and bursting with good health, opened the door and ushered him inside. "Oh, I'm so sorry, Officer," she said, surprising Paul-Henri. "You do look in woeful shape. I'm afraid the doctor is with a patient at the moment, can you wait for just a bit? Is there anything in the meantime I can do to make you more comfortable?"

Paul-Henri did not know what to say. He yanked down the hem of his coat and lifted his chest. "I'm not sure what you mean," he said. "I am here to see the doctor, yes, but on police business, not as a patient."

"Ah," said Robinette, looking skeptical. "You might want to let the doctor give you a once-over, while you're in there. Your color isn't good," she said ominously.

Unsettled, Paul-Henri took a seat in the small waiting area. He looked around at the minimal effort at decoration, suddenly wishing he could have a glass of something before going in to see the doctor. It had been years since he had had a check-up, and what if the doctor's wife had a talent for diagnosis? It would make perfect sense if she developed such an intuition, given that she had seen a parade of sick people coming into the office day after day for years on end. What if she could sense a dreadful illness on the verge of causing symptoms, something so dreadful that—

"The doctor will see you now," said Robinette, sticking her head through the door. "I've got a bit of pineau, if you'd like?"

The fact that she guessed what he had just thought did not ease Paul-Henri's anxiety. He nodded and took the glass as he went into Dr. Vernay's examination room.

"Bonjour, Officer Monsour," said Dr. Vernay over his shoulder as he washed his hands at the sink. "What can I do for you?"

"I appreciate your taking the time," said Paul-Henri, noticing a prickle at the back of his neck and assigning dire causes to it. He took a swig of pineau. "The gendarmerie is interviewing everyone in attendance at the Valette dinner, as you might expect."

"Of course, of course. Terrible business. Not really my line, you understand—I see people who are ill, sometimes tragically so, but by and large I deal with the living. For which I am grateful."

"Yes," said Paul-Henri, distracted by an itch on his left calf that he was sure was a developing hive. "So, first, just a general question—did you notice anything that night, anything at all that might be helpful to our investigation?"

"What sort of thing do you have in mind?"

"Oh, it could be anything really. An exchange between two people. A glance, even. A sense that there is something unexplained under the surface. An overheard comment that in retrospect seems troubling..."

Dr. Vernay held his chin in one hand, his usual posture for thinking. "I don't think there's a single thing," he said at last. "It was an unusual evening, as you know by now...a dinner party in which the hosts knew none of the guests. A bit strange, wasn't it? Of course we villagers were there in the usual high spirits, and I think it was coming off rather well despite the unusual circumstance, until...well, the horrible business with the nanny. What was her name again?"

"Violette Crespelle."

"Yes, right." The doctor nodded. "A lovely girl. Just tragic."

"Did you see anyone go into the library after the lights went out?"

"I'm sorry to say it was so dark I couldn't see my hand in front of my face. It was bedlam for a few moments, with people rushing around and knocking into furniture, until Pascal, I believe it was, managed to get the lights on again. Turns out some of our grown friends are afflicted with a fear of the dark," he said, looking amused.

"Pascal was the one to get the light on? Was Monsieur Valette with him?"

"I don't think so. I don't know where he was."

"And Madame Valette, do you know her whereabouts during the darkness?"

Dr. Vernay paused. He put his hands into the pockets of his coat. "As I said, I did not see her, or anyone."

Paul-Henri sensed the doctor had something more to say. "And what is your sense of Madame Valette, doctor?"

"Sense?"

"What kind of person is she? I know you did not give her an examination, it was a dinner party after all—but was there anything about her that, well, concerned you in any way? Or inspired some curiosity on your part of a, say, professional nature?" Paul-Henri understood that he was blatantly leading Vernay along, but they weren't in a courtroom after all, and the questioning was perfectly legal.

Dr. Vernay nodded slowly. "I think I see what you mean. Well, I don't like to...she's not one of my patients, so I *am* free to discuss…but nevertheless, it's not how I like to do things, you understand. I'm really not one for gossip."

"Gossip?" said Paul-Henri. "This is a murder investigation, doctor. Please, proceed."

Vernay looked uncomfortable, but eventually shrugged and said, "As long as you write down that this is definitely not a professional opinion, because without an actual examination and various modes of testing, what I am about to say qualifies as… nothing more than an impression. And not an informed one."

Paul-Henri gave a short nod and waited.

"Camille Valette did interest me, as a matter of fact, beyond simple social curiosity. At the start, I wondered about this dinner party for a group of strangers. I understand that the Valettes were new in the village, but most people would let social connections develop rather more…organically, I think we might put it. Don't you agree?"

Paul-Henri shrugged, but he thought the same. For a well-connected rich Parisian to have invited over a pack of strangers on the say-so of a waiter, also unknown to her, was pretty much unthinkable as far as he was concerned.

"So the fact of the dinner party piqued my interest, you could say," Vernay continued. "But then, there were some other moments, exchanges with various people…" he trailed off.

"Yes?"

"Well, again, let me state with some force that I am not a psychiatrist and so anything I might say on the subject has merely been gleaned from reading medical journals, not from clinical experience or specialized training. Barely worth more than the opinion of a random person on the street. But I did wonder, Officer Monsour—and perhaps we all did, who were invited on Friday night—why it was that a prominent, successful family such as the Valettes landed in Castillac? If they were much older and looking to retire, then possibly it would make some sense, though even that would be a stretch. But a man with his distinguished job, in the prime of life, with a young family—you do have to ask why, do you not?

"It occurred to me that the answer might be with his wife and not Monsieur Valette himself. And so with that in mind, I became somewhat more watchful of Madame Valette, and I noticed..."

Paul-Henri waited. He was generally a patient man, but the itch on his calf was distracting and unsettling, and he blurted out, "Yes? Noticed what, please?"

"I wondered if—pure speculation, I remind you—if perhaps Madame Valette might have received the sort of diagnosis that... that makes social settings problematic, if I may put it that way. And that perhaps Monsieur Valette wanted her hidden away in a little village where she might not have as much of a chance to do harm."

"Would you be more specific? What kind of diagnosis?"

"A personality disorder is what came to mind. Such persons can be...they can behave inexplicably," said Dr. Vernay. He dropped his voice almost to a whisper. "And they can be violent."

"Interesting," said Paul-Henri, reaching down to scratch his leg though he was certainly well-brought-up enough to know that scratching oneself in public, during a police investigation or anything else, was intolerably impolite behavior. "Can you tell me what she did or said to give you that idea?"

"Well, impulsivity is a hallmark of the condition, and the dinner party certainly qualifies, in my opinion. Then, when the storm hit and the lights went out, I saw no evidence that she was concerned about her children at all. Completely wrapped up in herself, was how she appeared to me. Oh, I sound like the worst village gossip! Really, it would make me happy if you would cross out everything I just said, Officer Monsour. It's nothing but the wispiest day-dreaming, no doubt brought about by the human insistence on finding reasons for everything, when sometimes there are no reasons."

Paul-Henri thanked the doctor, deciding to see how the itch

developed rather than ask for him to take a look on the spot. It had been a fruitful interview, no matter how much the doctor demurred, and Paul-Henri looked forward to presenting the chief with yet more evidence that there was a better suspect at hand than poor old Lapin. Even if he was a boor.

❧ 26 ❧

That Friday afternoon, Ben was off in Bergerac again, dealing with Bernard Petit. Molly walked with Bobo over to the renovation project and watched with satisfaction as several men began preparations for wall building, mixing a tub of mortar and arranging their tools just so. Enjoying the warmth of the late September day, she was tempted to go for a long, mind-clearing walk, but that would have to wait.

She needed to talk to Simon again. It would be much better to see him somewhere other than at his home, but Molly was in a hurry. If she could convince him to tell her why his wife had been in the psychiatric hospital—along with a few details, such as whether it had been a voluntary stay—Molly figured she would have a firmer idea about whether her hunch about Camille was right. So she went back to La Baraque and ate a piece of toast with Madame Sabourin's strawberry jam, put on a jacket and scarf, and rode the scooter to the other side of the village to the Valettes' manor.

She spotted Simon immediately; he was working on the ruin, shirtless, muscling a big rock into a wheelbarrow.

"That's pretty rugged work for an ENA," she said, with a hint of a smirk.

"You calling me soft?" said Simon, grinning. "I could tell you stories of data analysis that would curl your hair," he said. "Not that it needs curling," he added, looking at her wild mop, made wilder by the scooter ride.

"I'm sorry to show up unannounced," said Molly, liking him more each time she saw him. "But something's come to my attention that could use some clarification."

Simon looked at her with an open expression. "Yes?"

"It's about Camille," said Molly, lowering her voice. "And the *Hôpital Sainte Anne?*"

Simon made a small grimace. He wiped his brow with a handkerchief, and grimaced again. "It's not how it looks," he said.

"I'm not saying it looks any particular way. It's just...you understand my asking, I'm sure. It would be unforgivably nosy to ask such questions in any other circumstance. But was Camille... was she there of her own accord? It's important that Ben and I know."

"Yes," said Simon. "Very much so. It was...it was a moment of some distress for her, and..." He brought a hand to his face, and stroked his cheek with one finger as he considered what to say next. "She has always struggled with tremendous anxiety," he said. "And one day, it rather came to a head."

"And the diagnosis?"

"I'm not entirely sure she had one, at least beyond severely anxious and depressed." He took a deep breath and put one foot up on a stone. "I wholeheartedly supported her time in the hospital, but I can't say I have been impressed with the care given her. Mental health remains more mystery than anything," he said. He looked down at the ground for a moment before lifting his eyes back to Molly. "Now you see a bit better, I suppose, why the move to Castillac seemed a good idea?"

Molly nodded. "Yes, of course. I mean, I love this village with all my heart, so it's never surprising to me if anyone else is attracted to it. I...I moved here myself because I needed some emotional repair." She considered saying more but stopped herself. "The issue is...I think people are curious about the move because of *you*. A random American showing up doesn't inspire the same amount of curiosity as an ENA with a big-shot job at Byatt Industries. As I said, we don't see too many people with your accomplishments down this way."

He shrugged and turned his head away. At that moment, the light hit the side of his face and Molly saw a scar on his cheek she hadn't noticed before. It was about two inches long, going from his cheekbone toward his jaw, exactly where his finger had been stroking a moment before when he was thinking of his wife's hospital stay.

She cut him, thought Molly, simply, and in the instant of having the thought knew that she was right. Who knows what the circumstance was—maybe it had been an accident (though she bet not). Whatever the story was, Molly was certain that Camille Valette had taken a knife to her husband and left that scar on his handsome cheek.

It was not the time to press. Better to talk to Ben and the gendarmes, see if they could get confirmation from the hospital one way or another, and let the next steps proceed from there.

She stood in the driveway of the Valette home for another twenty minutes, bantering with Simon and enjoying herself perhaps more than she should have. It was appealing, a husband willing to cover for his wife that way, and in the back of her mind as they talked of local news and village goings-on, Molly was imagining the scene in which Camille had flicked the blade into her husband's face.

Had they been fighting? Or had she crept up and surprised him? And how on earth do you forgive someone attacking you like that?

She wasn't sure she would be capable of it, if she was honest.

Ben better stay clear of the cutlery, she thought with a little smile as she waved goodbye to Simon and set off for La Baraque.

🦋 27 🦋

The bawling was so loud the decanter on the sideboard rattled.

"Good God," said Simon, coming through the front door, scowling. "What is all that about?"

"It's Maman," said Gisele quietly. "With Chloë."

Simon shot his daughter a quick look of trepidation before bounding up the stairs three at a time. He burst through the door to the bedroom to find Camille still in bed, wearing the same Chanel quilted bed-jacket that she'd worn all week, leaning against a heaping pile of pillows with embroidered cases, her expression dour. Chloë stood at the foot of the bed, crying in great gusts.

"What is the matter?" he said in a low voice.

"She hit me, and I'm running away! I hate this family!" shouted the girl at the top of her voice, and rushed out of the room without stopping for any comfort from her father.

Simon took a deep breath. "Stop," he said, squinting his eyes at his wife. "I've told you countless times, you must *stop*."

"Do you think they should be allowed to be impertinent? I

should just let the girls, my own daughters, say and do anything they please? Is that what you want, Simon?"

"Of course not!" he said. "That's not what I'm saying at all and you know it very well! We've talked and talked about this, Camille. Your therapists—"

"You forced me down here so I can't see them anymore! It's your fault, Simon. All yours." Camille bent her head and made snuffling sounds. "You know I can't bear it when you shout at me," she said, groping blindly with one hand for a handkerchief.

Summoning every last bit of control, Simon walked through the bedroom to the bathroom, and began taking off his dusty trousers to get ready to shower.

"And now you're ignoring me, is that it?" said Camille.

As Simon stepped into the shower, he heard Raphael start to howl. He reached for the soap, a fresh bar of Marseillaise lavender, and inhaled its scent before ducking his head under the water, doing his best to block them all out.

Oh, what a loss Violette has turned out to be, he thought.

He tried to brush away the feelings of resentment and fury that were bubbling up inside, but he did not succeed, and the hot water did nothing to quell them.

"Come on, Molly—you're just guessing and you know it!"

She shrugged. "Well, maybe. Okay, of *course* I'm guessing. But—that feeling you get when you have an idea and you know in your bones it's right, no matter whether you have proof or not? I know you know what I'm talking about."

"Yes. And I admit, your intuition has a fairly good record." He reached out and touched her cheek. "I'm not dismissing what you say, not by any means."

"Thank you!" said Molly, pleased.

"But I still don't think we can go to Charlot with our suspicions. Not yet. For one thing, as I know I don't need to point out, all we've got is circumstantial evidence and suspicions. Even if Camille did attack Simon and slash him, that doesn't mean she strangled Violette. And second, Charlot doesn't know us at all. It's not like Maron, where we had history, and we knew going in that he valued what we had to say."

"Point taken," said Molly. "I suppose there's no way to get confirmation from the hospital that Camille was there because she attacked Simon?"

"Not legally. Privacy laws being what they are."

"Well, how about illegally, then? Aren't P.I's supposed to offer the odd bribe here and there? Don't people expect it of us, actually?"

"In TV shows, maybe. It would be different if the hospital were in Castillac. But up there, a suburb outside of Paris, we have no leverage, no contacts."

"Maybe Paul-Henri does."

Ben shrugged. "I'll feel him out."

They sat at the table, both thinking.

"You're still not really convinced, though, are you?" said Molly. "Is it because you don't really believe she stabbed Simon in the face, or because even if she did, that wouldn't be enough to make you believe she's the killer?"

"A little of both. Let's play the scenario out: let's say Camille is unstable and violent, and one day takes a knife to her husband. Maybe she was provoked, maybe she had some sort of psychotic episode. But either way, what does that have to do with the nanny? Attacking a spouse, to my mind, is entirely different from attacking anyone else. The potential for resentment and rage are so much greater."

"Disturbing words, coming from my fiancé," said Molly, deadpan.

Ben grinned. "I have heard that simply leaving the toilet seat up can eventually doom one to an early grave."

Molly was not about to get sidetracked. "But don't you see, if the marriage was a mess, that's even more reason why an unbalanced wife might kill the nanny. She would be furious and jealous in equal parts, and especially so, given who Simon is."

"Elaborate, please?

"I just mean he's a charming man. He likes women. I would not be surprised in the least to find out there was something going on between him and Violette—or that the nanny wished for something to be going on, and Simon led her on, or some such scenario."

"So you don't trust him?"

Molly laughed. "Trust him? Of course not! A young woman was brutally strangled in his library, of course I don't trust him."

"But you don't consider that *he* is perhaps the murderer and not his wife?"

"No. Well, I did consider it, we have to consider everyone who was in the house that night. He had means and opportunity, I'll grant you that. But where is the motive, Ben? Like I said, he loves women. I would imagine he rather misses having Violette around, whether there was anything between them or not."

Ben took a moment before saying anything. He knew he had nothing to worry about—at least he hoped he didn't—but hearing Molly speak so admiringly of Simon's charms was not his favorite thing. When the pang had passed, he said, "Maybe they were having an affair, Violette threatened to tell Camille, and Simon felt he had to shut her up?"

"Does Simon seem that unhinged or desperate to you? Untold legions of wives—and marriages—have survived infidelity without anyone getting murdered."

"Some marriages have no problem with it at all."

"Is that so?" said Molly, mischievously. "So in our case, if I—"

"*No,*" said Ben, reaching out to pull her closer. "I don't like to share."

Molly grinned. "Not my idea of fun either. Glad we got that settled."

Ben kissed her, then sighed. "I'm finding this case to be a little impenetrable. It seems, from the outside, as though it should be the easiest thing—a group of people stuck in the house when a murder is committed, most of them with no connection whatsoever to the owners of the house or to the murder victim. I know it looks right now that Camille is the obvious perpetrator, and I don't mean to be, what is that English phrase, sticks in the dirt?"

"Stick in the mud," said an unsmiling Molly, the charm of Ben's confusing that particular idiom having worn off long ago.

The truth was, she always felt irritated when she had an idea and couldn't convince him she was right, even though his insistence on evidence was absolutely proper—which only made it more annoying.

"Well," she said, brightening. "Let's not sit around all night arguing about Camille. It's Friday night, the gang will probably all be at Chez Papa. Shall we join them?"

Bobo lay down by the door with her head on her paws, looking as mournful as possible, so Molly gave her a liver treat on the way out the door.

"I don't know about you, but I find sleuthing exhausting, even when all I'm doing is sitting at the computer," said Molly as they got into Ben's car.

"Find out anything?"

"Well, I learned from that guest last Valentine's Day, remember Ira Bilson? He showed me how valuable a little internet detective work can be. People get online and think they're hidden, but oh are they wildly mistaken," she said with a laugh.

"So what have you found?"

"Nothing. Yet."

"I will tell you, I don't see the appeal of the internet, at least beyond business. Ordering things online and having them delivered, of course almost anybody would like that. Such a time-saver, among other things. But socially...I would so much rather talk to someone face to face. Facial expressions and even silences, in my opinion, can be so meaningful. But there are no silences in internet conversation, yes?"

"Well, kind of. If someone takes a long time to respond. But it's not really the same thing, you're right. No question that you lose some parts of communication that you have in person. It's sort of like writing a letter—not better or worse, just different. If you ask me."

"How about we ask the experts?" Ben said as they entered

Chez Papa to a chorus of bonsoirs. "Bonsoir, *tout le monde*," said Ben. "Molly and I were just wondering, how many of you spend any time online socializing? Not shopping, but chatting with people you know from real life or have met online?"

Everyone in the bistro raised a hand except Nico.

"Really!" said Ben, stunned.

"See? We're all trooping along here in the twenty-first century, and we've left you behind with the buggy whips!" said Molly. Nico looked faintly stricken and Molly assured him she was only teasing.

"I'm sure the internet is a great boon to the P.I. world, for sure," said Nico. "But I'd much rather get together with friends around a table than on a screen. The food's better," he said, reaching for the bottle of cassis before Molly had to say a word.

"A hundred percent agree on that score," said Molly. "I do wonder...do you think you are the same person, meeting someone online and getting to know them? Do we—on purpose or not—change who we are, in some way, since we aren't actually being seen?"

"I don't bring up my pot belly," said a man at the end of the bar, and everyone chuckled.

"I have met some people in political chat rooms," said Nico, "but the conversation is about ideas, it isn't personal. My own opinion is that we have to guard our privacy now more than ever."

Molly leaned her head to one side, considering her friend Nico, who had always had a secretive side. Some of his biggest secrets had been uncovered, but a lifetime of habit wouldn't be switched off that easily, she thought.

"Okay, second question," she said, raising her voice and addressing the room. "How many of you have googled someone you know, or searched for information online about your friends or family?"

Again, all hands raised.

"It's a different world," said Ben under his breath.

Perhaps, thought Molly. But if we get on top of it, this different world could be a tremendous advantage to Dufort & Sutton Investigations. Though how to do that is another, more difficult question.

❧

ALL MOLLY WANTED to do on Saturday morning was sit at her computer trying to find some scrap of something, anything at all, that might shine some light on Camille Valette and her penchant for violence. She tried several different search engines and got progressively more creative with her keywords, but after several hours of diligent searching she'd gotten exactly nowhere.

At nine o'clock she forced herself to step away from the coffee pot and the computer. It was changeover day, after all, and no matter how juicy the case or cold the trail, Arthur Malreaux needed to be seen off, Constance would be showing up any minute to do the cleaning, and a new couple was due to arrive later that afternoon. It was time to hop to it and get everything ready.

"Molls!" shouted Constance, having let herself in. Molly appeared from her bedroom, yanking a comb through her hair.

"Bonjour, Constance," she said, concerned at her friend's expression. "Is something wrong?"

"There sure is," said Constance, her eyes welling up.

Uh oh, thought Molly. What has Thomas done now?

"It's Madame Gervais," said Constance. She shook her head, her face crumpling.

"What happened?" said Molly, her heart sinking.

"She...she died last night. Or maybe this morning. I'm not sure exactly when. Her neighbor...Madame Gervais didn't answer the door, and so the neighbor let herself in, and she was...she was dead in her bed."

Molly swallowed hard, then again. Madame Gervais had made

it to one hundred and four years old and then managed to die in her own bed. Well played, thought Molly, well played. "I'm so sorry. I suppose we shouldn't be shocked, but that doesn't mean the news isn't awful."

"Well, I *am* shocked. I was pretty sure she was immortal."

"Kind of seemed that way. The streets of Castillac will not be the same without her."

"No, they will not," said Constance with a sob. "And I for one think you ought to go over there and have a look around. I'm not saying there was anything fishy going on or anything, but you never know, Molly. You never know. Someone could have sneaked in there and held a pillow over her head. You just don't know what horrible things people are capable of."

Molly sighed. Sometimes Constance took just a little too much energy to deal with. "I'm a hundred percent sure there was nothing fishy," she said. "Come on, give me a hug. I'm sad too. I'll really miss her."

They had a long, tearful hug, then straightened up and started gathering the cleaning supplies, both of them feeling as though some sweaty, productive work would make them feel better. Molly carried the vacuum cleaner to the pigeonnier, realizing she didn't know whether the Jenkinses were planning to stay another week. She could always put the new couple in the annex, so it didn't really matter either way, but she noticed that she was getting sloppy about some of the details of the gîte business and vowed to do better.

The Jenkinses were out, sightseeing at another church, no doubt, and Molly let herself in and vacuumed both rooms. They were tidy guests and there was not much to do. Molly scrubbed out the sink and made sure there was plenty of soap in the kitchen and bathroom, and then headed for the cottage, where she expected to see Todor and Elise waiting for her.

"I don't think we'll ever leave," announced Todor as she approached. He was smiling and opening his arms to the sky.

"Despite that sudden stomach bug, Elise and I have had the most wonderful time here. Wandering through the village feels a little like going back in time, doesn't it?"

"Yes," said Molly. "Even though obviously there are cars and mobile phones and all kinds of modern things around, very often if the light is right, you can look down one of the streets and feel as though you've stepped back to the Middle Ages somehow."

"It's those old stones," said Todor.

"I love them so," said Molly. She thought of Madame Gervais then, how she was so used to glancing down a street and seeing the old woman moving along with her shopping cart, stopping to talk to friends along the way.

"Is...I'm sorry to intrude, but is something wrong?" Todor asked.

"Umph, ah, something in my eye," said Molly. "Are you and Elise planning to be out sometime today? I can come back and do a quick vacuum then, if you'd like."

Todor went into a long description of all the things they planned to do before leaving, and ended by asking Molly if it would be possible to pay a little extra for the cottage and stay on an open-ended basis. "I'm not kidding about never wanting to leave," he said with a laugh. "Though of course that's only a daydream. We'll have to go back at some point. Perhaps next month? In the meantime, there are so many more pastries yet to try at Pâtisserie Bujold."

"A man after my own heart," said Molly, summoning a smile that was less glowing than usual at the mention of pastry, since that—like almost everything for the next several days—reminded her of Madame Gervais and an apricot tart they had once shared at the pastry shop.

Quickly she hustled off to the annex to wish Arthur Malreaux a happy farewell, but she found his room empty. He had left a thank-you note on the bed—not effusive, as that was not Arthur's way. But Molly understood that he appreciated the small help she had given him, even though the stories he had heard from Madame Gervais had not covered his relative with glory as he had hoped.

After a quick conference with Constance, Molly hopped on her scooter and headed into the village. She would be just in time for the tail end of the market, where she was hoping some in-person sleuthing would be a whole lot more productive than the online kind had been.

It would have been easy enough to get sidetracked by all the details of village life, including births and deaths, not to mention pastry and the changing of seasons—but not for Molly. Violette Crespelle's murder was always on her mind, the details flicking by in a constant slideshow as she tried to make order out of nothing.

❧ 29 ❧

On Monday morning, Molly stood in front of her armoire trying to find something to wear to Madame Gervais's funeral, her thoughts disordered and anxious.

"I never have anything to wear. I need to make a shopping trip, maybe to Bordeaux? But talking about buying clothes—or anything, really—seems so out of place, in the face of...hey! Did we ever ask Paul-Henri about Violette's family? And, this is a grisly thought, but what about *her* funeral?"

"I asked Paul-Henri a few days after the murder. Violette has a sister who lives in the States. Both Crespelle parents are dead."

"Oh. Not that I would want any parent to have to go through losing a child, but it seems even sadder that Violette doesn't have them to mourn for her."

"The sister has asked that the body be cremated, so I suppose there will be no funeral, or at least no grave-side ceremony. As for a shopping trip to Bordeaux, we can do that anytime you like. It might good for both of us to get out of Castillac for a day. We could stay over, eat a good meal..."

"How you tempt me."

Ben came up behind Molly and kissed the side of her neck,

which never failed to melt her. "I would like to tempt you to more than dinner, but if we're going to make it to this funeral, I'm sorry to say it's time to go," he said, kissing her one more time.

Quickly Molly combed her hair and massaged some product into it, threw Bobo another liver treat because now the dog expected one every time Molly went out, and was ready to go. They held hands once they got to rue des Chênes for the short walk to the cemetery. Before long they could see villagers walking towards the wrought-iron gates and a long line of cars parked along the road.

"Wow," said Molly. "Look at the mob!"

"Madame Gervais knew everybody," said Ben. "And just think: all of the people she knew as a child and even as a young adult are dead now, so this isn't even close to how many friends she had over her life."

They made their way under the arch that said "*Priez pour vos morts*," kissing their friends' cheeks along the way. Molly being Molly, she was taking special note of everyone connected with the Crespelle case: she saw Marie-Claire walking with Rex Ford; Dr. Vernay and his wife Robinette; Nico and Frances.

"Keep an eye out for Lapin and Anne-Marie," Molly murmured to Ben. "I'm really hoping he's come out of hiding."

Frances broke away from Nico and fell into Molly's arms. "Aww, I'm really sorry for your loss," she said. "And I hate saying that because it just feels like a trite thing to say, when I really want to say that I'm sorry to all of Castillac for losing this amazing woman, and I'm just so sad even though I can't actually say I ever had a conversation with her, thanks to not speaking French."

In answer, Molly hugged her friend. "She was one of a kind," said Molly. "Hi, Nico."

Nico kissed her cheeks, shaking his head. "I always thought I would die in my 20s," he said. "And when that didn't happen, I

—*merde*, I don't mean to be going on about myself. Today is about Madame Gervais."

"Well, yeah," said Frances, slipping an arm around him. "But you're allowed to talk about other things too, I mean jeez, come on. My sense of Madame Gervais is that she would appreciate people not getting too gloomy."

"Indeed," said Ben. "I expect Chez Papa to be packed after the funeral, with many spirited and long-winded toasts made."

They all smiled faintly in anticipation. Just then the hearse pulled up and the crowd quieted. A few young men Molly did not recognize acted as pallbearers, along with Edmond Nugent, who was so much shorter than the others that Madame Gervais's casket tipped dangerously to one side.

Molly scanned the crowd, looking for Lapin, but did not see him.

"What's Simon Valette doing here?" Ben said in her ear, giving his chin a little jerk towards the road, where Simon's head could be seen bobbing along above the stone wall as he made his way to the cemetery.

"No idea," said Molly. "I don't see Paul-Henri or Charlot here, do you?"

Ben shook his head.

The casket made its awkward way to the grave with hundreds of pairs of eyes watching.

Frances let out a noisy sob and Nico put both arms around her. "I feel like a fraud!" she shout-whispered. "I didn't even really know her!"

Molly shot her a look, then made her way behind the crowd to a higher spot where she could see better. There was Anne-Marie, dressed in a beautiful black suit...Molly tried to get closer to her but the crowd was too thick and unyielding.

A hundred and four, Molly kept thinking. That would mean I would still be alive in *2071*.

She stopped moving, dumbfounded. I already made a new life

once, she thought, but if my math is right, I might have time for several more new lives before it's all over. Then, as the coffin was lowered down, Molly bowed her head and thought of her friend, Madame Gervais. How her intelligence and good humor had shown in her bright eyes, how she did not shrink from truth, any truth, as she had recently demonstrated with La Baraque's guest, Arthur Malreaux.

I will miss her terribly, thought Molly, wiping her eyes, as over a hundred people were thinking exactly the same thing at nearly the same moment.

§✿

AFTER THE SERVICE, Ben and Molly were slowly making their way back to the road and on to Chez Papa for lunch when Molly's cell vibrated in her pocket.

"It's the Valette number," she said to Ben, furrowing her brow and then craning her neck to find Simon, but she was too short to see over anyone's heads.

"Âllo?" she said tentatively into the phone.

"Bonjour, Madame Sutton," said a young voice. Molly was barely able to hear; the voice was uncertain and the crowd had gotten talkative and loud.

"Bonjour?" she said. "Is this…Gisele?"

"Yes, madame," said the girl softly.

Molly put her hand over her other ear, trying to hear, but the girl said nothing else.

"It's nice to hear from you, Gisele. Can I—is anything wrong? Do you want me to come over?"

"No, it's not…not here. I was wondering if you would meet me, somewhere besides home? I don't know the village well, but there must be…"

"How about Pâtisserie Bujold? It's on the side of the village closer to your house, on rue Picasso. Just ask anyone you see on the street and they'll be able to direct you. Does that sound all right? I'm on my way right now."

"Merci," whispered Gisele, and hung up.

"I have to skip Chez Papa for now, I've got to make another stop first," said Molly to Ben. "See if you can find Simon in this throng," she said. "Find out what he's doing here, if you can find a way to ask without seeming too rude. It's not that I have suspicions or anything, it just…seems odd, so I'm curious about what he would say. Anyway, that was Gisele. She wants to meet, so I'm off—"

Ben nodded and waved, but Molly did not speed off like she wanted to; the way was clogged with people, none of whom appeared to be in any hurry whatsoever, but stood exchanging stories about Madame Gervais and talking about what they were going to have for lunch instead of moving through the gate and letting anyone else through.

"Pardon!" said Molly, over and over, making progress only by the judicious application of her knees and elbows, until at long last she was through the gate and marching down the road to the village, worried that Gisele would get to Pâtisserie Bujold first and wonder if she was being stood up.

Molly arrived breathless at the shop only to find it closed. Of course, she realized too late, probably every business in the entire village was closed while everyone turned out for the funeral. She paced in front of the door, her curiosity about why the girl had called nearly making her feel sick. She hoped Edmond showed up soon—she could desperately use an espresso and an almond croissant, having skipped breakfast in an effort to fit into her dress.

"Ah! The sun has truly come out, that I see you here, waiting on my doorstep!" said Edmond, from halfway down the block. "I thought you would be at Chez Papa, along with half the village. I am touched that you came here instead. And it is a lucky decision for you, Molly Sutton, because this very morning I happened to make the apricot with the layer of custard that you are so insane over."

"You just made a terrible day quite a bit brighter," said Molly, her mouth instantly watering.

Out of the corner of her eye she saw a child turn the corner, and quickly raised her hand to wave at Gisele. "This way, chérie!" she called. "I invited her to tea," she told Edmond, whose eyebrows were raised. "It's Gisele Valette."

"I know very well who she is," sniffed Edmond. "I was at the dinner, you know."

"Of course, sorry, I was only...I'm a little distracted," she admitted. "I need to have a tête à tête with Gisele for a few minutes. Can you find something important to do in the back, once we've got our pastries and tea?"

Edmond lifted his nose in the air with a scowl, but he nodded. "Girl talk," he sniffed.

"Come on in," Molly said to Gisele, who was lingering at the door as though she might bolt. "In my humble opinion, this shop is the best thing in Castillac, and all newcomers should be brought here on their first day. So we will do what we can to make up for lost time."

Behind the counter, Edmond's expression brightened. Molly and Gisele chose their pastries without much dithering. Edmond brought drinks to the tiny table in the corner and then dutifully disappeared into the back, leaving them in private.

"I'm glad to have introduced you to this place," Molly said confidentially. "That is, if you are a fan of pastry? I suppose there must be people somewhere who are indifferent to it, but even they might change their minds if they tried some of Edmond's. He is an artist, truly."

Gisele's eyes were wide and Molly could tell she wished the floor would open and swallow her right up.

"And also," Molly continued, "I'm so very glad you called me. Do you know—well, of course you don't know, what am I thinking?—I am about to be *forty* years old. True! Ancient, isn't it? My birthday is in a few weeks. But I haven't told anyone. Even my fiancé doesn't know. Do you think I should just get over myself and throw a big party? Do you like big parties?"

"Not really," said Gisele.

Molly waited but she said nothing further.

"Oh my gracious, I'm an utter blockhead...Gisele, I'm so sorry for babbling on about parties, when the last party at your house... it was...traumatic, is the only word. I know you must miss Violette tremendously."

The girl shrugged, but Molly was not fooled into believing the girl didn't care. "I hope you catch who did it," Gisele whispered. "I heard you are a famous detective, and I'm glad my father hired you."

"I'm glad he did too. And my partner and I are working very hard on the case." Molly paused and took a bite of the apricot pastry, savoring the burned caramelized bits and the vanilla cream. "I'm wondering, because you seem to be a person who notices things—might you possibly have something to tell me about the case? Something you overheard, or saw, or anything at all?"

Gisele shook her head. "No. I don't think so, anyway. I do like detective stories very much, and there was a show on TV we used to watch in Paris...but I know that's just pretend, and I don't really know what detectives do in real life."

Molly laughed. "It's far less glamorous than on TV, I can tell you. Often the best clues come from work that's painstaking drudgery, to be honest—going through someone's trash and finding receipts, interviewing people over and over until finally they mention the seemingly insignificant thing that turns the case around. You'd be surprised how often a case hinges on some small detail that everyone overlooks."

"But *you* see it," said Gisele, looking at Molly intently.

Molly shrugged. "I look for it," she said. "But even in the cases I've solved, who knows what I may have missed?"

"And have you solved every one?"

"So far. But it's not that many. Really, I've been extremely lucky, I don't want you to get the wrong idea about me, I'm not some Sherlock-level detective genius, I'm really not. Would you like another pastry?" she asked, seeing Gisele's plate was empty save for a few crumbs.

Gisele shook her head. She decided to be direct. "Gisele, you can be frank with me. Is there...a particular reason you called me?"

"I...I called because...well, I didn't *want* to call you, Madame Sutton, but you were so nice the other day, and with Violette gone...*please* don't tell my father or my mother. I don't think they'd like it at all."

Molly nodded seriously. "I am very, very good at keeping secrets," she said.

Gisele flashed a grin. Her two front teeth were a little bit crooked, which Molly found adorable. "I miss Violette," she said, still whispering. "I could tell her things. It made me feel better to talk to her when Maman..."

Molly felt a prickle on the back of her neck. "When Maman...?"

"Hits," said Gisele, barely loud enough to hear. She made a grimace that reminded Molly of Simon.

Molly breathed in sharply. She was not shocked to hear this news, but what in the world could she do about it?

"Oh, chérie. You and your sister don't deserve that."

Gisele shook her head, her eyes welling up.

"Does your father help?" Molly asked softly.

Again the girl shrugged. "He doesn't like it," she said. "But she's stronger than he is."

Molly thought this over. On one hand, it was hard to imagine that a man with Simon's charms, intelligence, and accomplishments could be overpowered by anyone. But on the other, Molly understood that those things might not be the best protection against violence. His good manners might, in fact, be his Achilles heel.

Molly brought her attention back to Gisele. She felt at a loss, wanting to offer reassurance but knowing there was little, if anything, she could do to help. Were there laws about this sort of thing in France? She doubted it, given that schoolteachers were allowed to whack their students in the classroom.

The only solution that Molly could see would be to prove Camille's guilt in the murder of Violette Crespelle. Of course no one would wish that their mother be arrested for murder, but at least it would put a safe distance between the vicious mother and the dear little girls, who deserved much better, as any child would.

"I didn't call you because of that," said Gisele, sitting up straight and looking at Molly with a serious expression

"There's more?"

"It's about the other night. I...I like watching people. And listening."

"You mean the night of your parents' party?" Molly got that tingly feeling she sometimes got, that meant something important was in the vicinity.

At least sometimes it was.

"Yes, the night when Violette was strangled," said Gisele matter-of-factly. "I took some notes about the things people were saying. Would you like to hear them?"

"Of course I would," said Molly.

"Well, that doctor? I missed the first part of it but he was saying something about how someone 'must have told you all kinds of stories from those days—students can be so naughty' or something like that."

"Who did he say this to?"

"Violette," Gisele shrugged. "And he said her last name reminded him of stuffing himself with pancakes."

Molly nodded, wishing the girl had something meatier to report.

"Also, the art professor patted her bottom as Violette went by, when she was chasing after Chloë. Like they were boyfriend and girlfriend? But they weren't. Violette told me she was too busy to have a boyfriend."

"I see. Anything else?"

"Chloë and I were under the table during the dinner, do you remember? I had asked Ophélie to pack us a little box of food and we spent all that time sitting next to everyone's legs."

Molly grinned.

"You see a lot down there," said Gisele.

"No doubt." Molly's tingle had gone away, to her great regret, as had her pastry and coffee. "Well, any other tidbits you have for me? I'm afraid I'm going to have to head home and see what kind of sleuthing I can do from my computer." They stood up. Molly looked around for Edmond but he was still sequestered in the back, and they went outside to the tinkling of the bell on the door.

"One more thing," said Gisele. "I don't know her name, but the woman with the stiletto heels, who sat next to the man wearing the rough boots?"

"Marie-Claire Levy? Next to Ben?"

"I'm sorry, it's hard to keep the grownups sorted out. I think so. Anyway, I heard her say something to that art professor after Violette went out of the dining room. She said, 'No one knows, just keep it that way.' Sort of quiet, so nobody would hear."

Molly had listened intently to all that Gisele said, but was becoming tired and distracted, feeling pressure from too many directions at once. "Sweet girl," she said, shaking Gisele's hand and then kissing her cheeks. "You have been a big help. I will go home and write down all that you've told me. And please know— you are welcome at La Baraque at any time. No need to call ahead."

Gisele nodded with a small smile.

"Do you need me to walk you home?"

The girl looked at Molly like she was insane. "What, Madame Sutton? I've been getting around my neighborhood in Paris by myself for ages. I can handle Castillac."

I bet you can, thought Molly, watching her stride down the sidewalk, both of them feeling sick at what she was going home to.

30

Anne-Marie Broussard had been married to Lapin for only a short while. She was not from Castillac but had met him at a flea market in Limoges and married him after a whirlwind courtship, much to the surprise of the Castillaçois, who had always known Lapin to be something of a weasel around women and who had never had a romantic relationship last as long as a month.

Yet the marriage, until the Valette dinner party, had been going extremely well for both of them. Lapin and Anne-Marie enjoyed spending time together; they got along without sniping or sulking, they were physically well suited to each other, respected each other, laughed and discussed politics without rancor—the list of their marital compatibilities was long and impressive.

And maybe that was part of the trouble, Anne-Marie thought, on day ten now of Lapin's disappearance. Maybe I started taking the whole thing for granted, started assuming that the marriage would just merrily continue on without my paying any special attention. Something must have been wrong and I didn't see it.

Restlessly, she tidied the house though it was already in

perfect condition. She walked by a mirror in the foyer and stopped to look at herself. She was middle-aged, her hair short and naturally curly. She was a bit thick through the middle and wrinkles were beginning to show on her forehead and around her eyes. Anne-Marie sighed, thinking of how Lapin would chase her around their house, singing arias as he grabbed for her, and how they would tumble onto the sofa laughing with disbelieving glee at how happy they were. What was she to make of those memories now?

And something else was bothering her. At the Valettes, Anne-Marie had for the first time seen her husband look at another woman with desire. The nanny had passed through the dining room at several points, both before and during dinner, and Lapin had not taken his eyes off her. Unsurprisingly, the new wife's heart had sunk. But surely, she told herself, this was commonplace. It wasn't as though she didn't admire Pascal when she went to the Café de la Place for breakfast—it didn't mean anything at all. She was not going to turn into a harping, jealous wife over nothing more than a glance. It was not who she was, she told herself at the party, and instead talked with animation to Nico, who was sitting on her left, and to Pascal on her right.

No, it was not Lapin's staring that had her worried, she thought as she polished the cherrywood dining room table—it was his taking off without a word when the lights went out. She and Lapin had been so close over the months; they had shared their fears and hopes and not hidden from each other. It was not even the running as much as not telling her anything about it, then or later on, when he knew she would be sick with worry. She could not believe—even after the days passed with no contact—that he had done anything wrong. He just couldn't have, it made no sense whatsoever.

Yet...where in heck was he?

WITH GISELE'S hurt expression fresh in her mind, Molly was determined to find some shred of evidence that could possibly get Camille removed from the Valette home temporarily, if not arrested. She had no idea what that might be, but wasn't searching when you didn't precisely know what you were searching for practically the main task of an investigator? Slipping on a jacket and leaving La Baraque with only a wave to Bobo, she jumped on the scooter and got on her way.

I don't even think of the Citroen coupe anymore, she realized, turning onto rue des Chênes. Months ago, the fancy car had needed a minor repair and been in the shop for a week, and after that Molly had almost always left it in the garage, preferring the wind in her hair and even the cold while riding the scooter.

This fleeting musing over transportation alternatives was the only distraction she allowed herself during the trip to the Valettes'. She decided that she would ask to interview Raphael, Simon's father. It was possible he might tell her something incriminating about Camille; perhaps his daughter-in-law let her guard down around him, discounting him because of his dementia and assuming he would be an unreliable witness.

At the Valettes', Molly parked the scooter and looked around the yard, seeing no one. She knocked on the heavy wooden door but there was no answer.

"Coo-coo!" she called out, having adopted the French manner of announcing her presence. She walked closer to the ruin, thinking she might have missed Simon, but he was not there. Circling around the house, she cocked her head to listen for the girls, but all was silent.

I can't imagine Raphael has gone out, she thought, and despite knowing full well she shouldn't, she turned the handle on the front door and pushed her way inside the house.

"Coo-coo!" she called, and listened.

She thought she heard something upstairs, like the legs of a chair scraping on bare wood. Slowly she crept up the stairs, praying Simon or Camille didn't appear. "Raphael?"

His door was cracked and sunlight poured through. Molly knocked softly, which pushed the door open wider. She saw him sitting in an armchair, facing the window. His shoulders sagged and he did not turn around at the sound of her knock or footsteps.

"Raphael? I'm sorry to bother you," she said. "My name is Molly Sutton. I was wondering if you would mind talking to me a little bit about the other night?"

The old man swung his head in her direction. His hair stuck up in back and he needed a shave, but Molly thought she saw a flicker of curiosity in his eyes.

"Who are you?" he asked, narrowing his eyes.

"I'm Molly Sutton. I'm a private investigator who also happened to be at the dinner party last Friday when Violette Crespelle was murdered." Maybe she should have been a little more circumspect, but she had a feeling that this was a man who appreciated straight talk.

Raphael stood up, and walked over to her. He was a tall man with a large frame, and he was not without physical power. "Who is Violette Crespelle?" he said.

Molly swallowed. "The nanny. The young woman who lived here, and helped take care of your granddaughters."

"Thieves," said Raphael. He stepped closer and took Molly by the shoulder, and kissed both her cheeks with some force.

"Did someone steal something from you?" Molly said, trying to take a step backward.

Letting go of her arms, Raphael leaned his head back and laughed. "Steal something? They steal everything, chérie, *everything*."

"Which things?" Molly wasn't sure why she didn't just give up and go home. He was obviously not in his right mind.

"My scissors," he breathed. "And my string. I've always told them that it's important to have string. Comes in handy. But these young people, what do they know of deprivation? They use a thing and throw it out. Everything is disposable."

"And then they come back to you for more because whatever they borrowed is gone."

Raphael looked at Molly with amazement. He had never been able to make any of them understand.

"Did you like Violette?" she asked, nonchalantly.

"Violette?" he said. He went to the table by his bed, opened a narrow drawer, and took out a cord. Molly thought perhaps it was a bootlace. Slowly he wrapped the cord around the fingers of his left hand. "Who are you?" he asked again, walking slowly toward her.

"Molly Sutton," she said, her voice unnaturally high. "I was wondering if you remember anything from the other night, the night of the terrible storm," she said, thinking maybe that the wild lightning and thunder might have made an impression on him.

He did not answer, but wrapped the other end of the cord around his right hand. He was an arm's-length away, staring into her eyes, searching.

"You don't know me," Molly said, trying to reassure him. "I'm sure it must be very difficult at your age—hell, at any age—to uproot and move to a new house, a new village. What do you like to do, Raphael? Do you like fishing?"

Why in the world am I talking about fishing, she thought, watching his hands pull the cord taut. Was it unconscious, or was he trying to frighten her?

It was working, intentional or not. Molly glanced behind her to make sure the door was open so she could dart through if need be.

"Fishing?" said Raphael wonderingly. "This house is full of thieves," he added in a harsh whisper.

"And a murderer?" Molly whispered back to him, taking a chance.

C hief Charlot, unlike her predecessors, spent most of her working time at her desk. She sent Paul-Henri out to do preliminary interviews for the murder case and to take care of the kinds of incidental problems that crop up in a small village. He took Madame Bonnay's dog back home, found Monsieur Vargas in the cemetery and returned him to his wife—it sometimes seemed to Paul-Henri that his main job at the gendarmerie was taking lost creatures back to their homes. Which he did not resent, to his credit.

"Have you driven past the Broussard house yet today?" the chief barked, startling him when he returned to the station.

"Not yet. I went by yesterday in the late afternoon. There was no car in the drive. Do you want me to ask Anne-Marie again if she has heard from him?"

"Of course that's what you should do," said Charlot, looking at him as though he had a screw loose. "But keep in mind that she might be an accomplice, and applying techniques of misdirection."

"Accomplice? How do you figure that?"

Charlot sighed. She pushed her chair away from her desk and stood up. "Let me take you by the hand, step by step. A woman was murdered. One person and *one person only* has disappeared and not been heard from. That makes him our prime suspect."

"With all due respect, so you've said, chief. And I agree that Lapin's behavior after the murder is suspicious. But how are you dragging Anne-Marie into it? Do you think she knows his whereabouts and is lying about it? Maybe she's a masterful liar, but she seems genuinely upset and concerned about Lapin's absence. On the verge of distraught, I'd say."

"And you believe this show of emotion? You do not think it can be faked?"

"Well, yeah, of course technically I suppose it can. I just don't believe it is in this case. Just because a thing is possible doesn't mean it's remotely likely. What possible reason would Lapin have for strangling that young woman, whom he'd never met before? Everyone at that party had the opportunity to kill Crespelle, so why aren't we focusing on the motive? Do you know about some connection between the Broussards and the nanny that you haven't shared with me?"

Charlot turned her back to Paul-Henri. "I'm waiting for the lab reports," she said. "We're virtually hamstrung until we get that information. It's impossible, working with these villagers who have no sense of urgency!"

Paul-Henri was used to Charlot ignoring his questions, but he tried once more. "What is the lab going to tell us beyond the fact that Crespelle was strangled? Do you have some reason to think Anne-Marie was involved, either before or after the murder was committed?"

Charlot ignored him again, causing an angry red to start creeping up his neck. She dropped back into her chair and picked up the phone.

"Put Nagrand on, it's Chief Charlot. Bonjour to you too… right…yes, that's exactly what I'm calling about."

Paul-Henri backed out of the office and took a brisk walk around the block to collect himself. The village looked as it always did, the old golden stones almost glowing in the sunshine, a cat wandering across the street, Madame Tessier sweeping the sidewalk in front of her house. It was hard to believe a place of such calm and beauty could also be vulnerable to such violence. When he circled around to the door of the gendarmerie, he had to force himself to go back inside, barely able to stand being in the chief's presence.

"Honestly, I don't know how anything gets done in this back-water," said the chief, striding out from her office. "Turns out the lab screwed up and that's why it's taken so long. Some of the samples were mislabeled and they've had to start all over again from the beginning."

Paul-Henri shook his head, not sure how she was able to make him feel that the lab mistake was somehow his fault.

"Nagrand says they still have enough of what they need. Should be any day now." She got to the door and then said over her shoulder, "Just because Lapin is the number one suspect doesn't mean I'm sitting back and thinking the case is finished. I'm heading out to talk to the people out at L'Institut Degas. Never trust an artist, that's what I always say, so I'm not going to give them any free passes."

"Why don't you trust artists?" asked Paul-Henri, truly baffled.

"Oh, you know how they are," said Charlot, leaving him just as confused. "And tomorrow morning, I plan to pay a visit to Molly Sutton. Private investigator, indeed. You might say it's the perfect cover if one wanted to go on a murdering spree."

"One death is hardly a spree. Are you seriously suggesting that Molly and Ben had something to do with the murder of Violette Crespelle?"

Chief Charlot just turned the corners of her mouth up as though she were smiling—which she was not—and left the station.

Paul-Henri sat at his desk for a good forty-five minutes before the redness on his neck dissipated, but his fury at having to serve under a woman he did not respect (and in fact loathed) was as intense as ever.

✌ 32 ✌

Rex Ford, longtime professor at L'Institut Degas, loitered outside Marie-Claire Levy's office, hoping to run into her as though by chance. His most promising student had been absent for the last two classes, and he wanted to ask Marie-Claire if the boy had called in with an excuse. An everyday sort of task, familiar to teachers of all levels—but Rex was famous for taking a simple thing and making it a thousand times more complicated: a useful trait in an artist, potentially, but one that made being his superior at work often tiresome.

Marie-Claire's assistant left to have lunch, but still Rex stayed in the corridor, pretending to study something in a notebook as the older woman passed by. Finally Marie-Claire herself emerged, looking well turned out as she always did, her hair in a neat chignon and a white silk blouse draping perfectly around the waist of her gray flannel pencil skirt.

"Rex!" she said, startled. "What can I do for you?"

"Oh, bonjour Marie-Claire," said Rex, as though surprised to see her. "Have you heard anything about the murder case?"

Marie-Claire shook her head. "Nothing that you don't know. I did hear that Simon Valette hired Molly and Ben, which I found curious. But I'm grateful about it, since I haven't heard a single positive word about our new chief of gendarmes."

"Nor I," said Rex, always pleased to join in on any complaining. "Do you know Charlot *bargained* at the épicerie? Well, you can't even call it bargaining—she just goes in, takes what she wants, and throws down any amount of money she pleases!"

"I've never heard of anyone doing such a thing."

"Nor I," said Rex. "I heard a group of vendors at the Saturday market talking about it. They want to do something to stop her, but they can't exactly call the gendarmes, can they?"

Marie-Claire shook her head. "Have you…has she contacted you, or Paul-Henri? I expected them to come around long before now. Molly stopped in days ago, but so far, nothing from the gendarmes."

"Haven't heard a word," said Rex. "Not that I expect them to be interested in anything I have to say. The lights went out, I saw and heard nothing, and that's that. Tough case, it seems to me."

"Yes," said Marie-Claire, sneaking a look at her watch.

"You don't…you don't think we should mention she was here?"

"No," said Marie-Claire. "I don't want the school mixed up in the middle of a murder case. It's not as though the fact that she happened to apply here had anything to do with what happened."

Rex cocked his head but said nothing.

"Well, I've got to push off, have a meeting in the village."

"Right, sure," said Rex. It was not until Marie-Claire was halfway to the village that he remembered he had forgotten to ask about his absent student.

THAT NIGHT, Paul-Henri Monsour spent a little effort on his dinner. He sliced a breast of chicken in half lengthwise and pounded the cutlets thin, breaded them, and fried them until the outside was wonderfully crispy. Then he made a quick sauce from the pan drippings, a dollop of wine, and a knob of butter, poured it over the cutlets, and sat down at his small table with a smile of anticipation.

He took a sip of a nice Bordeaux that had been something of a splurge on his salary; he picked up knife and fork, and then paused with them in midair. His stomach was roiling after another terrifically frustrating day at the station with Chief Charlot. It felt as though there was a pile of crabs inside his belly trying to eat their way out. He took another sip of wine and tried to calm down with no success, then slammed the knife on the table and snatched up his cell phone.

Paul-Henri scrolled through his contacts for some time, not able to remember who he was looking for until he saw the name. Yes, Adam Carron, that was it. An unpleasant fellow, to be sure, but the kind of man who knows how to play politics at work and is good at it. They had been at Officers' School together, and now Adam was comfortably ensconced at a relatively high administrative level, never having sullied himself with actual police work for more than a few months.

Paul-Henri wasn't positive Adam would remember him, but it was worth a shot. It hadn't been that many years ago, after all, and he thought Adam was likely to be the sort of person who remembers everyone, in case someday they might be useful to him.

He started to call but stopped himself. How to explain to someone who was not with Charlot, day after day, how colossally inept she was? How to get across that at that very moment she was bumbling through a murder investigation and Castillac's only hope for justice lay not with the gendarmerie but a pair of civilians (even if they did happen to be rather successful at their work)?

Paul-Henri set the phone down and picked his knife and fork back up again. Just contemplating making the call had settled his stomach somewhat, and he cut a piece of the cutlet and chewed with appreciation.

He just needed to bide his time. Adam Carron would help him, when the time came. He only had to wait and watch for the right moment, and deliverance would be his.

❦ 33 ❦

The next night, Molly invited the gîte guests over for an apéro, feeling a bit chagrined at how much of her time and energy had been spent on the Crespelle case instead of on them. She was still very worried about the girls, and her interview with Raphael had provided no information that was helpful.

Ah, poor Raphael, she thought. He's utterly lost, being in this new place. Impulsive, filled with understandable fury—but not dangerous, not really. All bluster, was her judgment of him.

Ben was in Bergerac trying to placate Bernard Petit, since so far the video cameras had recorded nothing of interest.

She hadn't needed to tidy up much, and after putting bottles and glasses out on the terrace, Molly had a few minutes to kill before the guests arrived. Sitting down at her desk, she tried for the third time to find a phone number for Violette's sister—and this time, hidden in Violette's Facebook postings, she thought she might just have it.

I shouldn't call now, she told herself, knowing she would risk being interrupted. But Molly told herself all kinds of things that she then went ahead and ignored, and this time was no different.

She clicked the numbers on her computer and in a wink a woman's voice came over the speakerphone.

"Hello?" said a faint voice.

"Bonjour, is this Sofia Crespelle? I'm very sorry to disturb you. My name is Molly Sutton, I live in Castillac—"

"Ech!"

"I...I'm so very sorry...about your sister. I am a private investigator," she said, always feeling silly to call herself that. "I am trying very hard to find out what happened to Violette."

No answer.

"Would you mind if I asked you a few questions? I know it's an intrusion."

"How do I know you're not from one of those papers?"

Molly paused, then realized Sofia was worried about the tabloids getting the story.

"Oh no!" Molly burst out. "I would never! Maybe I can email you, and tell you something about myself? I swear, all I want to do is find justice for your sister."

"A little late for that now, isn't it?"

"I don't think so, no. Wouldn't you be pleased if her killer went to prison?"

"'Pleased' is not the word I would choose."

"Right, that's...of course not."

"I appreciate your making an effort. But I must excuse myself now, thank you for calling."

Click.

Molly sat back in the chair, thinking. Impossible to judge anything about a woman who had just lost her sister to a violent act. It's no wonder she's suspicious. At least I have her number now. I'll try her again later, she thought, startling at the sound of someone rapping on the terrace door.

"Bonsoir!" cried the Jenkinses, peering through the glass door. They had showered and changed after a long day of sightseeing.

"May I make you a kir?" asked Molly, opening the door wide.

"And tell me what church you saw today, and what was interesting about it. I am a little embarrassed to admit that once I moved here, I stopped doing much sightseeing. It always gets put off to later, you know?"

"Oh yes," said Deana, taking a glass.

"I think if I lived here, I would never get anything done because I'd constantly be playing hooky to go look at one more thing," said Billy. "The culture is just so amazingly rich! The buildings are so old!"

"It is comforting, isn't it?"

"Yes and no. I do see what you mean, but it can also make me very aware of how fleeting our time is. The old stones aren't going anywhere, but us? We're here for a blink of an eye, and then gone..."

"Well, that's happy talk for cocktail hour!" said Deana, digging him in the ribs.

Billy grinned and kissed the side of Deana's head. "So today we drove down to Cadouin, to see the abbey there. We were not disappointed, I'll tell you that! It has the loveliest cloister—you know, an interior garden with a covered walkway all around."

"It's enough to make you want to be a nun," said Deana.

"Heaven forfend," said Billy, grinning again. "But seriously, I do know what Deana means. You can just imagine a life of contemplation, with simple work and in this beautiful serene place...it makes our hectic lives seem a little crazy."

Molly nodded. "What you just described? That's a lot of the reason I decided to leave the States and move here. I had a successful life, at least viewed from the outside. But all that hurrying left me feeling sort of empty."

"Cheers to a new life!" said Billy, and they clinked glasses.

"Do you miss home, though?" asked Deana.

"Oh yes. Absolutely. Not enough to consider going back for good, but I get pangs sometimes, even sharp ones. I mostly love being a fish out of water, but sometimes...you just want everything to be familiar and easy, you know? So, tell me more about the abbey. Is it very old?"

"Founded in the eleventh century, is that right, Deana? But the main buildings are gothic, built in the fifteenth and sixteenth centuries. Not terribly dark, not at all, but lovely. They've got a piece of a shroud that was thought to be Christ's, but turned out to be from Egypt in the eleventh century."

When they were on their second kir, Todor and Elise came over and joined them, and Molly and the four guests ended up talking and drinking on the terrace for hours, trading stories about traveling and exceptional places they had been. Dinner turned out to be olives and some garlic bread Molly scrounged up out of a stale baguette, but all of them went to bed happy that night.

Ben had sneaked into the house without disturbing them, and Molly was happy to climb in next to him as he read yet another volume of Napoleonic history.

"Should we talk about the case?" she asked, her eyes already starting to close.

"The Petit case is going nowhere."

"Crespelle?"

"Not sure what our next move is."

Molly nodded sleepily. "I talked to Violette's sister today. Do you think it's strange that she didn't come here?"

"What could she do?" Ben considered the question. "I can see it both ways, I suppose. Maybe they weren't even close—not all sisters are, of course. If they were close, she might want to see the last things her sister saw before her death, to be in the last place her sister had been alive. But on the other hand, I could see avoiding Castillac forever. I wouldn't relish a meeting with the Valettes, that's for certain."

"Camille, at any rate," said Molly, snuggling against Ben with her eyes closed.

"I don't see why you're so certain Simon is innocent. Sometimes I get the feeling you are quite vulnerable to male charms, chérie." He turned to see her expression but Molly had sunk into sleep, and was beginning, just faintly, to snore.

§•

EARLY TUESDAY MORNING, Simon was having a cup of coffee in the kitchen when Camille breezed in, dressed in a smart suit with an expensive handbag over one arm.

"Glorious morning," she said, giving him a quick kiss on the lips.

Simon maintained an even expression. "I see you're feeling better. Excellent! And looking quite chic, my darling. Do you have plans, or is that suit just for the Valettes to admire *en famille*?"

Camille peeled the top from a container of yogurt and dumped the yogurt into a porcelain dish, once belonging to one of the girls, that had bunnies around the rim. "I'm going into the village," she said. "I'm not going to allow this business with Violette to turn everyone against me. It occurred to me that as long as I'm acting like a hermit, people in the village are free to make up any kind of story about me they like. And the only way to counteract that is to show them who I am, in person."

"Brava!" said Simon, with well-acted enthusiasm. "I do wonder...not to be a pest, but do you think—for Castillac, after all —you might be just a little overdressed? We're not on the Boulevard des Capucines anymore, after all."

Camille stared at him. Her shoulders rose up around her ears and the corners of her mouth turned down.

"Of course, wear what you like, what makes you feel beautiful," Simon added, sipping his coffee. "I only bring it up because you are explicitly talking about wanting to make a certain impression, so...."

Camille ate a spoonful of yogurt, opening her mouth very wide so as not to disturb her lipstick.

"Are the girls up?" asked Simon, trying to change the subject.

Camille looked at him wonderingly and he realized his wife had not thought of them at all.

"I'll see to them," he said lightly. "They don't eat much before school anyway." He refilled his cup, kissed Camille on the cheek, and left the kitchen.

Camille stood for a long moment staring out of the window over the sink. Then she walked over to the counter and a wooden block that held a collection of Sabatier knives. She slid a six-inch chef's knife out of the block, tilted it in the light to see it glint, and slipped it into her handbag.

❧ 34 ❧

Molly was in the garden pulling weeds, where she did her best thinking. It was taking some discipline to focus on possible leads instead of mentally wringing her hands over the wellbeing of the Valette girls. For whatever reason, Gisele had chosen her to ask for help, and so far, she had managed nothing. Yanking up a particularly long and nasty root, Molly wondered idly about a wiretap. How hard were they to get in France? Would it ever be possible for a private investigator to get one legally? And even if it was obtained and put in place—was Camille chatty enough, revealing enough, to make it worthwhile?

Her cellphone buzzed and Molly sat back on her heels, tried to wipe the dirt off her hands, and dug it out of her pocket. A text from Lawrence:

raphael valette dead. thought you'd be interested

Raphael? *What?*

Molly was stunned. Not that there had been another murder —that was common enough, sadly. But Raphael? That...that made no sense. It didn't fit at all with how she saw Camille, or the Valettes as a family.

She jumped up and brushed off her jeans, then called Ben, who had gone over to check on how the renovation was going.

"Here's a shocker," she said when he answered.

"Yes?"

"Just got a text from Lawrence. Raphael Valette is dead."

"I'm sorry to hear that," said Ben. "I'm sure it's rather bittersweet for the family in a circumstance like that."

"What are you talking about? What could possibly be sweet about having a family member murdered, not two weeks from a different member of the household being strangled?"

"Murdered? You didn't say that, Molly!"

"I—well," she laughed weakly. "I guess Lawrence didn't say it either. I totally jumped to conclusions. Sorry! Maybe you could call Florian and find out what's going on?" She shook her head. "I guess I'm really on edge. I spent a couple hours this morning trying to find anything online that would help the case, but I'm getting nowhere."

"It is frustrating," he said.

"And...you're pretty iffy about Camille, aren't you?"

Ben didn't answer at first. "Well," he said finally, "of course I think that if she stabbed Simon, she's obviously not mentally well. And I suppose that could mean just about anything, but yes, it's a violent act and so, obviously, is murder. I don't dispute that she could have had motive, whether her fears were based in reality or not.

"But Molly, that adds up to a lot of supposition, a lot of jumping from one stone to another to get across the pond, if you see what I mean?"

"And you want a bridge."

"A solid one, made of concrete, if you've got one of those."

Molly sighed. "I'll keep looking. Let me know what Florian says?"

"Of course."

She threw a stick for Bobo for a few minutes, then took a long, leisurely shower, all the while combing through every moment of the Valette dinner party, hoping to see or hear something she had missed the first ten thousand times she had replayed the evening in her mind.

And once dry and clean, Molly sat back down at the computer, flipping through the same sites she'd looked at before and haphazardly trying new ones, desperately hoping for a bit of luck.

❧

BUT MOLLY'S natural inclination was not to sit at a desk staring at her computer screen. She much preferred to be out in the world, even if that only meant whipping down rue des Chênes on her scooter. So before long she stood up, deciding that at least she could finish her interviews with the dinner party guests. Just as she was headed out the door, her cell buzzed again.

"Âllo?"

"Molly! It's Anne-Marie. Just wanted to tell you that, thank God, Lapin has come home."

"Good! I hope he's given you some explanation for worrying you so?"

"Well, sort of. It's not exactly...I mean, all he says is that when the lights went out, he completely freaked out. Something about a punishment he used to get as a child? His father sounds like a real—"

"Yes, terribly cruel. But so...that doesn't explain why he was gone so long. The lights did come back on, after all."

"He was on his way back when he heard about the murder. He was sure that his disappearance would look suspicious."

"So he made himself look even more suspicious by staying

away? Lapin!" said Molly, shaking her head, but feeling a little sorry for him.

"I know. He's ridiculous," said Anne-Marie, but her voice was full of sympathy.

"I would let the gendarmes know. Better for him to make the first move, than that they hear it from someone else."

"Yes, good idea, Molly. I'll go around with him as soon as I can. Do you know...have you been working with Chief Charlot? Any tips on what we should say?"

Molly paused, taking a deep breath. "Charlot...she's not easy. She'll probably snap at you, say rude things to Lapin, accuse you both of who knows what. But look, we know Lapin didn't do anything wrong, so just hold your ground and eventually she'll have to let it go."

"Are you saying Lapin is actually a suspect?"

"That's what I hear, Anne-Marie. I'm sorry. We've tried to reason with Charlot, but she insists that his leaving puts him at the top of the suspect list. She doesn't have anything else though." Molly stepped outside and shut the front door behind her. "She doesn't, right Anne-Marie? I mean, I know Lapin is innocent, but do you know of anything Charlot might have gotten hold of, anything that would seem to be incriminating? I ask only because if all he did was leave, that's a pretty weak case for a chief of gendarmes to be making. Not without something in addition."

"There's nothing else, Molly. Nothing at all. That I know about," she added, a little weakly.

"Then don't worry. Ben and I will figure this out, and she doesn't have nearly enough to try to pin it on Lapin. I'll call you soon, and give Lapin my love. And a spanking."

🌿 35 🌺

Simon Valette stood in the midst of the ruin, surrounded by rubble and carefully sorted piles of stones, staring down the driveway where the coroner's van had traveled hours earlier, on the way to the morgue with his father's body.

Everything was entirely surreal. Death after death...and the feeling of unreality was compounded by the family's recent move to Castillac, where they experienced serial traumas but did not have the comfort of people and places familiar to them.

My father is dead, Simon kept saying to himself over and over, trying to believe it.

Camille was in the kitchen, planning dinner with Merla. After Violette's death, they had hired the cook to make dinner for the family twice a week, and thankfully the day of Raphael's death was one of the appointed days; Camille did not know her way around a kitchen, Simon was in no condition to do anything, and people, after all, needed to be fed.

"I think something in the peasant line," she said to Merla, who sat at the kitchen table with a notepad and pen at the ready. Merla was confused.

"Pardon?" she said. "Peasant line?"

"Oh, I just mean some sort of hearty dish, nothing fussy," said Camille, irritated. "How about a simple beef stew, can you do that?"

"Of course," said Merla, keeping her face unperturbed. "I've been meaning to ask about general preferences. Are there foods that anyone doesn't like? I know the young ones sometimes have—"

"The girls will eat what they're given," said Camille.

Merla nodded. "Are you...do you need any help with anything else, given Monsieur Valette's sudden passing?"

Camille looked up at the ceiling, thinking. They couldn't very well have a reception, because who would come? Not to mention that after the disastrous dinner party she had decided not to entertain for months, to let that memory fade a bit in people's minds.

"I'm...I'm not sure what the plans will be. It's..."

Complicated, thought Merla, but said nothing.

Home from school, Gisele and Chloë were in their room upstairs, building a fort with every blanket they could find. Gisele had dragged some high-backed chairs from somewhere to hang the blankets on, while Chloë had stolen pillows from all over the house, so that their fort was now, as they saw it, a sort of Arabian palace inside, with soft places to lounge and a feeling of princely grandeur. They were each sitting on a pillow, lost in thought, not taking the usual pleasure in their creation.

"He was horrible," whispered Chloë.

Gisele agreed, but said nothing.

"Do you think he fell?" asked Chloë. "I mean, I know he was old and everything, but I don't remember him falling before. I've heard about how old people fall sometimes. But..."

"All we know," said Gisele slowly, "is that *Grandpère* went over the railing of his balcony and then died."

"Do you think we're in danger?" whispered Chloë. "First Violette, now *Grandpère*...what if one of *us* is next?"

Gisele put an arm around her sister. "Don't worry," she said, though she was worrying intensely. "It's important to stick with what we know, and not start making things up. He probably slipped or something like that. You know how the tiles on the porch get slippery after a rain—maybe it was the same on his balcony. And he was so tall that the railing wasn't going to hold him back."

"Maybe he did a flip," said Chloë.

"Maybe," said Gisele, holding her sister more tightly.

Simon left the ruin and circled around the house to the side where his father's room was. He looked up at the door to the balcony, now shut. Then down at the ground, where the men from the coroner's office had struggled to get Raphael's body on a stretcher so they could lift him into the van.

"Rest in peace, father," Simon murmured. He tried to summon some earlier memories of their time together, before Raphael had begun to deteriorate. But Simon's mind was too fractured, too busy leaping from thought to thought with a kind of frantic desperation, unable to stay in one place for more than a moment.

He took in a long, slow breath, still staring at the ground where his father's broken body had been found. Was it over now? Any further loose threads to tie up, any tongues that needed to be silenced? He knew the inquiries and investigations would go on for an eternity, but that was almost a minor nuisance in comparison.

Could the deaths stop?

Was it over yet?

WANTING SOME EXERCISE, Molly walked from La Baraque to Dr. Vernay's office. For the entire half hour it took her to get there, she went over the details of the case for what felt like the millionth time, picking at all the questions that she and Ben had made no progress answering.

Had one of the Valettes gone to the basement that fateful night and replaced the fuse with a bad one? Did Violette Crespelle have any connection with anyone except the Valettes? Was Raphael capable of murder? Had Raphael been murdered himself—and if so, did that mean he did not kill Violette?

It was like being on one of those playground spinners, around and around and everything getting blurrier and harder to hold on to the more she thought about it.

As she proceeded down rue Malbec, Molly was tempted to stop in at the station to see Paul-Henri, and take the general temperature of the gendarmerie. Certainly Lapin's reappearance would put a stop to that ridiculous wild goose chase? And who knew where Charlot's suspicious eye might fall next? It made no sense to Molly that Charlot seemed to discount Camille; was it possible the two women had crossed paths before somewhere?

She shook her head to try to clear it. I'm making this more complicated than it needs to be, she said to herself as she arrived on the doctor's doorstep.

Smiling, with rosy cheeks, Robinette Vernay appeared quickly after Molly rang the bell.

"Bonjour, Molly! Wonderful to see you. I'm sorry you're not feeling well, come on in, please, have a seat and rest. Gérard is with another patient but I don't think it will be too long. What seems to be the matter?"

"Oh, I'm fine, I'm not sick—I'm here to talk to him about the murder the other night."

"Ah. Yes, well. It's really quite disturbing the way murder seems to flourish in our little village. Never seen the like. But I guess when you have a lot of new people moving in, people you don't know anything about..."

Molly smiled and raised her eyebrows.

"I didn't mean you!" said Robinette, her cheeks turning pink.

"It is almost as though you have always been in Castillac, Molly. And we are very lucky to have you."

The two women stood in silence for a few moments. Molly shifted from one foot to the other, impatient to see Dr. Vernay.

"You do look rather peaked," said Robinette. "Would you like a glass of water?"

"Really, I'm fine," said Molly, just as an old man came out of the examination room, followed by Dr. Vernay.

"Anything in moderation," the doctor called after the man, who chuckled to himself, nodded to Molly, and slipped out the door.

Dr. Vernay expressed concern about Molly's health, but once she explained why she was there, he led her into his office, which, like the examining room, was a homey place with thick rugs and many paintings on the walls.

"I must tell you, I found the other night to be quite unsettling," he confided. "Of course, a murder *is* unsettling, there's no avoiding it. Such a bit of sudden chaos, wouldn't you say?"

"That's a good way to put it," agreed Molly. "I guess you're a little more equipped than most of us to deal with death, or am I making an assumption there?"

Dr. Vernay leaned back in his chair and looked up at the ceiling. "It's true, many of us in the medical profession are dulled to it, as you say. But others—we got in this line of work to help people, to save lives. And so a senseless death like that of Mademoiselle Crespelle...it hits us hard. Very hard."

Molly nodded. As she tried to get her thoughts in order for the interview, her gaze wandered over the wall behind him. There were the usual diplomas, a painting of a horse galloping over a hill, and a portrait of a man who looked like he had eaten something bad. "Is that a relative?" asked Molly, with something like a smirk.

"Oh, yes," said Dr. Vernay, swiveling around to look. "Gustave Vernay. Somewhat dyspeptic, eh?" They laughed.

"And you went to university in Nice?" asked Molly, pointing at his diploma. "That must have been amazing!"

"Indeed," said Dr. Vernay. "Lovely city. I'm very fond of the sea."

"I'd love to ask you more about it sometime, I've been meaning to take a trip to the Riviera before long. But let's get the work out of the way, if you don't mind? A few questions about the other night?"

"Anything I can do to help, Molly."

"Did you notice anything on the night of the murder? Anything that seemed...out of place, curious? Maybe something that you brushed off at the time, but later wondered about?"

Dr. Vernay nodded as she spoke. He looked young for his age, which Molly figured was around early fifties, with an unlined face and hair that was only just starting to go a little gray at the temples. He put his hands in his pockets, looked up at the ceiling, and considered her question. Finally he shrugged and shook his head. "I've gone over it and over it. The thing is, the lights going out had such a dramatic effect. I myself was rather shaken by it for some reason. I jumped up from my seat at the table and was looking for my coat in the foyer, wanting above all to leave that house and get myself home. I've wondered since whether I was having some sort of premonition, or at least felt the presence of evil in some way...but no matter how hard I try, I cannot seem to identify exactly what it was that gave me that feeling."

"Did you have any such inklings *before* the lights went out?"

Dr. Vernay chewed on his lip. "I believe I must have, and the darkness amplified them. But as I said...I can't put my finger on what it was." He paused, brushing a bit of lint from his trousers. "I had been thinking...there was a person who—at any rate, I don't want to be simply gossiping about people without any solid reason for speaking. I'm afraid I may have sent poor Paul-Henri off in the wrong direction by rambling about some thoughts I had. I wish I could take it back now."

"What kind of thoughts?" asked Molly, perking up a bit.

"I shouldn't compound my carelessness by saying it all again," said Dr. Vernay with a sudden smile. "You *are* a relentless one, aren't you?"

"I try. Mostly I'm just very, very curious. I'll worm it out of Paul-Henri anyway, so you might as well tell me."

Chuckling, Dr. Valette leaned back in his chair again. "All right —but please, Molly, take this with an enormous grain of salt. On further reflection, I do believe I jumped the gun and wish I had said nothing."

Molly waited.

"All right. It's that—I wondered about...Camille Valette. Whether she was altogether of sound mind."

Molly moved to the edge of her seat. "Yes, she's crazy. But what *kind* of crazy, Gérard?"

"Again, I must demur. I've barely spoken three sentences to her, much less examined her. I merely thought that her relation to her children showed a certain...coldness...."

"Same," said Molly. "Same. And do you think that coldness could indicate a potential murderess?"

Reluctantly, the doctor started to nod, but then stopped himself. "Impossible to say. Almost anyone could be driven to murder, if the stars aligned the right way, wouldn't you say? As I said, I think I jumped the gun on that one. Please tell Officer Monsour so if you run into him."

Molly asked what he had thought of Simon and Raphael.

"Oh, Simon seems a nice-enough fellow. Quite sophisticated for Castillac, I'd say. Be surprised if this experiment of theirs lasts more than a year. As for his father, just a simple case of dementia and not much more to say about it. He might be capable of hurting someone, even killing them in a moment of unfocused rage, but not planning such a thing. No chance at all it was Raphael. Neat as it might be for you for the murderer to already be deceased," he added with a chuckle.

Sighing and feeling a pang of hunger, Molly asked a few more incidental questions, said her goodbyes, and made her way to Café de la Place to meet Ben for lunch. She hoped that the doctor's reluctant opinion of Camille might finally be the thing to sway him.

"You've been feeling better," Simon commented to his wife as he prepared to take a shower.

"Why do you say that?" she asked. Her tone was anxious and Simon turned toward her. He wished he had said nothing. "Why, Simon?" she said with urgency. "I think it is only that I am learning to fake it more successfully." She lifted her chin and turned away from him. "None of you in this family understands me. I am surrounded by people—by noise, by all these needs and wants and pressures—but I am utterly solitary."

"We all are, when you get down to it," said Simon quietly.

"No! I am more alone than all of you!"

Simon sighed a deep sigh. Not for the first time he regretted ever meeting Camille. But how was he to guess that that elegant young woman would turn out to be dangerously imbalanced, that her emotional state would zigzag by the hour so that no one in the house ever felt safe?

He dropped his clothes on the floor and stepped into the hot shower. He was filthy from working with the stones and the water pouring off him was at first brown and then gray. The water was very hot and soothing. His eyes closed.

He did not see his wife enter the bathroom. Or see that she had a knife in her hand, an expression of rage deforming her face.

ꙮ 37 ꙮ

W aving at Pascal, Ben came into the café and took a seat by the window. A cool breeze had kicked up and hardly anyone was having lunch on the terrace. Molly appeared a few minutes later and they kissed cheeks before settling in their chairs.

"I could eat a horse," she said. "Um, does Madame Longhale ever put horse on the menu? Because I didn't mean that literally."

Ben laughed. "I think she prefers beef and lamb," he said. "And duck, of course. All good cooks in the Périgord know their way around a duck."

Pascal arrived brandishing new menus. "Maman may have gotten a little carried away this time," he said to them. "She wanted to shake things up, said she was bored making the same thing day after day. So the entire menu is different."

"No beef stew?" asked Ben, stricken.

"Not for now," said Pascal. "Please excuse me, I've got a table I have to get to—" He made a short bow and hurried away.

"Now what in the world was that about?" asked Molly.

Ben looked up from the menu. "What?"

"Pascal. He's always the most charming man in the entire village—"

"Ahem."

"—excepting you, of course. Didn't you notice he seemed a little short with us? Not mad, but like...like he wanted to get away?"

"I didn't notice anything. I am busy mourning the beef stew I had planned to order."

"And—when he left, he made that excuse about another table, but he just ducked into the kitchen. Didn't go to another table at all."

"Hmm," said Ben, studying the menu with intense focus.

"Hmph," said Molly, opening hers and beginning to read. "I'm just saying that never once in the years I have lived in Castillac has Pascal not been warm and delightful when greeting me."

"Do you consider that rude?" Ben folded his menu and put it down.

"No, not rude. More...distracted. Wanting to get away from us."

Ben shrugged. "Maybe he's not in the mood for any talk about the investigation. It is true that when we're on a case, we hardly speak of anything else."

Molly nodded, unconvinced. "Maybe it's just Bad Manners Day here at the café...I see Boris whatever-his-last-name-is sitting over there. Do you know him? He's been driving a delivery truck for the renovation job. Do not like."

Ben dropped his napkin to the floor and sneaked a look when picking it back up. "Never seen him before. Must be new to the village."

"Is it totally selfish of me to wish the gates had closed after I got here?"

Pascal returned and took their orders with efficiency—a seafood quiche for Molly and roast pork for Ben—and headed back to the kitchen without any further conversation.

"See what I mean? The place isn't crowded. He's avoiding us!"

"Oh, Molly, you're like a dog with a bone," said Ben with a sigh. "It's just a moment in time. I'm sure it's nothing. Maybe he's coming down with a cold or has a blister on his heel. Could be a million reasons he doesn't feel like socializing today."

"Yes, if he were a normal person. But this is *Pascal* we're talking about." She took a deep breath. "Okay, okay, I'll drop it. You have anything to report on the Petit case?"

"Not a thing. It's crossed my mind that...that Monsieur Petit is not being entirely forthcoming with me."

"How so?"

"Well, as you know, I set up video cameras in strategic locations. As an aside, they were less expensive than you might think and I'm sure we'll have occasion to use them in the future. At any rate, they have produced absolutely nothing. I've watched a lot of footage of a cat wandering along the side of the house but not a single human except for the housekeeper and Petit himself. He has not reported anything else stolen."

"Can you think of anything else to do?"

"At this point, no. I'm all ears if you've got anything."

Molly was listening, but her eyes followed Pascal as he waited on a table in the far corner and went outside to check on one hardy couple seated on the terrace. She and Ben chatted about the weather, about some of the places the Jenkinses had told them about that they wanted to get around to visiting, and then, as usual, circled back to the case at hand.

"It's just unbearable to me that those little girls are being mistreated so," said Molly. "Did you get spanked when you were a child?"

"Oh, yes," said Ben. He shrugged. "We all did. It was unpleasant, no doubt, but since it was what almost all the parents did—and teachers too—it was just part of the world, if you understand me. I'm glad it's fallen out of fashion."

"I got the impression that what Camille is doing to her daughters goes beyond spanking. Gisele told me that sometimes her mother would put makeup on her to hide bruises."

Ben grimaced.

"I want to stop her."

"I know, chérie. I know."

Pascal delivered their plates with a flourish but did not stay to chat though Molly was looking at him quizzically. And then, in the most French of moments, as they ate the delectable home-made food, all thoughts of work, of murder, of any worry at all— everything fell away and their attention was utterly and completely on the succulent pork with crispy edges, and the pillowy scallops nestled in the most comforting chive-flecked custard ever to be surrounded by a buttery, flaky crust. Conversation was minimal, with Ben talking about his favorite dishes from childhood, and Molly scandalizing him by relating how much candy she had eaten once she was old enough to walk to the corner grocery by herself.

"Do you want coffee?" she asked him, feeling warm and nearly content after the meal.

"Actually, have it without me," he said, rummaging in his coat for his wallet. "I'm going to go see Paul-Henri, and I want to get over there right now, while he's in a good mood after lunch. See you at La Baraque?"

"Sure. Hope he gives you something decent."

"Probably it'll be a lot of complaining about Charlot, like last time. I get the feeling he thinks I'm connected to the gendarmerie somehow and will be able to do something to have her removed."

"He's a good guy, Paul-Henri. But maybe in the wrong line of work."

Ben nodded, put a pile of euros on the table, and left. Molly decided to see what Madame Longhale had made for dessert as she kept a close and suspicious eye on Pascal.

❦

THOUGH SHE WOULD HAVE PREFERRED to talk to him at the station, Chief Charlot was on her way to Lapin's shop, hoping to catch him inside and unwary. She had told Paul-Henri to demand he come in, but without any sort of actual legal pressure to force that, Paul-Henri had been reduced more or less to begging Lapin, which had not moved him even a little.

The village was all right, Charlot thought as she walked through the narrow streets to the shop. The people were just as ignorant as they were everywhere, no surprise there. Filled with smug overreachers like Dufort and Sutton, cheating merchants, and nobodies. She heartily wished her posting in Castillac would be over sooner rather than later, but knew from experience that trying to influence the whims of the gendarmerie was not a good or productive idea.

Just as she entered the Place, Ben Dufort came striding along on the same side of the street. It would be rude to cross over and avoid him, yet Charlot almost did anyway. The man was at the dinner party when the murder was committed, she thought. How dare he set himself up as an investigator, she thought, when he and that women he was living with (and don't get her started on that) had not proven their own innocence.

"Bonjour, Chief," Ben said, when they reached each other.

"Bonjour," said Charlot, her smile brittle.

"I'm glad our errant friend Lapin has finally come home," he said, shaking his head with a little smile.

"No doubt."

"I understand you will—or maybe you already have spoken to him, officially—but I wanted to tell you I talked to him, and it seems like it's a simple case of...well, neurotic behavior, I suppose you could call it. We in the village know his history, you under-stand—a cruel father Lapin had, very cruel. And so even now, as a

NELL GODDIN

grown man, sometimes his reactions to things are a bit...outsized, you could say."

"Could say, could not say...I am not so fussy with my characterizations, Monsieur Dufort. What I know from experience is that people do not abscond if they are not guilty."

Ben opened his mouth to respond but she talked over him.

"—I am not stating definitively that Monsieur Broussard, that you all insist on calling Lapin, killed Violette Crespelle. We are still, maddeningly, waiting for the lab report to come back. I am hoping that material from under the girl's fingernails will be useful. In the meantime, I am not willing to let your friend completely off the hook. He may or may not be guilty of murder, but I can bet you any amount he is guilty of *something*."

Ben looked at her, unable to find anything to say. He found her very unpleasant, and imagined shouting at her, though he kept himself in check.

"Well, I'm off," she said, nodding faintly and proceeding past him down the sidewalk. She went by the Café de la Place, seeing Molly Sutton inside, seated by herself. There's no getting away from these people, she thought with annoyance.

Lapin's shop was a five-minute walk from the center of Castillac, at the end of rue Baudelaire. Charlot spoke to no one on the way. She spent the walk ruminating over past grievances in what was a nearly lifelong pursuit of *pensées des escaliers*, when you come up with the perfect thing to say but you're already halfway down the stairs.

The sign hanging from the wall outside Lapin's shop said "Laurent Broussard" in stately gilt letters. Charlot pushed her way inside to the tinkling of a bell, and looked around for the owner.

The front counter was stacked with small cardboard boxes, and the two aisles on either side were jammed with furniture—a rocking chair, a console table that looked ancient, Louis XIII. Charlot sniffed, feeling a vague sense of disapproval that she couldn't quite pin on anything.

The shop was silent. Had he wandered off with the door unlocked? These villagers have no idea about security, she thought.

A rustling in the back, then footsteps, and eventually the large belly of Lapin showed around the side of a tall bureau as he made his way to the front of the shop. When he saw who it was, his face sagged.

"Bonjour, madame," he said, trying to pull himself together. "I believe you are the new chief of gendarmes? I am Laurent Broussard—everyone calls me Lapin—very pleased to make your acquaintance." He had often used kissing a woman's hand as a way to defuse an awkward moment, but it didn't seem right for the chief of gendarmes. He smiled weakly.

"Correct, I am Chief Charlot. Can you tell me why it is that everyone calls you Lapin? Why do they not call you your actual name, a name that you must approve of since you have put it on the sign of your shop?"

"It's—that's a long story, chief. Well, maybe it's a story that might...that might help my situation. I was born and raised in Castillac, you understand. I travel for my work but have spent almost every night of my life right here, in the very same house. The people...well, you see, in a village this size, we all know each other. A lot of us know each other pretty well, if you see what I mean." Lapin stopped talking and looked out of the window at a mother going by pushing a stroller.

Charlot looked askance, wondering if he was simple-minded.

"I guess some people might take offense, but I never did," he said, standing up a little straighter. "They call me Lapin because they think I'm a coward. A scared bunny. And I don't mind, because, well, it's true. As my recent behavior has amply shown."

Charlot blinked. "You're saying that your old friends call you a coward but you don't mind?"

Lapin shrugged. "Sometimes it's better to be seen for who you are. Sometimes truth—"

"Oh dear Lord," interrupted Charlot. "Tell me about the other night. At the Valettes' dinner party. Start at the beginning, if you don't mind."

She's not *that* bad, Lapin thought. "Would you like a cup of tea? Coffee?"

"I did not come to your shop looking for refreshment," she said. "Just tell the story. In your own words."

"Yes. All right," said Lapin, rubbing his hands on his belly. "It was a rather strange thing, the dinner party. An invitation out of the blue, you understand. I'd never met the Valettes, didn't even know of their existence. But when I got the invite, I talked to some friends, they'd gotten one too, so we decided what the hell —we'd go and give the thing a chance.

"Simon poured us a nice glass when we got there. By 'we' I mean me and my wife, Anne-Marie." He smiled, saying her name. "So, I don't know, we mingled around like you do at a party, talking to our other friends—I assume you have a list of who was there? I can say that I knew everyone, except for the Valettes, and poor Violette. The rest are people I've known all my life and can vouch for."

"I'm not asking for any vouching, Lapin. Just…tell the story."

Lapin took in a long, noisy breath through his nose. He closed his eyes. "All right. We drank the champagne in the foyer and before long moved into the dining room. People were a little subdued, since no one knew the host and hostess. It was awkward, you understand. I think the hostess was pretty nervous, understandably—it would be odd to give a party and know none of the guests, wouldn't it? Luckily there was some harmless drama thanks to the children—I suppose a big party like that gets them all excited. In any case, one of them was tearing through the crowd, and the poor nanny was chasing after her and losing her most of the time." Lapin chortled. "And there was another girl too, a little older. Serious. I'm not sure how they managed it, but they got themselves hidden underneath the dinner table during dinner. I know because I kicked one by mistake, and heard a yelp. Cute little girls. Do you have children, Chief Charlot?"

"Tell the—"

"Yes, yes. All right. Honestly, I don't have much else to tell. We were mingling, sharing a joke or two. Simon was friendly with the nanny, telling her not to worry about the children, he was sure they were out of harm's way. I thought that was kind of him. I do very much like to see fathers being kind, don't you?"

A muscle in Charlot's jaw twitched.

"Some of us had a quick word with Violette as she passed through—I did, I believe Ben Dufort did as well. Gérard—the doctor, you know—was going on about her last name, telling her how much he enjoyed eating crespelles on some vacation or other." Lapin looked up at the ceiling, chewing his upper lip and thinking. "The whole time the storm was getting worse and worse. You remember that night? It was crazy, the rain, the thunder and lightning...all through dinner it was practically all anyone talked about. I was facing the window and I kept seeing these jagged flashes tearing across the sky."

Lapin got suddenly quiet.

"Go on," said Charlot.

He sighed. "Don't know if you've ever had the pleasure of trying Merla's cooking? She's one of the best in Castillac, truly. Always thought it a shame she didn't have a little restaurant tucked somewhere, I'm sure she'd—"

"Please!"

"Yes. Well, we ate, we enjoyed the food tremendously. Things had gotten a bit looser, people were beginning to have a genuinely good time. And then...the lights went out."

"If you could be precise about who was where and what you saw at this time?"

"I'm sorry, that is impossible. You must understand, it was black as pitch, chief. You could not see your hand in front of your face."

"So what did you do, then?"

"I got up from the table, felt my way to the foyer, wrenched open the front door, and ran."

Charlot cocked her head. "Into the storm? Because...?"

"I can't explain it. I panicked. I...I didn't really know the extent of it until that night, but it turns out, I am deathly afraid of the dark. You just don't know what might happen. You don't know what people might do, given darkness that complete."

Charlot and Lapin looked at each other for a long moment. "I suppose it would have served the Crespelle girl well if she had felt the same," she said finally.

Lapin nodded. "I know it looks bad, and I'm terrifically embarrassed about running off like that. Especially for not calling Anne-Marie right away. But that's the thing about shame, it makes you want to crawl in a hole and disappear. It took rather a long time for me to work out that I had to come home and face things, one way or another. But I can swear to you that I never touched Violette! I would never, ever...I don't know what anyone in the village has told you, but it's probably all exaggeration anyway. I used to talk a big game about women and all, but the truth is... anyway, all I can say is, I very much hope you catch who did it because I don't like the idea of having sat down to dinner with a murderer one bit. I feel like I'm looking over shoulder every minute."

"I don't blame you," said Charlot. She craned her neck to see down the aisle on the left. "You wouldn't happen to have a small desk in this madhouse, would you?"

Lapin beamed, realizing that was the chief's way of saying he was off the hook, and noisily moved around several large pieces of furniture so they would be able to move to the back of the shop, where he did indeed have a small desk.

Not being arrested for murder and making a sale in the same day? Things might be turning around just a bit, he thought, looking forward to telling Anne-Marie at the end of the day.

38

It had gotten to the point that Paul-Henri woke with dread each morning, not wanting to go to work and have to face Chief Charlot. Every day she found something to pick on: the windowsills were dusty (they were not), his uniform was unclean (never!), he made too much noise typing on his keyboard (nothing he could do about that). He was afraid to breathe for fear of disturbing her—and needless to say, in that kind of atmosphere, there was precious little detective work going on. At least he was able to take care of the everyday work well enough, and heaven knows there was not usually much excitement going on at the Castillac gendarmerie.

But this month, they had a murder on the books. And to Paul-Henri's eye, instead of throwing all her efforts into the case, Chief Chantal Charlot seemed concerned with every detail about himself, the cleanliness of the station, and what shopkeepers charged for an array of inconsequential items. Her attention was taken up completely by everything in the world other than who had killed Violette Crespelle.

I'm waiting for the lab reports, she kept saying. Paul-Henri took forensics as seriously as any gendarme, but in the Crespelle case, he did not see how anything forensics had to say was going to crack the case. Okay, there was probably DNA evidence under her fingernails. Could be her own, or someone else's. That wouldn't prove the someone else strangled her. It would probably turn out to be one of the girls' anyway, he thought. Just a scratch while playing a rough game of tag, something like that.

Even though admittedly he himself had not been wearing out any shoe leather working the case, he was beginning to feel that unless a surprise video of the horrible act was discovered, the killer was going to go free. Seventeen people in the house, one strangulation.

No suspects.

Paul-Henri decided to delay going to the station and take a walk around the village first, checking in with various villagers. First he swung by Chez Papa, which didn't do a big breakfast business, but Nico was behind the bar serving coffee and croissants to a few people who dropped in on their way to work. Paul-Henri chatted with him for twenty minutes or so, trying to keep the conversation casual in the hopes that Nico would drop his guard for a moment and say what was really on his mind.

But what was on Nico's mind was only Frances, along with grieving for Madame Gervais. Paul-Henri gave up and kept going, stopping in at Dr. Vernay's next. After insisting to Robinette that he felt fine and was not coming down with dengue fever or anything else for that matter, he was allowed a few minutes with the doctor. Vernay expressed his sorrow for Madame Gervais as well, and for Violette Crespelle, remarking on what a delicious name she had and how he and Robinette had so enjoyed eating piles of crespelles when they went on holiday to Italy back in 2002.

Bored silly, Paul-Henri moved on, heading straight to Pâtisserie Bujold where he could see Edmond Nugent and get something delicious to eat.

"Don't see you in here often," said Edmond as Paul-Henri

entered the empty shop. "Figured you must be giving your business to Fillon," he added, lifting his nose in the air with a sniff.

"Oh no," said Paul-Henri. "It's not that at all. I know perfectly well that there is no place in Castillac to buy pastry except right here at Pâtisserie Bujold! Do you think me an utter Philistine?"

Edmond was momentarily off balance.

"You don't see me often only because I watch my waistline," said Paul-Henri. "If I allowed myself to come here as much as I like, I would need an entirely new wardrobe within a month."

Edmond chuckled. "So, I'm sure there are all kinds of bothersome rules about what you can say, but...has there been any progress on the murder? It does make the village unsettled, you know, thinking that someone like that...is loose."

"I did want to have a few words with you, if I might. The coffee éclair," he said, pointing at the row of identical éclairs in the glass-fronted case.

Edmond drew one out with a pair of tongs and slipped it into a waxed paper bag. "Ask away," he said. "Though I...I should admit that my own performance that night brings me no pleasure to remember. I howled like a small child when the lights went out. *Terrified.* And...well, I have thought that perhaps I did not make a fuss because I am a coward—though indeed that is possible—but because I sensed something terrible was happening."

Paul-Henri leaned forward, forgetting his éclair. "Can you close your eyes, think back on it, and remember what might have led you to that conclusion?"

Obediently, Edmond closed his eyes, holding onto the counter with both hands. He thought back to the night of the Valette party. Remembered how lovely Molly had looked, her red hair a crown of curls. How the little girls kept running through and getting underfoot, and the nanny in pursuit....

"Nothing, I'm afraid," he said after a few moments. "I can say that Rex Ford was coming into the dining room from the library when the lights came back on. Has he explained what he was doing in there, or whether he bumped into anyone?"

"I have spoken with him, of course. He says that he got mixed up in the darkness and was merely wandering randomly about."

"Hmph." Edmond knew for certain that the professor patronized Fillon, an unforgivable offense. He would not be sad to find out that Ford was guilty and would be carted off to face justice.

Paul-Henri took his first bite of the éclair and chewed slowly with his eyes closed. "You are a master," he said finally. "I have eaten éclairs from the top pastry chefs in Paris my whole life, and you, Monsieur Nugent, have surpassed them all."

Edmond beamed. "Perhaps you would like to take something home, something to brighten the last moments of a difficult day? I have no doubt that chasing murderers around the village is taxing work. Perhaps...the fig tart?"

"How did you know? That is one of my very favorites, and it's not easy to find. Yes, I will take two. And please, if you remember anything at all, you know where to find me."

"Glad to be of service," said Edmond. The junior officer has good taste in pastry, that is true, he thought. But a detective? Please. He is nothing compared to our Molly. Nothing.

39

Molly was never one to turn down chocolate in any form, so when Pascal told her his mother had made her famous chocolate torte with raspberries, she ordered it without hesitation. Seeing that the restaurant wasn't busy, she started to make conversation, but Pascal backed away and scurried into the kitchen before she could get out a word.

Something was going on, she was absolutely sure of it. People don't suddenly change into unrecognizable versions of themselves, for no reason. She wanted to know *why*.

But in the meantime, there was a cup of espresso and a big slice of the chocolatiest torte ever made, decorated with whole raspberries around the outer edge and a sauce spilled over the dense slice like a fruity red quilt. Molly took her time, taking tiny sips of the strong coffee and savoring every mouthful of torte while watching Pascal's every move.

There weren't many moves to be observed, though, since the room was nearly empty. He rang up a bill, took another diner some extra bread, stood looking out the window for five minutes, folded some napkins on a table in the far corner. Usually, if things were slow, he would come over to Molly's table and chat with her.

Flirt, really, she corrected herself. Because Pascal *was* a flirt, for sure, of the most harmless and well-intentioned kind. Could it be his new romance with Marie-Claire Levy that was making him act so strangely? Did he think that a bit of chatter with Molly would count as being unfaithful somehow?

Molly couldn't believe it. They weren't middle schoolers, after all. She watched as Pascal pretended to be doing something with a pile of ashtrays—she could tell he was pretending to be working, having performed that particular pretense herself once upon a time.

She signaled to him. "Pascal?"

"Check?" he mouthed, miming scribbling on a pad.

Molly nodded. And when he approached her table, she could see he was thinking he would toss the paper down and flee, but she was ready for him.

"*Pascal,*" she said, firmly grabbing his wrist. "Please. Stay still a moment."

He looked at her, crestfallen. "Oh, Molly."

"'Oh Molly' what? You've been acting like a nut since the minute I came in. What is going on?"

"I am the world's worst liar."

"Indeed. I would put that in the plus column, actually, but yes, you have no talent for dissembling at all. I suggest you don't join the…whatever the spy group is called in France?"

"The DGSE?"

"Yes. That. Okay, my dear friend, out with it. Is it something about the other night, the murder? Or something else? Has Frances caused some kind of scandal that hasn't reached me yet?"

"No, no, Frances is fine as far as I know."

"Because she's been known to…well, beside the point. Go on."

"I don't like to gossip."

"I've noticed that about you. It makes you something of an oddity in Castillac, as I'm sure you know."

"Yes," he said, bowing his head. Molly looked at his full head of nearly black curls, then at his handsome face when he lifted it again. "It's...all right, I'm only going to tell you this because I know Simon Valette hired you, and you should have all the information that might...might be relevant. Not because I want to talk behind anyone's back."

"I understand that," said Molly. "Please, sit. It's okay for you to sit down?"

"Of course," he said, pulling out Ben's chair and sitting heavily. He flexed his fingers and blew air into his cheeks, delaying and delaying.

But Molly was patient. She could sense that whatever Pascal was going to tell her was going to be worth waiting for.

"That night, at the Valettes'. It was insane when the lights went out, right? People were screaming and acting like they were being attacked by monsters or something. I'd never have imagined that a group of adults would be so undone by the dark." He took a sip of Molly's water. "So I figured I would help get the lights back on, if I could, and I left the dining room and felt my way along the wall until I got to the foyer."

Molly nodded, holding her breath.

"And...so this was right when Violette was killed, am I correct? Just then, during the minutes of darkness before the fuse was replaced?"

"Yes."

Pascal took a deep breath and held it. Finally he said, "When I got into the foyer, someone grabbed me by the shoulders. Pressed herself against me. And kissed me on the mouth."

Molly's eyes were wide. "And you have no idea who it was?"

"Oh, sure I do. It was Camille. She was wearing Opium, I noticed that when Marie-Claire and I first got to the house. Camille and I kissed cheeks—you know, we'd met before, and had quite a long talk—and I noticed then that she was wearing Opium. It's one of my favorites."

Molly smiled to herself thinking that not once had she had an

American boyfriend who would have been able to identify a perfume, any perfume, if his life depended on it. But her smile quickly faded as she realized what Pascal's revelation meant.

"So Camille...could not have murdered Violette," she said softly.

"Right," said Pascal. "I pulled away from her and went straight to the basement, and got the fuse changed in a minute or two, not more. The electrical box was ship-shape, and there was a box of new fuses right there. It couldn't have gone more quickly and smoothly once I was downstairs."

"And so...what...was there any acknowledgement later, between you and Camille, about what had happened?"

"No. None. Thankfully."

"Thank you, Pascal." She sighed, shaking her head. "I'll be honest, you've just blown a hole right in the center of our case, but I'm very grateful you told me. Wouldn't want to be accusing someone who could not possibly have committed the act."

"She was still in the foyer when I came back upstairs. Impossible for her to have circled around to the library, killed the girl, and returned, in the few minutes I was gone. I...I'm sorry I didn't tell you sooner. It's just...it's an embarrassing story for her, obviously, and I didn't want to tell it to anyone."

"Understood," said Molly, adding some more euros to the ones Ben had put on the table and standing up. "Thank you again. I need to be off—of course, I must tell Ben right away."

Pascal nodded, somewhat sheepishly, and watched as Molly flew out of the restaurant, hopped on her scooter, and sped away.

❧ 40 ❧

Telling Ben the news about Camille's alibi involved eating a dish of crow. Molly had no desire to put that on top of the lovely lunch she had just eaten, but what choice did she have? When she got home, she told him what Pascal had related about the kiss in the foyer, thinking she was doing a better job of hiding her disappointment than she was.

Ben was no dummy, and refrained from saying anything even in the neighborhood of 'I told you so.'

Nonetheless, Molly was mad at him.

"You know you want to say it, so just go on and say it," she said, knowing full well she was acting like a thirteen-year-old and not a grown woman only days away from turning forty.

"I don't know what you're talking about," said Ben, who again, was no dummy.

Molly sighed theatrically. "Well, ugh. Just *ugh*. I suppose all we can do is plod along?"

"In my experience, cases usually get solved by the long slog. So who's up next?"

Molly went to her desk and looked at some notes. "Rex Ford? Somehow I thought we'd talked to him already. You haven't?"

"No. I did have a chat with Nico after Madame Gervais's funeral. For a clever fellow, he's not all that observant."

"Or maybe just protective of his friends?"

"Even if one of them is a murderer?"

Molly shrugged. "I don't think he'd go that far, no. But he *is* extremely loyal. Would he lie to protect Frances? I have no doubt at all that he would."

"Have you ever noticed that when you get frustrated, you have trouble sticking to the matter at hand?"

She took a deep, slow breath, trying to decide whether to get huffy. She decided they couldn't afford it, not with the murderer not only on the loose but so far completely undetected. "Sorry," she said, and meant it. "Do you want to take Rex or shall I?"

"You, if you don't mind. I'd like to catch up with Lawrence and see what he has to say."

"You don't...?"

"Oh, no, of course not. But unlike Nico, he does pay attention to what other people are doing and saying, and unlike Pascal, is quite ready to dish it up."

"Did you hear back from your friend in Paris with any information about Camille's hospitalization?" asked Molly.

"No. I'll give him a call, too. Though I suppose it doesn't much matter now, does it?"

They kissed a distracted kiss and went their separate ways. Molly was grateful not to run into any of the gîte guests on her way out, feeling pressure to make some sort of progress with the case as soon as humanly possible.

She arrived at L'Institut Degas fifteen minutes later, her hair in a tangled cloud of frizz thanks to the humid weather, and strode down the corridor of the administration building looking for Ford's office.

The school was not large and Molly found the door without any trouble. "Rex Ford," said a gold nameplate, and under that, several drawings were stuck to the door with putty. One was pen

DEATH IN DARKNESS

and ink of a large beast, a fantastic sort of monster with crooked teeth and spittle flying out from its mouth. In its five or six hands it held tiny persons—women, Molly noticed, all of them—and appeared to be about to throw one into its cavernous mouth. She looked for a signature, and saw a tiny "RF" in the bottom right corner.

The next drawing was different in style and Molly checked for the signature first and saw that it was by "BN," probably a current student, she guessed. She rapped on the door.

A young woman answered, looking nervous. "Bonjour," said Molly, then looked over her shoulder at Rex, who was sitting behind his desk, leaning back in his chair.

"Bonjour, Molly," he said, sounding annoyed. "As you can see, I am meeting with a student at the moment. If you had only called first, I could have cleared my schedule or at least given a time when I was free."

"It's perfectly all right," said Molly, "I'll just wait outside until you're done. Is the appointment after this taken?"

Ford hesitated a moment. "No," he said. "That will be fine." The young woman closed the door.

Molly did not believe for one minute that Rex thought it was fine. She almost never called ahead when interviewing; of course it was better to catch people off guard, not give them a chance to work out their stories, or disappear entirely.

She did not suspect Rex Ford. She had known him long enough not to trust him exactly, but to believe she knew, more or less, what kind of man he was. She did not think he would kill a woman he had only just met, and she furthermore believed his story that he was coming into the dining room from the library because he had gotten turned around in the darkness.

Molly wandered up and down the corridor, letting her mind range over the details of the case. At one point, feeling an excess of snoopiness, she put her ear to the door and heard Rex saying something about how the ebauche had been poor and the paint was cracking, none of which made any sense to her but which she recognized as being about art and nothing sinister. After a few more circuits, the door opened and the student scurried off in the other direction.

"Come in," said Rex, gesturing to her to come inside his office. He was tall and rangy, and his furniture was too small for him.

"Thanks for seeing me. I'm a little behind, as you can probably tell. Fact is, the investigation was...well, it was headed one way and now is not. So Ben and I are trying to start over, as it were, and...." She trailed off, not wanting to talk about her failure as she attempted to organize her questions.

"Are you heterosexual?" she blurted out, then clapped her hand over her mouth because the words had flown out without thinking.

Rex Ford cocked his head. "What business is it of yours?"

"None," said Molly, swallowing hard. "It's only that when a young woman dies, you want to know...you want to know what the stakes are for everyone involved, if you see what I mean."

"Do you have any reason to think that Mademoiselle Crespelle's murder was sexual in nature?"

"No," said Molly, her voice small.

"Do you know what percentage of all murders are sexual in nature?"

"I don't, and Rex? I'd like to ask the questions, if you don't mind."

Rex smirked and gave a short nod as he settled into his chair, again leaning back precipitously, his eyes on Molly.

"First off, just generally: did you notice anything the night of the murder? Catch a stray comment, a look, anything at all that, looking back, you think might have some significance?"

"You've got nothing, is that how it is?"

Molly shook her head irritably. "Just please, answer the question."

He looked up at the ceiling and stroked his chin. "It was an awkward occasion, as you well know. I did not like either the host or the hostess. She was an utter mess, thinking about herself every second, and he..."

"He meaning Simon?"

"Yes. Fancies himself quite the...."

Molly waited. She saw a familiar expression on Rex's face, envy and spitefulness mixed; it was no surprise that he had not taken to the charming and accomplished Simon Valette.

"Yes?" she asked finally.

"You know, a funny coincidence. I was noodling around about it, couldn't quite place her—you know how it is, a person you meet seems familiar somehow, and you can't remember whether you've actually met them before or they only remind you of someone. Once I went up to Anthony Hopkins on the street in London and clapped him on the back, thinking he was an old friend—because he looked so familiar, you understand. He looked at me with horror and I realized too late that we had never met, I just knew him from the movies."

"Who was familiar? Camille? Violette?"

"Violette. And what a name, eh? Violette Crespelle. So...*romantic*, I suppose you could say. All those 'e' sounds tumbling along in a row. Quite poetic."

Patience had never been one of Molly's best qualities, and she felt it becoming thinner by the second. "And had you met her before?" she asked, pretending not to want to strangle him.

"Yes. Right here at L'Institut Degas."

Molly was confused. "But the Valette girls are far too young to be—"

"Quite. It was nothing about the girls. It was Violette herself. She applied for admission, and went through what I freely and rather proudly admit is a rigorous and arduous application process, including the preparation of a significant portfolio of course, as well as extensive interviews."

"When was this?"

"Oh, six months ago, I would say? Long enough ago that when I saw her at the dinner party, I couldn't place her for the longest time. We do get over a thousand applications, so I might be forgiven for not remembering all the faces right off, especially out of context like that. It would all be in the files somewhere, you can ask Marie-Claire. Or better yet, her assistant. She knows where all the bodies are buried." He smirked again, putting his hands behind his head and leaning back in his chair still farther.

Curious. So Violette Crespelle had been in Castillac before the Valettes moved here, thought Molly.

"And did Marie-Claire and you both interview her?"

"We did."

"And did you accept her to the institute?"

"No, I'm afraid we did not." Something crossed his face then, some worry or hesitancy, but Molly could not read its meaning.

Violette had been right in this very place, had possibly sat in the very chair Molly was sitting in. And been rejected. People apply and get rejected from schools all the time; it's perfectly commonplace. But...a coincidence, to end up in the same village a few months later as a nanny?

And if it was nothing, why had Marie-Claire lied about it?

❧ 41 ❧

There were still a few guests at the dinner that she had not spoken to. Her best friend Frances had been off on a jaunt for the last week, visiting Irish castles, if Molly remembered correctly. Frances was not known for her powers of observation, as her talents lay in other directions, but talking to her was worth a shot. If for no other reason than to follow the most basic investigative protocol of speaking to everyone who had been present at the scene of the crime.

Frances and Nico lived in a small apartment near the center of the village. Frances had always had money—first from her very wealthy family, and then money she made herself writing jingles for ad agencies. But after moving to France on a whim, she had fallen into a simple life with Nico that was not about having the latest clothes or fast cars, and so even though they could afford something much grander, they stayed in the small apartment, happy as peas in a pod as far as anyone could tell.

"Well, hello stranger!" said Frances, opening the door.

"I think you're the stranger," said Molly. "You've been traveling like mad lately. Having fun, or is there some other reason you haven't shared with me?"

Frances waved a hand in the air. "Always detecting, aren't you? Nah, you know me, I get restless. And Nico is so devoted to Alphonse that he won't ask for any time off to speak of, so I just go off by myself. It's all good." She flashed Molly a brilliant smile, her lipstick a dark red against her pale skin. Her jet-black hair had grown out to below her shoulders, and Molly reached out to tuck a hank behind her friend's ear.

"Anyway, I've missed you," said Molly.

"Same."

"You got time for a cup of coffee and a few questions?"

"How's the case going?"

"I thought it was going just fine, but I just found out that my main suspect has an alibi. So I guess you could say things are going pretty badly. Terrible, actually."

Frances went over to the kitchenette and bustled about with the coffeepot. "Well, you want my opinion? I think it was the old man, Raphael. And I heard he kicked the bucket, so really, there's not anything left to be done."

Molly tried to summon a smile but could not. When Frances said nothing else, Molly asked, "You're kidding, right?"

"No. Not at all. Don't you remember when he came into the dining room brandishing that fire extinguisher? He could have killed somebody with that thing, if he hit 'em in the head the right way. He was *so* hostile. I was afraid of him. Not you?"

Molly considered. "I can't say I was totally without fear," she said, thinking back to the interview when she had felt threatened. "But I've been around people with dementia before—my dad, remember? A lot of them are angry, and who can blame them?"

Frances shrugged. "All I can do is throw out my opinion."

"Don't get huffy."

"Never." She pushed the plunger on the French press and then poured out two cups.

"I went to talk to him. Was hoping he might, um, be lacking in filters and let something fly, you know? But I didn't have any luck. He kept going on about a missing pair of scissors. If we were dealing with a stabbing, that might have been helpful…"

"How's Ben? Has he got any big ideas?"

"Just between us? We're stumped. I was ninety-five per cent sure it was Camille, but turns out I was wrong. That means, I'm afraid, that the needle of guilt swings in Simon's direction."

"'I'm afraid'?"

"Of what?"

"No, I mean why did you just say you were afraid it might be Simon?"

"Oh. Not afraid that way. Well…hmm. I just meant that…you ask the most irritating questions!"

Frances grinned. "I do try my best. Always."

"I don't want it to be Simon, okay?"

"Charming fella, eh?"

Molly rolled her eyes. "Okay, yes, he is, to be honest. But I don't think it's just that. Maybe…maybe it's just my pride or something, but when I first met Simon, my take was that he is really a very decent man, down deep. How many men would leave Paris like that, a job that's the culmination of years of study and work, because a life in the country would better suit his family? Not many, I don't think."

"Women can be that ambitious too."

"Of course, I'm not saying they can't. I'm only saying it would be very tough for anyone to leave a life like that behind. And what does he spend his time doing? Breaking rocks like he's in a work camp." Molly smiled thinking about Simon sweating himself to death working on his piles of stone.

"You do have a weakness for—"

"Oh, shut up," said Molly, smirking back at her. "Got any pastry lying around? I'm feeling faint."

"I do not. I've been eating sour Haribo while I work, I think it's eating holes in my teeth."

"Sounds fun. All right, I suppose I should head home. I just wish I had a decent lead."

"You've got nothing?"

Molly just lowered her head. She tried to remind herself that cases were sometimes stubborn like this, and there was no way to speed things up—the facts of the case would become apparent, eventually. But she knew there was no guarantee. Whoever killed Violette could get away with it, and maybe this time, there wouldn't be any stroke of luck coming.

Frances smiled and patted her friend's shoulder. She wasn't all that keen about having murderers running around the village either, but at least she and Nico didn't feel responsible for uncovering evidence or catching anyone.

EACH DAY at the end of school, Gisele found her sister, which was usually not easy, as Chloë might be shinnying up the flagpole, streaking by in a race with classmates, or hiding in a closet in the science room. Once found, the little sister held hands with the older and they walked home. Gisele did not mind looking after Chloë, as other older siblings might have. Their mother had been inconsistent their whole lives—sometimes present and sometimes not, sometimes fierce and sometimes gentle; it had been natural for Gisele to take over some of the jobs a healthier mother would have performed herself.

It could seem as though the sisters had divided things up neatly: Gisele handled all the worrying, keeping track of what they were supposed to do when, while Chloë was all freedom and wildness. Not the fairest division, but that was how it was.

Their grandfather had been found dead in the backyard, beneath his balcony window, only the day before. Simon had told them they did not have to go to school but Gisele had insisted they should, wanting most of all to keep herself and Chloë away from their mother. Camille did best when life was on the boring side; any excitement, especially of an emotional sort like a death, tended to make things worse.

Including the beatings.

"Let's circle around like we did last time," Gisele said in a low voice. "Papa never suspected a thing. I want to go to the woods today and not go into the house until dinnertime!"

Chloë was surprised. Usually Gisele was all about washing their hands when they got home from school, hanging up their school-clothes, and other boring activities. They passed the manor, scampering past the driveway and not daring to peek to see if Simon was outside and had seen them, and on around the house, into the woods.

In late September, the air was still warm, and the leaves still green. The girls walked farther than they ever had before, looking for a good spot to camp for the rest of the afternoon.

"I wish we had a dog," said Chloë.

"We should ask Papa. You ask him."

"No, *you*," said Chloë automatically. "I think if we had a dog, we would always be safe, because the dog would love us and bite anyone on the ankle if they tried anything," said Chloë.

"Maybe," said Gisele. She stopped in a clearing and dropped her books next to a fallen tree that would make a good place to sit. Chloë turned an awkward cartwheel and let out a whoop.

"Ssh! If you make noise, Maman will hear and send someone to get us!"

Chloë rolled her eyes. "I'm going to stand on that log and do a back-flip!"

"Be my guest," muttered Gisele, pulling a small pad of paper and a pen from her bag. *Suspects*, she wrote at the top of the page, and then chewed on the plastic cap to the pen.

An hour went by as Chloë hurled herself from one end of the clearing to the other, practicing various gymnastic maneuvers, and Gisele took a few notes but mostly replayed the night of

Violette's murder over in her mind, going very slowly, like watching a tape in slow motion. Hadn't she seen or heard anything that could be useful to Madame Sutton?

Chloë flumped down on the fallen tree next to Gisele. "I miss Violette," Chloë said, barely louder than a whisper.

"Me too," Gisele whispered back.

Eventually they got hungry and headed for the manor, which did not exactly feel like home, not yet. Neither said a word as they made their way through the woods, feeling despondent from missing the nanny, not knowing what kind of mood their mother might be in, and not accomplishing a backflip or finding even the smallest nugget of evidence.

❧ 42 ☙

Molly was frantically going through the drawers to her desk, looking for the little notebook she had taken to the interview with Marie-Claire Lévy. It seemed like ages ago—and it was, in the weird world of a case, when time was alternately compressed, stretched out, and altogether unlike real life. Papers flew in a mini-tornado and she spilled a cup of coffee leftover from the morning...and just when she was about to give up, she spied the spiral top of the notebook sticking out from under a stack of bills she had been ignoring simply because there wasn't enough time in the day to get everything done.

She flipped through pages of random thoughts and notes until she got to the interview with Marie-Claire, dated September 22. The notes weren't extensive but appeared to cover the interview from start to finish.

no connection VC

There. Marie-Claire had definitely said that she did not know and had not met Violette Crespelle before the night of the Valettes' party.

Either she or Ford was lying.

"Ben!" Molly hollered, not having stopped to see if he was home.

He was sitting on the terrace finishing a ham and butter on baguette, drinking a glass of cider. "What's up?" he asked, knowing from her expression that she had news.

"It's...it's Marie-Claire. Or Rex Ford, I'm not sure which. Marie-Claire insisted she had no connection with Violette, but I found out today, from Rex, that Violette applied to L'Insitut Degas last spring. She came to Castillac for interviews—apparently the process is involved, not just a matter of a form sent in. She was here, Ben."

He nodded slowly. "Could they simply have forgotten her?"

Molly looked askance. "A young woman is strangled at a dinner party you were present at—a young woman you have met, talked to, evaluated her art—and that just slips your mind?"

"Okay. But we still don't know which one—"

"We don't know anything, let's not get ahead of ourselves."

"I want to tell you to calm down, but I'm afraid you'll hit me," said Ben with a slow smile.

"I'm just so frustrated! And angry with myself for not catching the lies. I think I went into Marie-Claire's office to talk to her that day without any objectivity whatsoever. I was thinking about her and you, if I'm going to be really honest, trying to keep myself from feeling jealous about your relationship."

"Molly, I—"

"Don't say anything. Please. It was ridiculous and I don't deserve to call myself a detective. I've embarrassed myself."

Ben got up and put his arms around her, saying nothing.

"So we have this lie, but what do we do with it?" she said after a few moments. "Any of us could have killed her. All we can do is focus on motive. Why in the world would Marie-Claire or Rex want to kill a prospective student at the Institute?"

"Did they accept her?"

"No, actually."

Ben heaved a sigh. "The thing's impenetrable," he said.

Molly paced the length of the living room, went into the kitchen, opened the refrigerator, shut it again, paced back to her desk. "Why would she lie if she had nothing to cover up? That is the central question here."

"Because she was scared to admit knowing a woman who was murdered? Maybe it was nothing more than a freakishly bad decision made out of fear."

"But why—that makes no sense to me, and are you sticking up for her?"

"No. I'm trying to explain why—"

"I made the mistake of not taking her seriously and here you are doing the exact same thing. It's no wonder the gendarmerie moves its officers around so often—it's absolutely true that we don't want to suspect our friends. Or girlfriends," she added, knowing full well she was behaving badly but unable to stop herself.

"Oh, Molly."

"Don't 'oh Molly' me. I'm not accusing you of anything I haven't done myself. We are failing at this case, Ben. Failing hard." She walked to the door to the terrace. "I'm going to check on the renovation and take a walk to clear my head. In the meantime, figure out what the hell Levy's up to, will you?" She tried for a smile but it came out a little strange looking, called for Bobo and set off for the broken-down barn, feeling sick to her stomach at the thought of what else she may have missed.

BEN TOOK the time to finish his glass of cider without rushing, as he considered Molly and what she had said. He had dated Marie-Claire briefly—not for long, but it had been just before he and Molly had started seeing each other. It was not Molly's jealousy that bothered him; he knew she'd snap out of it before long. It was Marie-Claire and her lie.

Did he know her the way he thought he did?

Did any of us really know each other at all?

Ben drained his glass and took it and his plate into the kitchen and put them in the dishwasher before setting out after Molly. He wished he had a tantalizing tidbit or two to dangle in front of her, something that would steer her attention in the direction Ben thought it belonged: Simon Valette. So far he had not managed to dig up anything even slightly dodgy about him, but that didn't mean it wasn't there.

He could see Molly from a distance as she talked to one of the workmen at the old barn, her hands waving in the air and Bobo jumping up on the man excitedly.

She has a blind spot when it came to charming men, she'd shown this over and over, Ben thought. And now that her first horse in the race had pulled up lame, she was determined to avoid looking at Simon and instead go after Marie-Claire, who as far as Ben knew, was as harmless as a house cat.

"Chérie," he called as he got closer, as Molly stood looking at a beautifully restored wall and the masons got back to work.

"She lied," said Molly, shrugging her shoulders. "How about if you get the job of finding out why?"

"All right," said Ben, trying to catch her eye. But Molly shook her head quickly, thanked the workman, and waved a hand in the air before heading back to the house. Mon Dieu, she can be stubborn, he thought as he followed behind.

"I'm going to see Paul-Henri," he called out, loud enough for her to hear.

"Thought you did that already." Molly paused to let him catch up to her.

"Got sidetracked. I'll tell him about Camille's alibi? Seems only fair to share any exculpatory—"

"Yes, of course. But leave out the business with Marie-Claire, will you? I'd like to figure out what's going on first."

Ben hesitated, then nodded. "If I had to guess, I think now that Lapin is out of the woods and Camille is off the list...the attention of the gendarmerie will be aimed at Simon. He is the most—"

But Molly was in no mood. "Let me know if he has anything," she said, and walked quickly in the direction of the woods, Bobo bounding behind her.

❧ 43 ❧

Paul-Henri had just gotten back to the station after speaking with Merla, Ophélie, Edmond Nugent, and Nico, and was gratefully sinking into his chair, very pleased that he had the place to himself, when Ben strolled in.

"Ben," he said, teeth gritted, though he did want to speak to the former chief.

"She's not here?" asked Ben, gesturing to his former office.

"No. No idea where she is or how long she'll be. You want to talk? I think we should go somewhere else. I don't even want to think about what she would do if she saw us talking all cozy-like."

"That's fine. I have something for you this time. Don't want you to feel like you're doing all the giving." He smiled, seeing fear flash Paul-Henri's face. "Are...are things that bad?" he asked gently.

Paul-Henri shook his head. "Nothing I can't handle," he answered. "How about the alley off of rue Malbec? There's an empty garage back that way..."

The men left the station and ducked down the alley and into the garage. It smelled musty and they could see dust hanging in the air.

"It's about Camille," said Ben. "Turns out she has an alibi. I know that was the suspect we were pushing the hardest, but Molly and I have had to let that go. She did not do it."

Paul-Henri brushed the front of his uniform. "What sort of alibi?"

"I don't like to say."

"If you want to be helpful, you must say, Monsieur Dufort."

"Please do keep this to yourself. I mean to the gendarmerie—I know you will have to tell the chief. Camille...she grabbed someone and kissed him, in the foyer, at the precise moment that Violette was being strangled."

"Which someone?"

"Is it really necess—"

"Of course it is!" said Paul-Henri, nearly losing his temper. "Just give all the facts, if you please!"

"Pascal Longhale."

Paul-Henri's eyebrows flew up.

"*She* grabbed *him*," said Ben. "And he is not a gossip, despite having grown up in Castillac, so he didn't say anything at first. Molly pried it out of him."

The two men stood for a moment, thinking.

"In light of this, I would bet a rather large sum of money that Charlot will go after Simon," said Paul-Henri.

"I thought as much."

Paul-Henri shrugged. "He makes her feel inferior. She is feeling the pressure of having no suspect while the village becomes restive. Perhaps she's even thinking Simon has gone on quite the murderous spree, having also killed his father because he was inconvenient."

"What? How can—"

"I didn't say she has the slightest bit of evidence of any of it. But of all the things that the chief gets excited about, actual evidence does not seem to be on the list."

"What do you think of Simon?"

Paul-Henri was momentarily taken aback by being asked for his opinion. "Well, I...it's certainly possible, wouldn't you agree? Maybe Camille discovered him and the nanny in a compromising position."

"But why kill her? The cat would already be out of the bag."

Paul-Henri opened his mouth to say something but stopped himself.

"Maybe she was blackmailing him," said Ben.

"That's what I meant to say."

"I don't think Simon did it."

"Neither do I! He would've had to be very quick on his feet, for one thing, to get from the foyer around to the library. Unfortunately Merla and Ophélie can't give him a solid alibi. They were not in the kitchen the entire evening, as one might have hoped. They stepped out for some fresh air even during the storm, saying the kitchen is poorly ventilated and got uncomfortably stuffy, and Ophélie says they also went into the large pantry from time to time—at any rate, there were opportunities for someone to cut through the kitchen and get to the library and Violette. Without having to go through the dining room at all."

Ben nodded, trying to imagine it. It was so strange, having been present himself at the scene. Every time he tried to remember, all he could see was that terrible darkness, impenetrable as a shroud of the blackest velvet. "What were you saying about Raphael's death?"

Paul-Henri rolled his eyes. "Well, on orders from the chief, I spoke to Florian Nagrand. He says it's possible that the elder Valette was pushed from the balcony, but there's no way to be sure. Chief Charlot interprets that as a decent possibility, and has a theory that the old man saw something—either the night of the murder or some other time—and that Simon needed him out of the way."

"But Simon moved his family to Castillac partly to rescue his father from a nursing home. That makes no sense at all."

"It does if you understand he's playing the long game," said Paul-Henri. "If you tell everyone you're doing this selfless act of moving your mentally ill father into your home, nobody's going to suspect you if the old fellow ends up with a broken neck."

Ben took a long breath in through his nose and sneezed. He was thinking about Gisele and Chloë, and how badly things would go for them if their father were arrested.

The two men shook hands, promised to meet again if either one got hold of any new information, and set off in different directions.

❧

ONCE THE SUN WAS DOWN, the air was cooling quickly. Gisele and Chloë had been home from school for hours, playing in Gisele's room. They left the door open because a closed door was one of their mother's triggers, and they had long ago learned that closing a door was not worth a beating.

They were huddled over a board game, never Chloë's favorite enterprise, but Gisele had prevailed. They startled at a knock on the open door and looked up to see their mother in the doorway.

"Bonsoir, Maman," said Gisele.

Camille sighed. "Tell me truthfully," she said. "Do you like your new home in Castillac? Do you think we should stay here, or move back to Paris?"

Chloë stiffened. She hated when her mother asked her questions like this, questions that to Chloë belonged to the parents, not to her. She shrugged, hoping her mother would accept that as an answer.

"I like it," said Gisele. "But I miss my friends."

"Of course you do," Camille said, her voice kind. Then she drifted out of sight down the corridor, and the girls heard her heading downstairs.

The sudden and unpredictable kindness of her mother made

278

Gisele angry. If she would just stay the same, the girl thought, then we could all work out what to do. But she shifts this way and that, changing so fast, it's impossible.

"Chloë," she said, picking up the dice and rolling them. "Would you like to go on an adventure?"

Chloë leapt up from the floor and knocked the pieces around on the board game. "Yes! Let's leave this instant! Where are we going?"

"I think we're old enough to be on our own, don't you? Just for a little while?"

"Yes, of course I do! Are we going to New York?"

"I don't think we have the money for plane tickets."

"Well, Africa then?"

Gisele smiled. "How about we just get out of here, out of this house, and worry about our final destination later?"

"What about Papa?"

Gisele shrugged. "He'll manage without us. He'll just keep building that dumb wall."

Chloë had rarely heard her sister speak with an edge of bitterness and she found it fascinating. "Let's pack!" she said leaping about the room and flinging Gisele's things up in the air.

It wasn't a perfect solution, Gisele thought as she pulled a small duffel from under her bed. But there had been two deaths in less than two weeks, and if she could, she was not going to allow either of them to be next.

❧ 44 ❧

Chief Charlot drove quickly along the back road that wound from Bergerac to Castillac. She had spent the morning in meetings with the chief of the Bergerac gendarmerie, withstanding all manner of slights from a man she deemed not fit to polish her shoes. But Charlot wasn't any more surprised by his incompetence than by his mere existence; it was the norm, sadly enough for the state of the country, she thought as she whipped around a tight curve and sped up on a straightaway.

By the time she reached Castillac, she had forgotten about the Bergerac chief entirely and was gearing herself up for a fight with Florian Nagrand's lab. It was unconscionable, having to wait so long for a couple of simple tests. She was beginning to believe that she could count on nothing working in a satisfactory manner in this godforsaken backwater the gendarmerie had sent her to. Clenching her teeth, she parked neatly and climbed out of the police car, not admitting to herself that she quite relished the thought of a shouting match with someone at the lab.

"Paul-Henri!" she said upon entering the station. "I didn't expect you to still be here. It's quite late, after all."

"I wanted to give you this in person," he said, handing over an envelope.

""Have they not heard of the internet around these parts?" she mumbled to herself. Tearing the envelope open, she narrowed her eyes while reading the results, leading Paul-Henri to wonder to himself how he had never noticed how much the chief resembled an angry rodent.

The angry rodent let out a stifled sound—was it a laugh, or a cough? Paul-Henri was not sure. "Well?" he said.

Charlot handed him the report. "Finally they give us something we can work with. Two DNA matches. Let's go."

"Go where? I don't see—"

"No? Do you have an excuse for why his skin was under the fingernails of a young woman who was strangled?"

"Of course it bears more investigation. But I—"

"You drive." She tossed him the keys and her eyes were glinting with pleasure at the thought of handcuffing one of the men on the list, who had looked down his nose at her from the very first.

With the excuse of a quick run to the toilet, Paul-Henri managed to text the news to Ben, though he felt no confidence it was going to help in the least.

❧ 45 ☙

Molly was having a kir after a long day of frustration and lack of progress. She sat at her desk, surfing the internet with a vengeance. Questions abounded: why had Violette chosen to apply to L'Institut Degas, of all places? Had being rejected been a terrible experience, worse than usual somehow, and did it have anything to do with her death? Was Marie-Claire involved? Molly read through pages of Violette's Facebook posts, and though she was beginning to feel that she knew the young woman a little bit, she could find nothing about the art school or anything the least bit suspicious.

She leaned back in her chair and looked out the window. Maybe she should go back to running her gîte business and gardening, and give up this whole private investigator foolishness. Clearly, with those earlier cases she had just gotten lucky, and now that a murder was truly thorny, she was lost.

Ben came through the front door looking at his phone. "Text from Paul-Henri. DNA Lab report is in at long last." He turned his phone so she could read Paul-Henri's text.

"Simon did not do it," said Molly quickly.

Ben's eyebrows flew up.

283

"Well, they did live in the same house," she said. "He could have scratched her while they were playing with the girls or something. It's not freakishly weird to have someone else's DNA on you when you share a house."

Ben put his head to one side. "Really? That doesn't make you wonder even a little? You're that convinced of his innocence?"

"I am." She felt like throwing something, breaking something. Now it wasn't only that she hadn't caught the murderer, but an innocent man was at risk for being arrested, because she couldn't figure out what had happened. "Dammit, Ben! If I just knew where to look, but I'm...I'm as much in the dark as we all were the night of the murder!"

He came up behind her and rubbed her shoulders, which usually she loved but at that moment did not. She jumped up from her chair and paced the living room. "Charlot's definitely going after Simon, isn't she?"

"I don't know. I haven't heard anything more from Paul-Henri."

"They're probably pulling into the Valettes' drive right now. She's infuriating!"

"Want another kir?"

"Yes! I want five kirs! But I can't, there's not a moment to be lost, only—only I have no idea where to go or what to do."

"Molly, listen to me. If Simon is not guilty, then even if Charlot arrests him prematurely, it will come to nothing. DNA under Violette's nails is evidence, let's not pretend it isn't. But it's circumstantial. It's not going to put him away, not unless Charlot has something else she hasn't told anyone."

Molly turned back to her computer, idly flipping from one website to the next. "Oh." Molly looked stricken suddenly. "Oh!" And she grabbed her coat and was out the door before Ben had time to say another word.

✻ 46 ✻

She was missing half of what she needed to know, Molly was quite clear on that. All she had was a shred, a thread, a barely visible filament connecting the murderer to the victim.

But it was there. A whole lot better than nothing. And Molly was going to have to make it pay off somehow.

She rang the bell at Dr. Vernay's office, and as usual, Robinette answered the door quickly.

"Bonjour, Molly! You look a bit agitated, may I get you a cup of tea?"

"I'm fine, Robinette. I'd like to speak to Gérard, please."

"He's with a patient at the moment."

Molly came inside and the two women looked at each other for a moment before Molly's attention sailed off and she was lost in thought.

After ten minutes, Robinette touched Molly on the elbow. "Molly?" she said, gently. "You're a million miles away. I don't think you even saw Gérard's last patient leave. You can go in now."

"Thank you." Molly walked into Dr. Vernay's office, struck as she was each time by how homey yet interesting it was: the

285

portraits, the stuffed civet, the whole enterprise so unlike the visually sterile doctors' offices back in the States.

"Molly," said the doctor with a wide smile. "How good to see you looking so well. You're absolutely blooming!"

Molly gave a short nod. She was at a loss for what to say.

"I'll tell you, Gérard, I'm surprised to hear you say that, because this case I'm working on is causing me to lose sleep like I never have in my life."

"No leads?" he asked.

"None. I had been so positive that Camille was guilty, but that's turned out to be utterly wrong. I guess I'm...really doubting my powers as a detective."

Dr. Vernay leaned back in his chair and put his hands behind his head. "You're sure about Camille? As I shared with you, I had some reservations—"

"She has an alibi. Rock solid."

"I see. Ah well, I'm sure when the next case comes along, you'll be back in fine form!"

Molly let her eyes wander up the wall behind the doctor, to the framed diplomas. "So tell me more about the university in Nice. Were you happy there?"

Dr. Vernay did not answer immediately. For the first time, Molly thought she could see him thinking through what to say.

"It was a long time ago now," he answered finally, trying for a light tone that did not entirely come off.

"Do you keep up with many of your friends from those days?"

"Like I said, a long time ago."

"I hope you won't find it unforgivably nosy of me, but I'm wondering—I'm at such a loss about this case, and you're the only person I've discovered so far to have any connection with the Crespelles at all." She tucked one hand into her coat sleeve and crossed her fingers. "And you know, so often it turns out that the crimes of the here and now have their origins in something that happened long ago."

Vernay smiled again, drumming his fingers on his leg. "Connection?" he asked. "I don't know what you mean."

"Yes. Well, your university," said Molly, gesturing to the diploma. "It's such an interesting insignia the school has, wouldn't you agree? The colors are so perfect for Nice, that turquoise and yellow, so sunny and lovely. I've never been there, but that insignia seems to suit the city well, at least as I imagine it. That's why it caught my eye."

"I don't pay attention to school insignias."

"I know what you mean. Who cares, really—it's the education you're after, right?"

"My reputation—"

"You cured me from that horrible Lyme disease, and I haven't forgotten for a minute," said Molly, keeping her voice light.

Vernay's face relaxed a bit but his fingers kept drumming.

"Violette's father, was it, who you were friends with? Biagio Crespelle? A long time ago, as you say. Thirty years, give or take?"

"No idea what you're getting at, Molly. I'm sorry I don't have any way to help you on your case, but I'm afraid I do have patients to see—"

"I glanced at Robinette's scheduler as I went by, looks like you're all clear for the next few hours. You know, of course I was once a college student myself. Can you just imagine me and Frances at that age? Oh, we got into all kinds of trouble. I remember one party, mixing drinks in a garbage can if you can believe it. Something so American too—it was ice cream, vodka, chocolate syrup, and Kahlua, if I remember right."

Molly seemed to be lost in her happy memory but she was watching Vernay carefully. "We thought we were smarter than everyone—especially anyone older than we were," she chuckled. "Was it the same in France, or maybe still is? I mean at that age, thinking you know it all?"

Vernay shrugged and looked out of the window. "Just kids," he murmured.

"What kind of a man was Monsieur Crespelle?"

"He wasn't anything!" blurted Vernay. "I barely knew him! It's not—he was an annoying twit, if you must know. He has nothing to do with anything, which is why I didn't even think to mention it."

"But you mentioned it to Violette, the night of the party, isn't that right?"

Vernay blinked rapidly. "No. I don't know. I might have. So?"

"It's an unusual name, Crespelle. A tasty name, if I may say so. Although Biagio—to my American ear, that's very exotic. You must have been surprised to meet your old friend's daughter out of the blue like that."

"I haven't said anything about knowing anyone." He laughed unconvincingly. "It's certainly interesting watching you work, Molly. I never realized the degree of imagination involved...pure fantasy in this case. Now again, I don't mean to be rude, you know you've always been one of my favorites...but I have some things do to this afternoon, a few...things..."

"You're a terrible liar."

Vernay's face sagged.

"I'm sure it was a sudden impulse, something you immediately wished you could take back?"

She thought she had him. For an instant she almost heard his confession, the words rushing out before he could stop them, filling in all the gaps in what she had imagined.

But Vernay collected himself. He rearranged his face to something resembling politeness, and refused to say anything more. Molly asked a few more questions, trying to show the man as much sympathy as she could muster, but eventually gave up and left the office, because what other option did she have?

WHEN SHE STEPPED out onto the sidewalk, Molly instantly saw

Ben across the street, not doing a very good job of looking inconspicuous. He and Paul-Henri were pretending to read the same newspaper, halfway behind a tree.

"What in the world," said Molly, unable to keep from smiling as she crossed the street to them.

Ben shrugged. "I'm just glad you're okay. You left with a particular look in your eye that I recognized."

"What are you talking about? What look?"

"Like you were running headlong into a murderer. *That* look. I texted Paul-Henri and we tailed you to the doctor's. Not one of the top ten places I thought you'd be going, I'll admit. Are you— do you really think that Dr. Vernay—?"

"What happened in there?" asked Paul-Henri.

"Let's walk," said Molly, and the three of them set off towards Chez Papa. "To be honest, I think...well, I know it's a shock, and he's practically like family to most of the village and all...but I'm fairly sure..."

"He's the killer? Dr. *Vernay?*" Ben asked, incredulous.

Molly nodded. "I know it sounds crazy. But follow my thinking: there *has* to be a linkage somewhere. It makes no sense at all that a stranger came to town and got brutally murdered out of nowhere, with no motive. Either there was something really bad going on in that family, and therefore it was one of the Valettes, *or* one of the villagers knew Violette before the night of the party. Had some connection to her, somehow, someway."

Paul-Henri nodded. "This is the kind of police work that—"

"How does any of that lead to Vernay?" asked Ben.

"He knew Violette's father, he's admitted that much. I was hoping I could get him off balance, maybe he'd blurt something out, explain what went wrong in the friendship or whatever it was that led to murder all these years later. But he wouldn't admit to anything else. I got close. Damn close. But I...I couldn't think of any way to put more pressure on him, so finally I took off."

"More details, Molly," said Ben. "How did you connect them?"

They were a half block from Chez Papa. Molly had a sudden urge for a plate of hot and salty frites, but did not want to have this conversation in the bistro where anyone could overhear them. She stopped and pulled the other two into the narrow space between two buildings. "Here's how. Vernay went to the University of Nice. Apparently they have a good medical school there, the diploma is right there on his wall. Has a yellow and blue school insignia."

Ben and Paul-Henri waited, looking baffled.

"Violette had an active Facebook page, where she kept up with a lot of old friends and family. I don't know if you do Facebook, but people have their own pages, and most of them have a big photo across the top. Violette is in the photo, smiling—and behind her, on the wall, is a University of Nice school flag, or whatever you call it—the same yellow and blue insignia. But she did not go to that school—her father did. And right at the time when Vernay was there."

"Excuse me, Molly. A fair coincidence, I guess you could say, but isn't it a big jump to think it is meaningful? Many thousands of students go to that school every year, do they not?" said Paul-Henri.

"Yes, yes, no doubt. But there's one more thing. It may not sound like much, but fellas, you have to admit that clues have been pretty scarce so far. We've got to grab onto any little thread we find, no matter how tenuous it may appear."

"I'm just not seeing it, Molly," said Ben, frustrated that he couldn't quite grasp the story Molly was trying to tell.

"Did you know that Gisele and Chloë were under the dining room table the night of the party? While we were eating, they were under there having a picnic."

"I don't see—" started Paul-Henri.

"—and Gisele is a thoughtful kind of girl. The kind of kid who pays attention to grownups and what they say to each other. She notices things. And so she told me what she had heard, either before we sat down to the table or during the meal. Much of it was useless, as you might imagine. But there was a snatch, just a snippet she overheard—I paid no attention at first, I was distracted by Camille—that Vernay said to Violette as she went through the dining room looking for the girls. Something about the old days, and stories about naughty students."

Ben and Paul-Henri said nothing. They waited.

"That's it?" said Paul-Henri finally.

Molly looked at Ben. "Don't you see? The 'old days' are the student days of Vernay and Violette's father, who were at the University of Nice together. Vernay made the connection because the name 'Crespelle' is, if not odd, at least a little attention-catching? Lord knows Vernay mentioned it enough times, going on about Italian pancakes. I think he was trying to cover up..."

"Cover up what?" asked Ben.

"That's the thing—I don't know! He knows I suspect him, it was right out in the open...but he didn't crack. Even though he's not good at lying. Even if he didn't do it, he's holding back *some*thing."

"So I was right, you *were* headed straight into the arms of a murderer."

"What was he going to do, strangle me in his office with Robinette right there? I don't think he's that crazy."

"Molly, if you're right about him, he strangled a young woman he had just met only steps away from fourteen people sitting at dinner."

"You have a point."

"I'm going to rush to the station and tell Charlot what you've told us," said Paul-Henri. "Maybe it will at least slow her down as she rushes off to arrest Monsieur Valette."

Molly blew out a big breath of air. "Sorry that I failed to bring it home," she said to Ben as they watched Paul-Henri jog off to the station.

"Maybe it's all just a misunderstanding, and he did not confess because there is nothing to confess to," said Ben. "Marie-Claire and Rex Ford were in no rush to say they had met Violette before, either. But I accept their explanation of being freaked out by the coincidence and wanting to protect L'Institut Degas from another scandal. It was poor judgment, to be sure.

"At any rate, I understand your desire to look for connections...and I think you're right to look," he said quickly, seeing her expression. "How about for now, we get some frites, and talk some more" he said, taking her arm and steering her into Chez Papa.

❧ 47 ❧

Chief Charlot had called Paul-Henri and gotten no immediate answer, which was clearly a problem and something he would have to answer to once she had made the arrest. She turned the police car into the Valettes' driveway, looking forward to confronting Simon. Not making an arrest, she wasn't that impulsive…but who knew how the questioning would go this time, when she applied a bit more pressure?

Simon opened the door at her knock, his expression stony.

"Have I caught you at a bad time?" she said, in a syrupy-sweet tone. "Good. That's usually quite helpful." She slipped into the house though Simon had not gestured to her to enter or even moved out of the center of the doorway.

"Haven't I answered all of your questions?" he said.

"Oh now, you must understand, Monsieur Valette, that with an active murder investigation there is literally no end to the questions. No end at all, until we catch who did it. But we'll start this session with a little something different: I've received some news to share with you."

Simon walked heavily into the living room. There was no

sound of girlish chatter, no clattering coming from the kitchen; the house felt like a morgue, silent and cold.

"Your DNA was found underneath Violette's fingernails," Charlot told him with triumph. "Would you care to elaborate on how that might have come to be? I'll just make myself comfortable," she said, sitting down on an enormous velvet-covered armchair that made her small body look almost doll-like. She peered closely at Valette but did not see any signs of fear or guilt, but rather a deep weariness instead.

"All right," he said to Charlot.

She noticed how different his face looked, now that he was not trying to be charming. Simon did not look handsome and virile but rather worn, diminished. It was exhausting, living with a woman who literally went for the knives whenever she was feeling stressed. When she attacked him in the shower, he had easily caught Camille's wrist and no one was hurt that time. It had not been a close call. But the effect of her violent unpredictability and not knowing what to do about it—it was debilitating.

With some effort, Charlot managed not to stroke the handcuffs on her belt in anticipation. "Go on," she urged.

Simon sat down on the sofa across from her. "I did leave something out before," he said, in a flat voice. "It is true that Violette and I...were not having an affair. We were not lovers."

Charlot managed to keep disappointment out of her expression. "What then?" she said finally.

"We were not lovers *yet*. We were in that delicious stage of seduction, in which one comes closer and the other steps away, then the positions reverse, every time we get closer and closer, almost close enough that our lips touch—and then dash away again, excitement building all the while..."

He stared down at the carpet. Charlot wondered that he had not insisted on someplace more private to have such a conversation.

"The day of the party, I met up with Violette by accident several times. No—truly, it *was* by accident. There was no need for specific intention," he said, with the first hint of a smile. "I mean only that in the course of the two of us moving about the house, doing whatever was necessary on that particular day, that at least twice we ran into each other in the corridor upstairs. Alone.

"The first time nothing happened. A burning look, nothing more. Exciting, to be sure. Almost excruciatingly so. But we did not touch. However, the second time..."

Charlot moved to the edge of her seat. "Yes, monsieur?" she whispered.

"You must understand. I have known my wife nearly my whole life. It was one of those marriages that come to be because the world you live in expects it, cannot see any other possibility at all for the two people except to carry out the world's dream about who they are. And on the whole, Camille and I...we have done all right. We *try.*"

"And how does Violette fit into this trying?" said Charlot.

Simon's face lit up for a moment as he told her how he had met the nanny in the corridor the second time, had embraced her, held her tight, kissed her on the neck, the ear, and finally—ecstatically— on the mouth. How the passionate young woman had reached under his dress shirt and scratched him almost hard enough to draw blood.

"A tiger," he murmured, overcome with one of the waves of grief that never seemed to stop for long.

Charlot hated him for that last comment. How dare he? "It hasn't been that many days. I suppose you can show me the scratches?"

Simon stood up and unbuttoned his shirt. His muscles were well formed and his skin a dark brown from all his work at the ruin, but Charlot did not notice any of that. She was focused on the scratch marks, four parallel stripes on each side of his back, where fingernails had ripped across the skin and just barely not caused him to bleed.

A tiger, indeed, thought Charlot with distaste, and no small amount of dissatisfaction.

"And let me see your arms and hands?"

Simon's face was still stony as he presented his bare arms, palms down, and then flipped them over so she could see both sides. There were scratches here and there, a cut on his left forearm, but Charlot could see it would be difficult to prove that they had been made by fingernails and not the stones he worked with day after day.

Perhaps the lab had made an error. Perhaps, if she failed to find the culprit, her time in Castillac would be cut short, as the gendarmerie demoted her once again. The first she would cheer, but the second....

She needed Molly. There was no avoiding it any longer.

"BUT DOESN'T she have piles of guests? Won't they see us and tell?" Chloë said as she and her sister passed the cemetery on the long trudge to La Baraque.

"We're not going to break into one of the gîtes!" said Gisele, shaking her head at Chloë's silliness. "She told me that she's having part of it renovated. It's a ruin, like what Papa works on, and she's making it into more gîtes, but they're not finished yet. And it's after dark on a Friday so nobody will be there now. We can camp through the weekend while we figure out our next step."

"I thought you were big pals with Madame Sutton."

"She is a friend. I think you'll like her, too."

"Then why are we hiding? Can't we just ring the bell and she'll give us dinner?" Chloë never liked missing a meal.

"I don't want her to get in trouble. Can you imagine what

Maman would do if she found out we'd run away to Madame Sutton's? She'd probably—"

"Hack her to bits?" said Chloë.

"At the very least, torture us about it for months. And here in Castillac it's not as if she has to worry about what her friends might think, because she hasn't any."

Chloë changed the subject. She asked what her sister's favorite pastry was at Pâtisserie Bujold, and whether she thought the history teacher was stupid. Before long, La Baraque came into view, though it did not look like anyone was home.

"We'll go past it and circle back, just like we do at home. It should be pretty easy to find the renovation site—it'll be a big stony mess just like at home."

Chloë never liked admitting she was afraid, and she kept her mouth shut. But she did allow herself to slip her hand into Gisele's as they walked farther into the darkness.

48

On her way back to the station, Chief Charlot looked through the big window at Chez Papa and saw Molly and Ben sitting at the bar. Though she had never wavered in her opinion that the pair should not have accepted the job investigating the murder when they had been guests at the Valettes that terrible night, the chief admitted to herself that she was stuck.

Terribly stuck, which was a painful situation to be in, at a new posting, her job insecure, where everyone in the village and the national gendarmerie would be judging her every move.

And what a crazy place Castillac was turning out to be: a junk dealer who fled the scene, didn't turn up for over ten days, and as far as she could tell, had no connection to the case whatsoever. A pâtissier who screamed like a baby when the lights went out. A couple of snobbish academics, a pair of private investigators who thought they were better than everyone in the gendarmerie put together, a frivolous bartender and his even more frivolous partner who always painted her lips like she was a movie star.

A pair of fancy Parisians who looked down their noses at everyone. A doctor.

Charlot pushed open the door and made her way to the bar.

She didn't want to do it, but what choice did she have? If she was going to avoid being drummed out of the gendarmerie, she needed Sutton. Better to face it and get it over with.

"I'd say 'bonsoir' but it's not especially *bon*, is it," Charlot said gruffly to Molly. "And I'd be willing to bet you're feeling the same."

That was the most human thing Molly had ever heard Charlot say, and she smiled while holding on to suspicion. "Excuse me for jumping right in, but did you by any chance just come from the Valettes'?"

"I did," said Charlot. "Bring me a martini, extra dry, olives," she said to Nico, whose eyebrows zoomed up as he nodded. Drink orders, as any bartender will affirm, are telling of character, and he wasn't often surprised by a customer's choice.

Charlot sighed. "I want the killer to be Simon Valette," she said simply.

Molly was nearly won over by this. "I totally get it," she said, and with some effort, said nothing else, hoping the chief would keep talking. Ben judged the situation for a moment and then got up. He sauntered down to the end of the bar and engaged Nico in conversation about rugby.

"I admit, I didn't want the killer to be Simon," Molly said, confidentially. "As you know, my pick was Camille. And I was crushed to find out I was wrong."

"We've got DNA from only two people. But Simon has some convincing evidence that points to a different sort of relationship. Not killer and victim," said Charlot.

"More like...lovers?" asked Molly.

Charlot waved her away, not wanting to relive the vision of Simon's scratched-up back.

"Of course," added Molly, "DNA isn't completely conclusive."

"You mean Violette might never have had a chance to scratch the person who killed her."

"Yes. And she might have scratched someone who didn't kill

her, like Simon, it sounds like. Still, it's not nothing, either. We have two positive samples, and one man has been crossed off the list..."

"Correct," Charlot said, nodding.

It was a conversation in which much of what was said was not spoken aloud. Sentences were begun and not finished, and meaningful looks exchanged. They found they understood each other better than they expected.

Eventually Charlot said, "I think we should go forward, Madame Sutton. I only wish we had sat down like this many days ago."

Molly nodded. "So do I. We do want the same thing, after all."

"What do you say we go pay the good doctor a visit, just the two of us?" Charlot proposed.

Molly beamed. Paul-Henri would be furious at being snubbed but she would just have to smooth that over later.

"Watch our backs," Molly said quickly to Ben as they left the bistro. "I don't think there's any real danger, but you never know, right?"

❧ 49 ❧

It was dark. They expected Dr. Vernay to be home with his wife, as on any normal evening. Chief Charlot and Castillac's most famous detective made their way through the quiet streets of the village, each trying to think of some conversational gambit that might trip up the doctor.

In the back of her mind, Molly worried that Ben did not seem convinced she had it right; it *was* precious little to go on, and anyway, the doctor was such a respected member of the community. Was it arrogant of her to suspect him? Unfair? Did it put too much emphasis on a forensic test when labs could and did get things wrong all the time?

She would just have to see how it went. And whether she could get him off balance just long enough to get at the truth.

They rang the bell. Robinette appeared so quickly it was as though she had been waiting for them.

"Bonsoir!" said Molly. "So sorry to barge in at this hour, I hope you're not sitting down to dinner?"

Robinette looked at Molly strangely, since by most French person's reckoning, it was nowhere near late enough for dinner.

"We were having an apéro in the living room. Would you like to join us?"

"This is not a social call," said the chief, moving past Robinette and inside the house.

The doctor met them in the foyer. He recovered quickly, but Molly thought she caught a flash of fear cross his face when he saw who it was.

"I've got some news, doctor," said Charlot. "Your DNA was found under the fingernails of Violette Crespelle. I know you examined her once her body was found, but unless you took one of her lifeless hands and dragged it along your skin, this warrants an explanation."

"Of course I took no such liberties with her body, and I'm appalled that you would suggest so."

"I do not expect that you did. I only stated the only case for innocence to point out exactly how ludicrous it is. So please, explain it some other way. How exactly did your DNA end up under the young woman's fingernails?" Charlot was enjoying his discomfort.

Molly looked at Vernay and could practically see the armor going on. They would get nothing out of him this way.

"Dr. Vernay, could I trouble you for a glass of water?"

He startled, then smiled at her. "What, do you mean to say that grilling me has worked up a thirst?" He started to call Robinette but decided to get the water himself. The kitchen was just off the living room, with the sink in full view.

Molly quickly whispered to Charlot. "I have an idea. Follow my lead?"

Charlot was taken aback. Follow the lead of a civilian, and an arrogant one at that? Her thick brows came together and her mouth turned down.

Vernay was back with a glass of water and handed it to Molly. "Are you sure I couldn't get you both an apéritif? Doctor's orders?" he added, with a false smile.

"No, thank you," said Charlot. She opened her mouth to continue, about to ask for the doctor to show them his hands, wrists, and arms to see if they were scratched up.

But she paused. Perhaps there was time for that, and she could first see what Sutton was up to. If it was a failure, then Charlot could hold it over her head into eternity. And if it worked, well, they were in this together, weren't they?

And also true: the chief was curious.

Vernay had been prattling on about a homemade apéritif he had gotten while traveling, and how much good it did for poor digestion.

Molly interrupted him. "That's all good to know, doctor, but we're here on a rather pressing matter. I know the chief was asking you about your DNA, but it is actually the DNA of Simon Valette that concerns us most."

"Can we trust you to keep this to yourself?" jumped in Charlot. "Simon is our prime suspect." She looked at Molly to make sure she was on the right track.

Molly nodded. "But we're looking ahead, post-arrest, and there are complications."

"Almost always are," added Charlot.

Vernay nodded though he had no understanding of what they were getting at.

"The problem is this," explained Molly. "If we arrest Simon Valette, the two girls will be left at home with Camille. You've said yourself you thought she has a personality disorder, I believe? That she has been or could be violent?"

Vernay nodded again. His stomach was churning.

"So obviously we can't leave the children alone with her, with no nanny or father for protection. Camille will need to be properly diagnosed and the girls removed from the home."

"But where will they go?" asked Vernay.

Molly shrugged. "That's up to Chief Charlot—I'm not familiar with the French system. An orphanage, I guess, or some kind of foster care? Terrible situation, no doubt about that. One parent too mentally ill to care for them, and the other in prison."

Charlot couldn't help feeling satisfaction as she watched Molly's ruse have its effect. The doctor looked heartbroken and anxious all at once.

"So here's how you could help, Gérard," said Molly. "We know how you delivered most of the babies in Castillac after all, and how you've devoted your life to making people well, most of all the children. We know you'd like to help with Gisele and Chloë even though they are new to Castillac."

"Of course, of course," the doctor said, hoarsely.

"We will need official certification of Camille Valette's mental state. You might need to testify in court, but that won't present any kind of problem, will it?" said Charlot, playing her part beautifully.

Dr. Vernay went to the sofa and sat down. Then he stood up. "You're sure it was Simon who did the murder? Camille—"

"Camille could not have done it," said Molly. "Can't be two places at once."

A long pause. "The older child has told me some things..." said Molly, with mixed feelings about breaking Gisele's confidence. "I'm sure a lot of children are beaten by their parents. It's not fashionable now, but of course millions have grown up and not been broken because of it. I'm afraid, though, that Camille doesn't just lose her temper and spank. There's more, the sort of things that can cause deep emotional problems in children. But..." she added, with a flash of inspiration, "I don't have to tell you what it's like to be raised by someone that disturbed."

Dr. Vernay jerked his head up. "What do you know about that?" he said.

Molly went with it. "About mothers with a touch of insanity?"

He laughed harshly. "A touch? My mother was far worse off than that, I can tell you."

Charlot was impressed, seeing Molly react so nimbly.

"And Camille was bad off as well, wasn't that your professional opinion from the beginning?"

"Those girls..." Vernay's voice broke, almost imperceptibly.

The women waited. They watched with fascination as Dr. Vernay paced around the room, one moment looking furious and the next on the verge of tears.

"The girls are young, but who knows, maybe at least one of them will be resilient, and her life won't be a complete disaster," said Molly, prodding.

"No," he whispered, finally sitting down in a chair and putting his head in his hands. "No. I can't."

Charlot walked to him and touched him on the shoulder.

"It was impulsive of me," he said, barely audible. "I would...I would take it back if I could."

"I understand," said Molly. "I'm sure you would." She was suddenly overcome with sorrow at what had happened, and how many lives had been affected.

And for what?

Charlot tugged at the collar of the doctor's jacket. His head bowed, he slipped it off, then rolled up his shirt sleeves.

On one wrist and forearm were the scratches Violette had made as she tried to stop her attacker. The scratches were deep, making lines of blood just under the doctor's skin as though someone had attacked him with a dark red marker.

❧ 50 ☙

The next night was Saturday, just over two weeks since the Valettes' ill-fated dinner party. Molly spent the afternoon taking a long walk with Bobo into the deep forest to the north of Castillac. She needed to clear her head of visions of bad mothers and children in pain, of the agony of mental illness, of death. Of course it went a long way to have caught the murderer and gotten a confession out of him, but even so, it did Molly's heart good to see Bobo joyful as only a dog can be, bounding ahead and circling back to check on her, lapping furiously at streams and only occasionally barking when high spirits overtook her.

It was starting to get dark sooner, right on the cusp of October. Some people dreaded the dark winter months, but this year, Molly looked forward to plenty of quiet time at home with Ben; perhaps she would think of some parties to throw to liven things up in the village a bit. She got home tired from the long walk, and muddy and sweaty.

She came into the house from the terrace, which was lucky for everyone since it meant she didn't see all the cars parked along rue des Chênes, which might have given everything away.

"Surprise!" shouted thirty-five people—thirty-six if you

include the young man from the caterer, who stuck around after making the delivery even though he knew neither the host nor the guest of honor. The Mertenses and Jenkinses were there, looking merry and holding birthday presents.

Molly dropped the pinecone she was carrying, her eyes big. "What?" she said.

All thirty-six boomed out with "*Bon Anniversaire*," and she got tears in her eyes. Ben came for a kiss and she hugged him, burying her head in his shoulder while she collected herself.

"Happy forty," he said, kissing the top of her frizzy head.

"How did you know?" she said wonderingly.

"You're engaged to a private investigator," said Ben, rolling his eyes. "Do you really think that little of my powers?" Everyone laughed. "And let me take this moment," he added, tightening his arms around Molly, "to tell everyone that Molly has agreed to make me a happy man. We're getting married!"

Shrieks from Constance and several other quarters, and the couple was briefly mobbed by guests wanting to give congratulations. Molly was aware that it felt good, having the news out in the open, with no lingering superstitions causing any trouble.

The party took off, with Lawrence making Negronis for anyone who was willing, Frances and Constance serving heavy hors d'oeuvres, and everyone talking about every detail of the case of Violette Crespelle.

"I still can't believe Gérard is guilty of anything," said Manette, her friend the vegetable seller. "You know he delivered all of my children, and was going to deliver this one, too?" She patted her huge belly and shook her head.

"I know," said Molly. "He was so wonderful when I was sick with Lyme that it took me a long time to think about him with any objectivity. If I had known earlier about the kind of household he grew up in, knowing the effect that can have on a child, maybe that might have helped? But honestly, I doubt it. It's very difficult to override your experience with someone, either good or bad. Maybe especially when it's good."

"But why did he do it—that's what everyone wants to know," said Lapin, holding a beer in one hand and his arm around Anne-Marie.

"It's a long story," said Molly.

"Well, get on with it, then!" said Marie-Claire, standing next to Pascal.

Molly took a sip of her kir. It was utterly delicious, as always. "He sort of broke down when Charlot and I told him that the Valette girls were going to an orphanage."

"They *are?*" said Lapin, horrified.

"No, no, it was just something I said to put pressure on him."

"You're very bad, Molly," said Lapin. "A bit frightening, if I'm honest."

"The girls did run away from home—that horrible Boris What's-His-Name found them at the worksite last night, but they were unharmed, just hungry. Though I worry very much about them still. Their mother...."

"Come on, Molly, get back to that in a minute—we want to know about Vernay—"

"What happened was...the whole thing was a, just a very unfortunate combination of mistakes and bad timing. See, Vernay went to the University of Nice with Violette's father. Something happened during their time there, something Vernay was deeply ashamed of."

"If you think you're going to get away with not saying what it is, you are sorely mistaken," said Lawrence.

"He failed out of medical school," said Molly.

The room went quiet.

The first sound was of close to thirty-six people taking a sip of their drink, all at once.

"Failed out of medical school?" said Edmond Nugent. "But he performed *surgery* on me! It was outpatient, to be sure, but there was a scalpel involved! Oh my heavens," he said, looking for some-place to sit down.

"So he's been faking it all this time?" said Lawrence.

"Pretty much," said Molly. "But a faker with some knowledge and talent, I think we'd all agree."

"I suppose he studied extra hard to make up for it," said Ben. "Kept up with the current science and techniques, that sort of thing."

"What an irony, that the best doctor in the village is a liar and a fraud," said Lawrence.

"*And* a murderer," added Molly.

"I'm still not seeing—what did Violette have to do with any of that?" asked Constance.

"So..." Molly continued, after snatching a *gougère* from the tray Frances was holding. "Obviously, Vernay spent his life in terror that his secret would come out. Very few people knew, and one of them was his former friend from the University of Nice, Biagio Crespelle."

"The nanny's father." said Ben.

"Right. Vernay said that he managed to hide his failure from most of the people he knew, but Biagio found out somehow. He promised not to tell anyone, but of course, Vernay was uneasy about it anyway."

"Did Violette make the connection between her father and Vernay?" asked Lawrence.

"I don't think we have any way of knowing," said Molly. "Biagio passed away five years ago. We don't know if he told his daughter about it, or if he took Vernay's secret to his grave."

"So you're saying the murder might have been for nothing," said Edmond.

Molly and Ben nodded in unison.

"I still have questions," said Marie-Claire. "How in the world did he manage it? The lights weren't out for that long. It seems like such a freakish thing, his slipping in the library and doing the deed so quickly."

"You have to understand that Gérard had been living with this fear for decades. A sort of constant controlled panic just under the surface, knowing that all would be lost if anyone ever found out the truth.

"So when he realized that Violette was Biagio's daughter, he totally lost it. Internally, I mean—he was overcome by fear. Somehow, as we all saw that night, he managed to hold it together during the first part of the dinner. I didn't notice anything off, did any of you?"

The friends who had been there shook their heads.

"But Dr. Vernay was planning. All during the salmon rillettes and the lamb, he was planning. He told Chief Charlot and me that earlier in the evening he had picked a length of string off the floor, partway under the dining room table. Maybe the children were using it for a game, who knows, just a length of string, harmless enough in itself.

"And as he ate, he had one hand in his pocket, turning that string around his finger. Thinking about Violette, and how she had the power to smash his life into a million pieces. He watched her carefully as she came in and out of the dining room, looking for the girls. He saw her go into the library just before the lights went out.

"And so, the instant we were all in darkness, he jumped up and reached her in a matter of seconds." Molly paused, looking around at the guests. "This isn't exactly party talk, is it?" she said, feeling sad for Violette, the village, and even for the doctor.

"Molly!" shouted at least four people.

"All right. Well, he got to her, got behind her, pressed on her carotid artery. Meanwhile people in the dining room were calling out, even screaming—there was no question whatsoever of any noise giving him away. Violette fought him—scratched him up pretty badly on one arm—but stopping the blood flow to the brain works quickly, and she passed out. By the time Gérard brought the string from his pocket, she was unconscious.

"The whole thing, amazingly enough, took only a handful of minutes. The doctor had time to return to the dining room and take his seat before Pascal got the lights on again. And that was that. I'm just lucky I noticed that school insignia on Violette's Facebook page, and put it together with the one on Vernay's diploma."

The crowd murmured agreement, and after a few moments someone put on some music—the blues, Molly's all-time favorite.

"Well, happy birthday," said Lawrence, giving Molly a peck on both cheeks. "Sure has turned out to be a stroke of luck, having you in Castillac. We'd all have been slaughtered in our beds by now, what with all the killers we seem to attract."

Everyone laughed and poured another drink, but the thought was a bit unsettling, if one allowed oneself to think about it for long.

ALSO BY NELL GODDIN

GLOSSARY

1

La Baraque..........................the shed or shack
gîte.......................................holiday accommodation, usually for a week at a time
rue des Chênes....................street of oaks
Gendarmes..........................police
gendarmerie........................building where gendarmes live
apéro...................................cocktail

2

foie gras..............................goose liver

3

chérie..................................dear, sweetie

5

épicerie...............................small grocery
au revoir..............................goodbye

7

bonsoir................................good evening

317

8
pâtisserie.............................pastry shop
pâtissier..............................pastry chef
L'Institut.............................Institute
13
Pain au chocolat..................chocolate croissant
14
notaire................................government official
mon Dieu.............................my God
17
partout................................everywhere
20
primaire...............................elementary school
25
toute le monde.......................everyone
26
Priez pour vos morts..............pray for your dead
merde...................................poop (vulgar)
30
En famille.............................family all together
32
pensees des escaliers.............thoughts on the stairs (after-thoughts)
50
gougère................................cheese puffs
Bon anniversaire..................happy birthday

ACKNOWLEDGMENTS

The crack team of Thomas Glass and Nancy Kelley continues to give excellent critiques of early drafts. And Joan Cramer of 4eyesediting.com did an astonishing job of editing and proofing.

Kathy Church found some inconsistencies right at the last minute—thank you! I raise a brimming glass to you all!

ABOUT THE AUTHOR

Nell Goddin has worked as a radio reporter, SAT tutor, short-order omelet chef, and baker. She tried waitressing but was fired twice.

Nell grew up in Richmond, Virginia and has lived in New England, New York City, and France. Currently she's back in Virginia with teenagers and far too many pets. She has degrees from Dartmouth College and Columbia University.

www.nellgoddin.com
nell@nellgoddin.com

Made in United States
North Haven, CT
14 November 2024

60325506R00195